And Then She Flew

jen labesky

For my mom – The perfect example of grace, strength and love.

And for my dad – Thank you for building my wings.

PROLOGUE

May 28, 1977

Her father's head snapped up at the sound of her mother's pointed stilettos on the top step. Anna giggled as she watched her father, Raymond Cunningham, PhD, tenured English professor... at complete a loss for words - his extensive vocabulary wiped clean.

Lord help me, he thought. *She's wearing that dress again.*

Katherine's eyes met her husband's.

"You look..." He hesitated, juggling adjectives in his head, grasping, dropping, grasping again – searching for just the right word to describe his wife as she descended the staircase. "Amazing," he finally coughed out. An inadequate description perhaps, but even while his mouth failed him, his eyes spoke eloquently, glistening as they followed her graceful movement to the bottom step. Raymond had been held captive in Katherine's trance from the moment he first laid eyes on her. Even after a decade of marriage, seeing her this way still reduced him to a bumbling toddler. He reached up to straighten his tie, to smooth his hair, then down to check his zipper. He stuffed his hands into his pockets to contain them.

"Thank you," Katherine whispered, her eyes burning into his, lingering for a moment – an unspoken promise. She draped her shawl around her shoulders, trapping the ends of her feathered blonde hair, as she made her way to his side.

Raymond pulled his hands from his pockets and gently lifted her hair,

1

freeing it from the shawl, allowing it to fall like silk down her back, releasing the aroma of her lilac shampoo. He closed his eyes and breathed in the familiar scent. *I'm home.*

He opened his eyes and placed a soft kiss on the side of her neck, then trailed his fingertips down her arms.

Katherine inhaled sharply. Raymond's touch sent ripples through every inch of her body. She turned slowly, allowing him to admire her in the red dress with the daring slit up the leg. The slit stopped short of indecency, exposing just enough of her toned leg to constantly pull her husband's hungry eyes toward her thigh. She had chosen the red dress tonight precisely because of the effect it had on him.

His eyes pleaded.

"Later," she whispered, then turned her back to him and smiled at the babysitter. "Stephanie," she said, "Thank you for coming."

Stephanie stood paralyzed as she watched Raymond's eyes devour his wife's backside. She blushed. After ten years of babysitting for the Cunninghams, Stephanie was well versed in the house rules, but she had never been able to brace herself for the electricity between the enchanting couple.

"As always," Katherine said, "you're welcome to anything in the kitchen."

Stephanie nodded, unable to speak.

"We shouldn't be too late." Katherine passed a suggestive glance over her shoulder toward her husband before kneeling in front of their ten year old daughter.

Her eyes glistened as she held Anna's precious face between her palms.

Anna gazed into her mother's eyes, mesmerized.

"I love you Sweetie," her mother said. "Have a great night with Stephanie." She kissed Anna's forehead softly then stood and stepped back to allow her husband a moment with their child.

Raymond crouched down, wrapped his arms around his daughter and squeezed, gently at first, but with each breath she took, he tightened his embrace – a boa constrictor. She kicked him playfully in the shin, and he

2

released her, holding up his hand for a high-five. Anna's tiny hand pressed into his; he clutched it and brought her open palm to his lips. "I love you baby," he said, then took his wife's hand, and they disappeared together out the front door.

~

Anna peeked out from under her covers when she heard the car pull into the driveway. The glowing red numbers on her clock read 10:42. Stephanie thought Anna was sleeping. She always thought that, but the truth was, every time her parents went out for the night, Anna would read to her tattered stuffed bunny under the covers with a flashlight until her parents arrived home. She would wait for the comforting sound of the key turning the deadbolt and the joyful dance of muffled voices thanking Stephanie and dismissing her. Even at ten years old, Anna still played possum when her parents crept into her bedroom to kiss her goodnight. She loved inhaling the heady scent of secondhand smoke that clung to their clothes, the scent that told her that her parents were home, and she was safe.

She clicked off her flashlight and tucked it under her pillow, curled up on her side and squeezed her eyes shut, anticipating the jingling keys and happy voices…

Nothing.

She pulled her knees to her chest and waited…

Nothing.

A chill raced up her spine and her eyes began to burn. She pulled her knees in tighter and waited…

Where are they?

She opened her eyes and rolled onto her back. Her bed began to spin beneath her. "Mommy?" she whispered. She squeezed her eyes shut to stop the spinning and felt a tear slip down her cheek. "Daddy?"

A firm rap on the front door jolted her upright; her pink bedspread fell around her waist. *They must have forgotten their house key,* she thought, clinging to her bunny and to hope as her bottom lip began to quiver.

A deep voice pierced the walls of her bedroom.

She slid out from under her covers, petite bare feet tiptoeing toward her bedroom door over cold, century-old pine floors. She didn't feel the cold beneath her feet; she didn't feel anything. She cracked the door open and pressed her ear to the space between heaven and hell, knowing in her soul that her life would never be the same if she opened that door. She had no choice.

The foggy conversation pulled her over to the top of the staircase. She looked down and saw her father's best friend, Officer Kurt Malone, propped against the door jamb, his peaked cap in his hand over his chest, a woman in a dark suit at his side – the two of them silhouetted by a backdrop of flashing red lights.

The wood bruised Anna's palm as she gripped the banister tightly. She curled her toes around the edge of the top step and leaned forward, desperate to understand the words of the man who was like a second father to her.

Officer Malone fell silent when he saw her. There were no more words. His eyes, streaked blood-red, told Anna what her ten year old heart already knew.

And then she fell.

ONE

May 28, 2002

Anna skipped up the brick walkway gripping a bouquet of freshly picked dandelions in her fist, the loose satin ribbon on her pink dress trailing like butterfly wings at her back. Her mother smiled and stood from the porch swing, then knelt and extended her hand. Anna stepped onto the porch and held out the flowers.

The sky flashed red, scalding her pupils, branding her mother's silhouette on her retinas.

She dropped the dandelions and clawed at her eyes, frantically wiping at the red ash. All she saw was red.

"Mommy!" she shouted, falling to her knees and feeling her way toward the porch swing. Twenty-five years flashed by behind her eyes – images of a woman staggering, bottles of booze and voices of men, expressionless faces of children, strangers, patients...

Anna grasped the edge of the porch swing and pulled herself to her feet. She ripped off her suit jacket and pressed the silk to her eyes, scrubbing her vision clear. The swing hung motionless.

"Mom! No!"

She yanked off her leather pumps and hurled them at the swing. Red dust floated to the floorboards. She kicked the front door open and staggered inside.

"Mom, where are you?"

Red lights flashed in the street, and the door slammed shut behind her. She turned back toward the door, threw it open and sailed onto the lawn. The crumbling sidewalk fell away at her heels as she raced barefoot toward the creek, her silk pants snagging on the overgrown hedges as she passed. The flashing red lights illuminated then darkened the night in turns. The stars burst into crimson flames in the sky as Anna's bare feet sank into the soggy earth at the creek's edge.

She dropped to her knees and grabbed a fistful of mud. Smearing it across her chest, she threw her head back and inhaled the red mist rising from the creek. She closed her eyes, crawled into the blood-red water and collapsed onto her back. The icy current rose around her. She took a deep breath and waited for the water to fill her lungs.

It would all be over soon...

"Dammit!" Anna's eyes shot open. She wiped her sticky hair from her forehead and glared at the flashing red numbers on her alarm clock. She hadn't had a full night's sleep in twenty-five years. The nightmares stalked her; there was no escape. The dreams followed her in every waking moment, planning their assault, waiting until she drifted off to sleep before ambushing her. The first one had come when she was just ten years old, on the night of her parents' funeral, and she had spent the next few nights wide awake. Eventually her young body had rebelled, dragging her into dreamland, so she had learned to live with the nightmares like her own second shadow. But while the nightmares were different every night, the message was always the same - Anna was alone.

The clock read 3:47, and she knew it was futile to stay in bed any longer, especially today. She threw back the pink bedspread, pulled on her jeans and grabbed the fleece blanket from the foot of her bed. She forced her bare feet toward the kitchen and put the teakettle on the stove. As the water heated, she took one of her mother's teacups from the cabinet and held it up, admiring the two doves hovering weightlessly above the willow tree. She pressed the cool porcelain to her cheek and envisioned her mother carefully laying out her prized

Blue Willow china for her dearest friends.

Her mother had always pretended not to notice when Anna and her best friend, Sandy Malone, tiptoed down the stairs in their pink silk nighties. The two girls would perch themselves silently in the hall, peeking around the corner into the dining room, eavesdropping on their parents' conversations, yearning to join the party. Katherine would glance over and catch Anna's eyes every time, winking before turning back to the Malones.

The girls would spy on their parents from their not-so-secret hiding place, watching as Katherine breezed from the kitchen to the dining room, her cheeks flushed with joy as she doted on her guests, topping off their coffee, offering seconds, then clearing their plates before offering one of her mouth-watering chocolate cakes for dessert. Anna would take note of exactly how her mother served each dish, and the way her eyes would smile at the sight of her friends enjoying the meal she had lovingly prepared.

When their eyelids grew heavy, Anna and Sandy would creep back upstairs and crawl into bed, side-by-side, tucking Anna's beloved Fuzzy Bunny between them as they drifted off to dreams of the chocolate cake that would be left over in the morning. Anna's mother always made extra for the girls and would allow them to have cake for breakfast "just this once."

A deafening shriek jerked Anna back to the present; she reached for the teakettle to silence it. She dropped a tea bag into her cup and poured the boiling water, then lowered her body onto a chair at the kitchen table – the same table where she had enjoyed so many lively breakfasts giggling at her father's silly antics while her mother rolled her eyes and tried to stifle her grin.

Anna located the familiar scars in the tabletop and traced them with her fingertips – "12x9=108" – bubble numbers scribed by an overly enthusiastic nine-year-old pressing her pencil down a little too firmly.

"Oops, sorry Daddy," she had said.

"It's ok baby. It's just a table. What matters is that you got it right!" He slapped her five. "Smart *and* beautiful, just like your mother."

Anna dropped her forehead to the table with a "thud." The sound reverberated throughout the kitchen until it dissolved into the oppressive silence. *I'm nothing like her,* she thought. Anna was an apparition, nothing more, going through the motions, clinging to the hope that there was a reason for breathing. No one saw her – *really* saw her. No one had in years…

September, 1977

Anna clutched her plastic tray as she wove around clusters of gawking fifth-graders toward the empty table in the corner. Everyone stared, but Anna was invisible. Sure, they could see her skinny legs and her tangled curls, but they couldn't see her shattered heart, and there was no way she would let them see her cry.

She kept her eyes on her tray, watching the foul creamed spinach slosh around, threatening to spill over and contaminate her pizza. She heard the whispers as she passed. She kept her eyes on the spinach. Her hands trembled as she lowered her tray onto the table; the swampy green goo splashed over the edge onto her pizza. "Great," she whispered. She collapsed onto a metal chair facing the wall and focused on the buzzing of the fluorescent lights.

Danny Everett watched her. He saw the shimmer of tears lining the lower rim of her blue eyes. He heard the whispers too. *Why can't they just leave her alone,* he thought.

Anna knew they were staring at her. She didn't care. What did they know? She didn't need them. She wiped at her eyes with the back of her hand, then tore the tainted edge off her pizza and dunked it into her spinach. *Why does Aunt Teresa make me buy lunch,* she thought. Anna's mother had always made her lunches – PB&J or ham and cheese sandwiches cut into the shape of flowers or smiley faces with holes for the eyes and mouth.

She inspected the charred slice of pizza, then took a bite and began to chew; the crust turned to paste on her tongue. She dropped it onto her tray and opened her chocolate milk. The buzz of hushed voices encircled her like a swarm of angry bees. She shook her head and focused harder on the buzz of the florescent lights, blocking out the bees, humming along with the soothing miracle of electricity and illumination. The bees grew angrier, their buzz deafening. Anna closed her eyes and clung to the buzzing of the lights.

"Anna Cunningham... mom and dad... dead."

Anna pressed her palms to her ears.

"Glad it wasn't me."

She pressed her palms harder, hummed louder, and tightened her grip on the peaceful buzz of the lights...

"Sometimes I wish my parents were dead."

She lost her grip.

She whipped around in her chair and glared at the boy who had uttered those words. His cheeks flashed red and he turned away, cupping a hand beside his mouth as he whispered something to Sandy Malone.

Danny sprang to his feet; his scrawny knees trembled beneath him. He curled his lips around his bulky braces and balled his hands into fists; his heart pounded and his fingernails cut into his palms. He took a deep breath and puffed out his chest...

Then he sat back down.

There was nothing he could do and he knew it. That kid was nearly twice his size.

Just leave her alone, he thought, glaring at his tray.

Sandy glanced up at Anna, her eyes exposing her conflicted heart. She wanted to comfort her best friend; she wanted to tell all the kids to shut up... She looked down at her lunch instead – a peanut butter and jelly sandwich cut into the shape of a heart.

Anna picked up her tray and marched to the trashcan. She tilted the tray, tipping the chocolate milk, and watched as it carved a tiny canyon through the spinach and trickled off the edge. She dropped the whole tray in the trash and walked to the back of the cafeteria, pressing her body against the wall as the swarm of bees was called to line up for recess. She took her spot at the end of the line - a calf being led to slaughter. She followed the herd outside and made her way to her solitary haven at the far side of the smoldering blacktop.

The sun bore down hard on her shoulders as she dug the toe of her pink Converse All Stars into a crumbling patch of asphalt, cracking off a chunk, sending it tumbling over the edge into the grass. The other kids played kickball or hopscotch, climbed the monkey bars or pumped back and forth on the swings.

Danny leaned against the old pecan tree trying to think of something to say to her. He wanted to reach out, to let her know she wasn't alone. He wanted to make her smile again... the way she used to.

Sandy watched her from the top of the slide, but when Anna looked her way, Sandy slid down and ran off to join the kickball game. Anna kicked harder at the crumbling asphalt, breaking the whole corner free.

At the shrill call of the whistle, Anna took her spot at the end of the line. The girl holding the door looked away when Anna walked past.

Whatever, Anna thought, scowling at the floor as she marched to her classroom. She slid into her chair and leaned her elbows on her desk, cradling her head in her hands. When Mr. Humphries called on her, Anna looked up at the clock. *Just let me disappear God,* she thought, watching the twitching second hand chisel away time, waiting for the bell that would free her from this jail cell. *So I can go home to prison,* she thought.

Mr. Humphries turned away from her and called on Danny.

When the second hand clicked to the twelve, the bell blared. Anna swiped her backpack off the back of her chair and sprinted out the door.

Danny chased after her, hurrying down the sidewalk to catch up with her. "Anna," he called out, his voice cracking.

She didn't turn to look back.

Sweat beaded on her forehead as she counted, "one thousand two hundred six, one thousand two hundred seven..." The number of steps between school and her house hadn't changed, but everything else had. She unlocked the front door and kicked it closed, then raced up the stairs to her bedroom. She locked her door, sat down on her pink bedspread and pulled her homework from her backpack.

"If Johnny leaves school at 3:30, walking at a pace of four miles per hour, and his home is a half mile from school, what time can his mother expect him home?"

"Never," Anna grumbled, crumpling the worksheet in her fist and tossing it over her shoulder toward the trashcan. It bounced off the edge and fell to the floor. She flopped down onto her back and forced herself to hold in the tears. "What good will crying do?" she whispered to the star shaped stickers on the ceiling.

"That one is Orion, the mighty hunter," her father had said, pointing up at the adhesive constellations as he tucked her in just five months earlier. "Greek mythology has many tales about Orion. Some believed he was killed by a giant scorpion, and his girlfriend, Artemis, asked Zeus to place him in the stars so she could see him forever."

"How did he do it?" Anna whispered. She wished she had thought to ask. Maybe she could get ahold of this Zeus guy and see if he could put her parents in the sky too.

The front door slammed, startling Anna from her musings. She covered her face with her hands. *Great,* she thought. *She's home.*

Slurred voices echoed throughout the house. Anna didn't recognize the male voice – she never did. It didn't matter. Even though the voices were different every night, they all said the same things. She heard two sets of feet stagger up the stairs, a hard thump against a wall, and then the familiar squeak as bodies collapsed onto the bed in the next room. She grabbed her pillow and buried her head.

TWO

May 28, 2002

Anna raised her head from the table and rubbed the sore spot on her forehead. *That's going to leave a damn bruise,* she thought. She brushed her hands up and down her arms to create heat as she stood, but she felt nothing – nothing but cold. She wrapped her blanket around her shoulders and carried her tea to the front porch.

The moonlight mocked her, and the lonely silence of early morning seemed appropriate for the occasion. She raised the teacup to her lips, then set it on the small glass table, cursing herself for once again allowing her tea to cool too much. She pulled the blanket tighter around herself and settled onto the porch swing.

The weathered wood slats creaked and moaned, tired and angry, as they endured her weight. She wondered, as she did every year for the past twenty-five years, if the slats would hold. Every May 28th, on the anniversary of her parents' death, Anna would sit out on her porch swing – always on the right side, leaving her mother's spot vacant, just in case. Each year the creaking grew a little louder, a little more irritated. Anna knew that one of these days the rotting slats would no longer support her. As a psychologist, she earned more than enough money to have the swing replaced, but that would mean letting go of what little she had left of her mother.

She ran her hand down the arm of the swing, the wood rough beneath her fingertips, paint flakes cutting into her palm as she searched the sky for Orion.

You've deserted me too, she thought.

Lifting her bare feet off the ground, she shifted back and let the breeze rock her gently as she strained to recall the sound of her mother's voice...

Nothing.

But the words her mother had spoken so many times remained fresh in her mind.

"Life," her mother had said, as Anna's tiny feet dangled from the porch swing, "is all about love."

Anna laughed to herself now as she considered how sentimental her mother had been in this respect.

"Life is love. Family is love. *You,* my sweet girl, are love."

Yeah right Mom, Anna thought. *If you could see me now.*

Anna had spent the last ten years observing, day in and day out, as couples in therapy tore each other down, cut each other off and pretty much did everything they could to make life hell for each other. *How am I supposed to love that, Mom?*

But the answer forced its way into her mind, and she sighed. "I know, Mom," she whispered. "I remember." She closed her eyes and surrendered to the memory.

May, 1977

Anna's mother turned to her and smiled. "Close your eyes, Sweetie," she said.

Anna looked up at her mother, then closed her eyes.

"Now," she said, "I want you to imagine you're standing in a room with no windows and no lights." She paused, allowing her daughter time to construct the image in her mind. "What do you see?"

"Darkness?" Anna asked.

"Yes," her mother said. "Now, imagine you're holding a lantern."

Anna pictured the silver lantern her father carried along the trails when they took nighttime walks at the cabin.

"Now light it."

Anna lit the lantern in her mind.

"What do you see now?" her mother asked.

"Light," Anna whispered.

"Exactly," her mother said. "That light represents love. If you walk into that dark room without it, nothing changes. But when you bring in the light, the darkness doesn't stand a chance."

Anna opened her bright eyes and stared at her mother – the wisest woman alive. She wrapped her arms around her mother's waist and leaned into her, feeling a soft kiss on the top of her head.

"There's more," her mother said. She asked Anna to hold up her right hand.

Anna sat up tall and raised her hand.

"I want you to make me a promise," her mother said.

Anna nodded.

"Promise me, Anna, that no matter what happens in your life, you will always put love first. Love for yourself, for others and someday for your own family."

"I promise," Anna said, her heart fluttering at the thought of one day becoming a mother herself.

"You first," her mother said, lifting Anna's chin and gazing into her blue eyes. "Because you have to love yourself first if you hope to share love."

Anna promised - the same way she recited the Pledge of Allegiance every day at school. She felt like a woman inducted into a sacred sisterhood, honored to be entrusted with her mother's divine secret to happiness. She pledged allegiance to her mother's example, and at ten years old, Anna had every intention of making her mother proud.

May 28, 2002

"Fairytale bullshit," Anna muttered. "Sorry Mom."

She rubbed the sore spot on her forehead again, then let her hand fall limp onto the wood slats. "I'm nothing like you."

She lowered her feet to the floorboards and pushed off, feeling her hair, still damp with sweat, rise and fall with the motion of the porch swing. She lifted her feet back onto the swing, pulled her legs close to her body and sighed, accepting the silence. She ran her fingers over the hole in the knee of her jeans, tugging out a few frayed ends and releasing them, watching them drift to the floorboards.

"Anna."

Her head jerked up. A chill raced up her spine, and she felt the blood drain from her cheeks. She sucked in a breath and scanned the perimeter of the yard. She listened for the voice she had heard… or had she?

No, she told herself. *You're imagining things.* She released her breath as the swing slowed to a stop. She rolled her shoulders to shake off the eerie feeling and reached for her tea. Raising it to her lips, she allowed her gaze to rest on her mother's lilac bush, standing frail but fighting for life. Anna marveled that the lilac was still alive in spite of her neglect. She considered the many similarities between herself and the lilac bush, and the main difference – one of them *wanted* to live. The lack of buds this far into spring meant that, again this year, the lilac would remain flowerless; it hadn't bloomed in twenty-five years, but it had never given up.

Anna closed her eyes and imagined the sweet perfume that would permeate their home as her mother ran from room to room, throwing the windows open wide each morning. She longed to inhale the intoxicating scent again. *Maybe next year.*

She opened her eyes and surveyed the battered yard. Everything had shone a blinding green when her father was alive to tend it. He would come home from work early once a week and spend the rest of the afternoon mowing and weeding and seeding and watering. Then he would step inside smelling of dirt and sweat and freshly cut grass, and Anna's mother would place her hand firmly on his chest and push him back out the door to hose him off. He would race over and seize Anna, lifting her tiny body up in front of his own – a human shield. Anna would squeal when the icy water doused her, and her mother would redirect the spray toward her father's face. In the end, her father would be clean, Anna would be giddy, and they both would be soaked. It had become a tradition.

But as the years passed without him, the grass had become a crusty blanket around the lilac bush, encroaching on the driveway, smothering the brick walkway that led up to the front porch. Patches of parched earth claimed more and more of the yard each year. Anna understood. She too had once glowed. She too had once reflected all the love and attention she had received, yet now she felt the merciless cold and neglect drying her out, smothering her, claiming more and more of her each year.

The wooden slats moaned as she let her bare feet fall and slid her stiff body off the porch swing. The chill pricked her spine again, and she glanced around the yard one last time before carrying her teacup inside.

Maybe it's time for me to see a psychologist myself, she thought, shaking off the chill. She paused in the doorway. "Come and get me," she said. "I dare you." *At least I wouldn't have to go to work today.*

THREE

Sandy woke at 4:00 a.m. out of instinct. She slipped from her bed without a sound, like a leaf falling silently to the ground in autumn. *Please don't wake up*, she thought as she carefully pulled the covers up and smoothed them, nice and straight on her side of the bed, just the way he liked them. She tiptoed to the bathroom and showered by the faint blue of the nightlight. She didn't dare turn on the overhead light.

After a three minute shower, she toweled off and stood in front of the mirror. The blue glow from the nightlight accentuated the shadows under her eyes. She parted her hair down the middle and combed it straight. Leaning toward her reflection, she spotted a grey hair and plucked it from her scalp. Mitch detested grey hair, and lately Sandy worried that if she continued to pull them, she would be bald within a few months. But Mitch would never allow the luxury of a salon visit to have it colored, and her grocery budget was tight already. No, hair dye was out of the question.

She tugged the remaining hair back tight and tied it off in a ponytail. Averting her eyes from the bruises on her ribcage, she slipped into her turtleneck and denim jumper.

A silent ghost, she padded down the hall, peeking into the bedroom her two boys shared, then stopped to check on her daughters. Little Libby smiled in her sleep. *So peaceful,* Sandy thought, hesitating a moment before turning away. She closed the girls' bedroom door softly. *I wish every moment of their lives could be that peaceful.*

Sandy did all she could to give her children a childhood like the one she had enjoyed. She made their favorite meals, picked dandelions with them at the park, cut their sandwiches into hearts – all the things her own mother had done for her. But the one thing she couldn't do was give them a father like hers.

With a sigh, she entered the kitchen to prepare her husband's breakfast. Her four precious children would sleep another two hours, but Sandy had only fifteen minutes before Mitch would appear in the doorway expecting to be served. She had to work quickly, but quietly – oatmeal, fried eggs sunny-side-up with the yolks slightly runny, bacon warmed but the fat still rubbery, just the way he liked it. She took two oranges from the bag to juice for him and noticed with a slight panic that only two remained. She had already exhausted her meager grocery allowance. *Maybe I could ask mom,* she thought, but then there would be questions Sandy was not prepared to answer. *No,* she thought, *I'll have to find another way.*

The eggs sizzled, and she hurried back to the stove to tend to them.

Mitch entered the kitchen as she scooped the eggs from the frying pan. Her back was to the doorway, but her heart jumped and her hands began to shake at the sound of his footsteps on the linoleum. *Darn it!* She was late.

He said nothing, but the loud scraping of his chair sliding out from the kitchen table told Sandy she was in trouble. His chair was to be pulled out for him before he arrived, his napkin and silverware neatly arranged beside his plate of warm food. She heard the wooden chair creak under his weight, and turned to place his plate on the table, reminding herself not to raise her eyes to his. She studied the arrangement of food, silverware, napkin... *the juice! Darn it!* She stumbled toward the counter on wobbly legs, grabbed the first of the two oranges and sliced it in half, then grabbed the second one.

The impact lit a fire at the small of her back; the orange fell from her hand and rolled out of sight. She held her breath. The plate lay in pieces on the linoleum at her heels, its edge having left an instant bruise on her spine.

"Stupid bitch," Mitch mumbled as he stomped over to the mudroom and threw on his peaked cap. Sandy kept her eyes trained on the yellow Formica countertop. "Guess I'll have to go to Marcy's Diner to get a decent meal. Again." He slammed the door as he left.

Sucking in the sob that clawed at her throat, Sandy allowed herself to breathe again. She quietly bent over to pick up the pieces, scooping up the food and the tears, and dumped it all in the trash.

~

Anna pounded the steering wheel. "Get off the road, you moron!" Her hair whipped her cheeks as her car slammed to a stop. It never failed - every time she was running late, some idiotic college student would cut her off, darting out in front of her, then drive at a snail's pace. By the time Anna pulled into her parking space at the clinic, she was fighting back tears. *God I don't want to be here.*

Her moping patients grated on her nerves; the tone of their voices scraped her eardrums raw. Sometimes she would poke her fingers in her ears then pull them out to examine them, just to make sure she wasn't bleeding out through her ear canals. *Would that really be so bad,* she thought.

Day after day she sat in her leather armchair and focused on the "tick tock, tick tock" of her grandfather clock, as her patients droned on and on, and she would think to herself, *two dollars, four dollars, six dollars...* as each minute passed. Anna entered her office like a robot every morning, steeling herself to endure the monotony and collect the $120 hourly fee.

This morning consisted of an alcoholic who refused to admit his disease, even while his wife and daughter were slipping from his life, a man who just liked to hear himself talk, and a couple going through a divorce. Anna would have given her right arm to have had a man love her, even if the love had died – to have the reassurance that as a woman she was, at some point at least, reasonably loveable.

Mom was crying and dad had his head turned toward the window. Junior and his sister played Go Fish in the corner of the room, oblivious to the animosity between their parents. Anna didn't doubt that this couple's pain was real. *Sometimes it really is better for an unhappy couple to part ways,* she thought. But still, this morning all she could do was stare at the couple and wonder what it felt like to have been loved, at least once. She sighed.

"I think it would be best if the children stayed with me in the home they've always known. Don't you agree, Dr. Cunningham?"

Maybe I'm not the best therapist for this couple, Anna thought. She yearned to tell these people that if they wanted out of the marriage, they were going to have to exhaust every option before she would give them the ok. *Not that they need my permission,* she thought. No, therapy for this couple was not a way to save the marriage, but merely a way for them to ease their guilt, to tell themselves and the world that they had tried - "We even saw a psychologist. We just couldn't make it work."

"Time's up for today," Anna said, a cassette tape worn out from repeating those same words over and over every day for ten years. The bewildered couple glanced at one another, their argument about custody still hanging in the air. They stood and handed Anna a check that cleared their conscience, and she scheduled them for the same time next week.

After ushering them out, Anna closed her door and collapsed into her armchair. She had passed countless hours in this chair contemplating her life, and this hour was no different. Would she ever have the chance to fail at marriage? What was it about her that made her so impossible to love? And, more importantly, why would anyone pay good móney to talk to her, of all people, about their marriage? She couldn't possibly be objective.

A knock at the door made her stomach lurch, and she suddenly regretted the bagel she had scarfed down on her way in. She knew who it was – no need to ask.

"Hello," a raspy voice called, scarred and charred from decades of chain-smoking. Dr. Ronald Patterson was the managing partner of the practice, and he never let anyone forget that crucial fact. Twenty years Anna's elder, he always spoke to her as if it were his lot in life to mold her into someone completely different than who she was. In spite of all the psychologists at the clinic being on a first-name basis, Ron Patterson insisted that everyone in the practice call him "Dr. Patterson" - his way of reminding them of his clout, Anna supposed.

"Hello," he called again.

She could remain silent, pretending not to hear, but Dr. Patterson would barge right on in anyway. "Come in," she said. She reached for a patient file and began making notes to avoid having to look at his bobbing head as he spoke in his sandpaper voice, his slimy eyes suffocating under pillows of grey skin.

"Don't you have any patients scheduled?" he asked, shoving her door open. Dr. Patterson loved to imply that Anna's patient load was completely insufficient to merit her position at his practice. Anna glanced up as he scanned every inch of her body except her eyes. She cringed.

"Not during my lunch hour," she muttered through clenched teeth. He knew that Anna took lunch at the same time every day – she never strayed from her schedule. Nevertheless, he seemed intent on taking advantage of every opportunity to imply that she could be working more *efficiently*, as he liked to say.

"Alright then," he said, looking her over once more before backing out of her office and closing the door.

Anna released the pen she was strangling and let it drop onto her desk.

Dr. Patterson had a way of saying relatively benign words while conveying a completely malignant message. He had asked her out a few times when she first joined the practice which, in addition to bordering on sexual harassment, was also a revolting thought. She had tried to be polite when she turned him down, and after a while he stopped asking. She knew he had never forgiven her though, and he got his revenge at every possible opportunity.

A few weeks after his last overture, for instance, Dr. Patterson had eyed Anna from head to toe and arrogantly proclaimed that her appearance was "too young and unprofessional, a bit like a floozy," and that "no one would ever respect someone who looks like that." Anna knew it was just sour grapes, and she honestly didn't give a damn what he thought of her appearance. It didn't take a psychologist to see through Dr. Patterson.

Shaking off the shivers the man's stares always left on her skin, Anna whispered a quick "thank you" that he hadn't pressed further. She saw no need to explain that she had no more patients scheduled for the day. She had made it a point to take the afternoon off to visit her parents' gravesites, as she did every May 28th. *"How inefficient,"* he would have said. Dr. Patterson would never have understood. He was incapable of understanding, which was the thing that perplexed Anna most about him. Cold, heartless and more than a little creepy, how had that man succeeded in creating and maintaining a successful practice? Why would anyone want to return to him after the initial visit?

She waited until she heard him close his office door before collecting her things and sneaking through the waiting room and out the front entrance.

The cemetery lay across the street from her office, perhaps a subconscious reason she had wanted to join this practice. Maybe she had secretly hoped that her parents might overhear the work she was doing and celebrate her successes with her. But the proximity of their gravesites had merely served as a reminder of how few successes she had actually achieved in her work. *And in my life,* she thought, her eyes beginning to burn as she stepped onto the sidewalk.

~

Ron Patterson pulled his ashtray from the top drawer and set it on his desk. He leaned back in his chair, stretched his arms wide, then folded his fingers behind his head. A copy of the *Bloomfield Times* lay open beneath a bowl of peanuts in front of him. Leaning forward, he lit a cigarette and took a long, slow drag as he scanned the article detailing the most recent news on the attacker:

"Serial Rapist Remains At Large – Bloomfield Police are following up on hundreds of leads received from the public and asking that anyone with information come forward, even if the information seems insignificant."

"Imbeciles," Ron muttered. "The Bloomfield Police couldn't catch a stray cat, let alone an experienced criminal." Ron Patterson understood the mind of a criminal. He had spent ten years working as a correctional psychologist at the state prison. At first it had unnerved him when he found himself aroused by the stories of the criminals he counseled, but after a while, he convinced himself that he just had a knack for empathy. The tales of armed robberies and assaults entertained him, but the wife-beaters and rapists were his favorite. He felt himself tingling when his patients would recount their acts, and he would ask them to retell them over and over, convincing them that reliving their crimes would aid in their rehabilitation. But when the administration caught wind of his methods, they discretely offered him an early retirement package – at the age of thirty-eight. So he had opened a private practice. The patients weren't nearly as interesting, but it paid the bills.

He heard Anna lock up her office and close the front door. *Where the hell is she going,* he thought. Anna never left her office at lunchtime, except to heat up her chicken noodle soup in the break room.

He took one last drag of his cigarette then crushed it in the ashtray. Standing slowly, he pulled his master key from the pocket of his blazer, and crept out into the empty waiting room. He glanced around to make sure all the office doors were closed, then slid the key into Anna's lock and slipped into her office. After locking the door behind himself, he took a seat at her desk and flipped through the pages of her Day Timer, checking over all her appointments, searching for a clue to where she had gone. When he saw that she had nothing written in for the rest of the day, he felt heat creep up his neck. *Where the hell did she go?*

He turned the pages to the coming weekend to confirm that she had nothing planned for Friday or Saturday night. The pages were blank. That satisfied him. He couldn't stand the thought of her with another man. She had rejected him, and she would soon realize her mistake, but there was no way Ron Patterson would tolerate Anna dating. He would keep her on call every weekend, if that's what it took.

Careful to leave everything just as he had found it, he closed her Day Timer and went back to his office. He paced the spacious room before sitting down at his desk.

Who the hell does she think she is, he thought. *That little tramp thinks she's better than me, and now I've got to track her ass down.* He checked his schedule – three more appointments. He groaned. *It'll have to wait.* He placed the ashtray back in the drawer. *But I'll find her, and when I get my hands on her and the jerk she's with...*

Leaning back in his chair, he closed his eyes and pictured Anna wrapping her sensuous legs around some fool in a lunchtime tryst...

His eyelids flew open.

No. That just won't do. He popped a peanut into his mouth and crushed it between his teeth, shell and all.

~

Anna walked slowly, deliberately placing one foot in front of the other, studying her leather pumps as she crossed the street, silently begging someone to plow her over in their SUV... No such luck. Instead, she heard horns and cursing as she continued onto the grounds between the weathered stone pillars that, instead of welcoming her, created a somber air of eternal cold. She rubbed her arms for warmth and stepped off the paved path onto the grass. The heels of her leather pumps sank into the soil; she slipped them off and tucked them under her arm.

The earth felt moist beneath her feet. She paused and surveyed the rolling acreage. Vases of vibrant flowers adorned most of the gravesites, but Anna never brought flowers on her annual visits. *What's the point,* she thought. *As if they can smell them?*

She lifted her face to the sky as she made her way to the weeping willow that guarded her parents' sacred resting place.

The weeds had grown high around both her parents' headstones, even though every other gravesite was meticulously manicured. Anna made a mental note to call the caretaker.

She dropped her pumps, kneeled and began ripping at the weeds. *How is it that nature always seems so fertile wherever my mother is,* she thought. Anna's mother had always seemed to enjoy weeding her flower beds. She never got annoyed when a new weed popped up. She would simply smile, greet it calmly and say "prepare to die." Then she would pluck it and add it to her compost.

"Prepare to die," Anna mumbled, digging at the roots with her fingers; she couldn't muster the smile.

After she had cleared the weeds, she slipped her hand into her pocket and pulled out a tattered sheet of loose-leaf paper, then lowered herself onto the cool earth. She inspected the folded sheet as she turned it over in her hands, and the chill raced up her spine again. Her breath caught in her throat. She cautiously raised her gaze, her heart pounding through her ribcage.

A young girl was leaning against the wrought-iron fence at the edge of the cemetery, watching her. When the girl saw Anna look up at her, she smiled and waved, then skipped off.

Just a harmless little girl, Anna thought, releasing her breath. *You really need to get a grip.*

She shook her head and looked back down at the folded sheet of paper in her hands. After carefully unfolding it, she set it in the grass in front of her and studied the penmanship, each letter perfectly formed cursive bubbles slanting slightly to the right.

She took a deep breath and closed her eyes.

A soft hand caressed her shoulder, and the minister's voice echoed in her mind –

To everything there is a season

And a time to every purpose under heaven:

A time to be born, and a time to die;

A time to plant, and a time to pluck up what is planted;

A time to kill, and a time to heal;

A time to break down, and a time to build up;

A time to weep, and a time to laugh;

A time to mourn, and a time to dance.

– Ecclesiastes 3:1-4

"You ok, sweetheart?" Cathy Malone whispered, squeezing Anna's tiny shoulder gently.

Anna didn't respond.

Her mother's best friend tightened her grip on her shoulder as the service drew to a close. Then everything went silent.

"I have something I want to share," Anna whispered, brushing Cathy's hand away.

Everyone watched as the timid ten-year-old approached the caskets, unfolded a piece of paper, and began to read the words she had written for the occasion – the words of a heartbroken child:

"Morning sun, take me with you on your flight.

Let me drift across the sky with you all day.

Let me turn yellow, orange, then red with you at dusk,

And when you go, let me fly away with you.

Don't leave me here to spend the night alone."

The paper had become brittle over the years, and a corner cracked off as Anna refolded it. Most of the words had faded, and it seemed to disintegrate a little more each year. Though she had memorized the poem long ago, she still read straight from the sheet every time.

"I miss you," she whispered, then stood and walked barefoot and numb through the gate, across the street and to her car.

FOUR

Anna turned the key in the deadbolt then paused and turned toward the porch swing. Every once in a while she would see it move, swaying back and forth ever so slightly despite the absence of a breeze. When this happened, she would allow herself to believe that her mother was with her.

She stood frozen, staring, waiting...

The swing hung motionless.

Anna sighed. She opened the door and entered the empty foyer, void of the jackets and sweaters that had once hung layer upon layer from the iron pegs. Glancing over at the walnut clock on the fireplace mantle, she suddenly wished she had scheduled more patients for the afternoon. She rubbed her cold arms. *What am I supposed to do now,* she thought.

Even though the day had warmed significantly, the walls of Anna's home seemed to embrace cold, holding it tight within its bones. She wandered into the kitchen and opened the refrigerator – nothing but half a bagel, condiments, and milk two weeks past its sell-by date. She stepped into the laundry room and transferred a load from the washer to the dryer, pressed the start button, and leaned her back against the machine to feel a little heat. Sliding down onto the cool tile floor, she dropped her head into her hands. "I miss you guys," she whispered, feeling the tears prick the backs of her eyes.

"Walk."

Anna's head sprang up. "Mom?"

"Walk."

One simple word in her mother's voice. She wanted more. She *needed* more.

"Walk."

This time it was unmistakable. The tears came now, and Anna wrapped her arms around herself, imagining her mother's arms holding her tight. She waited for the word to come again, hoping to memorize the sound of her mother's voice to hold onto forever...

Silence.

She waited...

Nothing.

Anna sighed and wiped the tears from her cheeks. "Get a grip," she said. "First you think someone's watching you, and now you're hearing voices." But still, she waited...

Nothing.

"You're officially schizophrenic," she said.

She shook her head and stood, walked to the foyer and slid into her pumps.

As she stepped out onto the porch, she glanced over at the porch swing, her heart a butterfly in her chest, finding a small sense of delight in doing as her mother had told her.

Anna's was a quaint neighborhood of gingerbread Victorian houses, an Easter basket of pristine debutantes posing elegantly atop lush green lawns. The historical homes had all been fully restored – life-sized dollhouses with white trim and pastel wood siding. Each house boasted twin oak trees standing sentinel on either side of brick walkways, tire swings hanging from the branches of many. Those oak trees had witnessed births and deaths; a few might have even known life before electricity. *I can only imagine what stories those trees could tell*, Anna thought, as she moved slowly down her own smothered brick walkway toward the sidewalk. Anna's neglected home was an eyesore - the rotten egg in the basket, her two trees leafless, her own tire swing brittle and faded – an ecosystem of stagnant water, moss and mosquito larvae. Anna was grateful that none of the neighbors ever approached her about the condition of her home, grateful that none of the neighbors approached her at all.

She stepped onto the sidewalk, right foot, left foot, right foot... repeating her mother's command in her head, *"Walk."* She kept her eyes to the concrete, following the cracks like miniature canyons, wondering if she stepped into one, would she plummet to the center of the Earth? *That would be nice,* she thought, smiling to herself as she closed her eyes and imagined the weightless sensation, free-falling toward the sweltering core. She felt her body ignite as the iron ball grew closer and closer...

And then she tripped.

"Dammit."

She opened her eyes and kicked at the bump in the sidewalk. That bump was etched in her memory from afternoon walks with her mother as a young child, napping in the red Radio Flyer wagon. Every time her mother had pulled the wagon over that bump, Anna's hazy head would thump against the side of the wagon. The bump grew every year, the root of an invincible oak tree fracturing the concrete, winning the battle of man versus nature. Anna kicked the bump once more as payback before continuing on.

"Good day," a nameless neighbor called.

"Hi," Anna mumbled without looking up. Anna hated walks. When she walked, she wanted to be left alone with her thoughts. She didn't want to chat with people who had families over for cookouts, people who posted banners above their front doors when babies were born, people who had shiny tire swings hanging from their oak trees. No, walking was not Anna's thing. But she had heard her mother's instructions and she would not disobey. She marched on past the neighbor, not caring to know his name, but feeling a little guilty that he had probably known hers all her life.

Her dream the night before pulled her toward the creek at the end of the street, and she shook her head to release the image of the red flashing lights. *Not enough water in here to do any real damage*, she thought, as she dipped the heel of her leather pump into the water. She pulled her foot back and bent down to pick up a few stones. Running her fingers over the stones, she thought of the sunset hikes, walking hand-in-hand with her father along the trail to the lake by the cabin.

"It's all about choosing the right stone," her father would say as he sifted through and picked out the best ones for her. He would count how many times her stones would skip before sinking, high-fiving her when she broke her own personal record. Then he would give it a try – His stones always sank on contact, and Anna would hold her head up a little higher knowing she could do something better than a grown-up. Of course, looking back on it now, Anna realized that her father's stones had skipped seven or eight times when he was teaching her, but once she had mastered the skill, he had suddenly lost his ability. That was how he was though, always building her up in her own eyes.

A smile crossed her face in spite of her mood. Discarding the misfits in her hand, she located just the right stone – flat and smooth with rounded edges, just like her father had taught her. She gave it a toss.

It sank.

"Must have been a flawed stone. Try again," her father would say, then he would sing to distract her from any possibility of self-doubt. *"Dear face that holds so sweet a smile for me…"*

Anna closed her eyes to allow her father's voice to blossom in her mind. *"Were you not mine, how dark this world would be…"* His deep tone swirled inside her and she felt her shoulders relax. She leaned her head back and allowed the sun to warm her face. *"I know no light above that could replace…"* His song wove its way into her heart, filling her… *"love's radiant sunshine on your face…"* She began to sing along with him in her mind, her own soft voice amplifying, the two melodies twisting and turning in a magical dance as the two became one. The lyrics softened her heart as they spun their way into the center of her soul, the beautiful harmony of her father's strong voice blending with the innocent voice of a child, and for a moment, Anna didn't feel so alone.

And then the chill returned.

That's not my voice! Her eyes sprang open. The bliss was broken. She turned downstream in the direction of the voice and felt the chill again. The young girl from the cemetery was on her knees at the edge of the creek, dipping something into the water, singing to herself.

Is this little girl following me?

Anna's curiosity forced her body into motion and she moved closer, humming the tune along with the girl as she approached.

The girl looked up at Anna and smiled, then focused back on the task at hand – catching tadpoles.

Anna sat down a few yards upstream and watched, recalling her father bringing her down to this same creek to catch tadpoles every spring. They would place their captives in a fish bowl and transport them home so they could observe as, little by little, the tadpoles grew legs and their tails began to vanish. Once their conversion was almost complete, Anna and her father would carry the little froglets back down to the creek and release them so they could rejoin their long lost friends.

Anna sat spellbound, watching the child carefully catch each tadpole in her net. She imagined approaching her and asking to borrow the net. They would splash each other and giggle; they would slosh through the muck, sending the tadpoles in the creek fleeing for shelter. They would sing songs, skip stones, and Anna would have a friend.

Get real, she told herself. Instead, she picked up a stick and poked it into the dirt, trying to dig up more memories of a life that had been filled with laughter and excitement and love.

The girl never looked up again, so Anna assumed she didn't mind the company. She wondered if the child lived in the neighborhood; judging by her brand-name shorts and high-end pink windbreaker, Anna could tell she had caring parents. *She's probably got a shiny tire swing too,* Anna thought.

Finally, when the sun dipped below the horizon, Anna stood and walked back home, leaving the girl by the creek.

She traded her soiled silk pantsuit for sweatpants and a T-shirt, then turned off the lamp beside her bed. With a sliver of jealousy, she imagined the little girl snuggled up in bed, her loving parents tucking her in at this very moment.

~

Satisfied when he saw Anna's bedroom window darken, Ron Patterson tossed his cigarette butt out the window and drove home. He had forgotten that today was the anniversary of her parents' death, which had explained the vacancy in her Day Timer. Once he realized what day it was, he had known exactly where to find her. But she had spent so much time sitting by those headstones that Ron had run out of smokes.

After she left the cemetery, she had driven home, then walked down to the creek where she sat in the dirt for hours. Lucky for Ron though, because it had given him time to sneak away to buy another pack, happy to find her in the same spot when he returned. As sexy as she was, the woman had absolutely no life, and that was exactly the way Ron liked it.

He strolled around the perimeter of his bedroom studying the newspaper articles and photographs taped to the wall. "Anna Cunningham inducted into Psi Chi." "Professor Raymond Cunningham's daughter awarded Psy.D, Graduates Summa Cum Laude." Ron had found those two on microfiche at the library. He uploaded today's photos to his computer and printed out his favorite one - a picture of Anna on the floor with her back to the dryer, crying. He had risked the neighbors seeing him to get this shot, but it had been worth it. He enjoyed seeing her cry. *Serves her right,* he thought as he taped the photo to the headboard beside the picture of his mother. The resemblance between the two women always made his heart beat a little faster.

He lay down on top of his sheets and stared up at the ceiling. The questions knocked, and he allowed the door in his mind to inch open… *How could you, Mother?*

"No," he snapped, slamming the door on the memories. He leaned over and turned out the light beside his bed. "Sweet dreams, bitch."

FIVE

December, 1984

"Mom."

Cathy Malone rolled over and tried to focus her groggy eyes on her teenage daughter cowering beside her bed. "What is it, honey?"

"Mom," Sandy whispered. "Can we talk?"

Cathy absorbed the desperation in her daughter's eyes. *This is serious,* she thought and pushed herself upright. She grabbed her robe from the chair beside the bed and followed Sandy into the hallway.

"I didn't want to wake Daddy," Sandy said, leaning into the wall for support. "I'm sorry to bother you."

Cathy sighed and reached for her daughter's face, touching her cheek tenderly with the back of her fingers. After months of closed doors, Cathy felt relief that her daughter was finally confiding in her again. "Sandy, you are never a bother," she whispered.

Sandy pulled away from her mother's touch. *Not until now,* she thought. "Mom," she said, pausing for a moment to calm herself. "I need to tell you something."

Cathy took her hand and guided her down the stairs to the couch in the living room. She lowered herself next to her daughter, holding her hand as she waited for her to continue. She knew this had something to do with that Mitch kid. Sandy had been so wrapped up in him lately that she rarely came home before midnight. *Does that kid know that Sandy's father is a police officer,* she thought. Of course he did, and Cathy suspected that was part of the allure - a bad boy and a cop's daughter.

"Mom," Sandy's eyes searched her mother's. *Oh Mom, please don't hate me.* "Mom, I'm pregnant."

Cathy felt her heart launch out of her chest. She searched for words, but none came. Her mind raced, a slide show of images – Sandy packing up her Taurus and heading off to college, Sandy in her cap and gown at her graduate school commencement, Sandy walking down the aisle in a flowing white wedding dress – the visions slid through her head then faded, one by one. She stared into Sandy's terrified eyes. She would not let her daughter down. "I..." *Come on. You can do this.* "I... Sandy... honey..." The tears betrayed her. She tried to wipe them away, but they wouldn't stop. "Oh honey," Cathy said, and pulled her daughter into her arms.

May, 2002

Sandy held the key between her lips as she stretched out on her belly to reach the metal box under Craig's bed. She had tucked it back against the wall, behind the dirty socks and piles of dusty comic books, knowing that her son wouldn't venture that far under his bed, and certain that Mitch would never enter the boys' room. She grasped the box between her hands and pulled it to her. After brushing the dust bunnies off the bottom, she inserted the key in the lock and opened the lid. She pulled out the stack of bills and counted them slowly, one by one – *four hundred twenty-two dollars.* Then she sorted the coins into neat piles and added those to her total. *Seven dollars and sixteen cents.* She sighed. *Not nearly enough.* She tucked the money back inside the box and slid it under the bed, scattering the socks around it.

She was taking a huge risk sneaking a few dollars here and there from Mitch's wallet while he slept. *Good Lord, if he caught me.* Sandy shuddered at the thought. It had taken her over eight months to come up with a mere four hundred twenty nine dollars and sixteen cents, and she wasn't sure how much longer she could wait, how much longer she could endure his brutal pounding in bed, how much longer until he snapped.

She stood and tucked in the corners of Craig's sheets. *My sweet boy rips the bed apart when the nightmares come,* she thought. With a sick feeling in her gut, she smoothed the threadbare bedspread then straightened the sheets on Todd's bed. After tidying up the girls' room, she tackled the hall bathroom. She screwed the lid on the toothpaste and lowered the toilet seat, scrubbed the bathtub and sink, then carried the soiled towels to the washing machine. The dial had broken off months ago, but Sandy knew better than to complain to Mitch about it. The washer had been his mother's – Mitch's only inheritance after his mother overdosed. He had told Sandy that she should be grateful to have a washing machine at all.

Sandy pulled the dripping clothes from the washer and dropped them into the plastic laundry basket before putting the towels in to wash. Luckily the sun was out, so she would be able to get two loads on the line today.

"What do you need a dryer for?" Mitch had asked her, the one and only time she mentioned it. Her hands had been chapped and scabbed from hanging laundry all winter, and she had asked him about saving up for a dryer.

"Just something modest," she had said.

"Do you think I'm made of money?" Mitch had snapped. Sandy didn't respond; she kept her thoughts to herself.

She set the basket in the grass and pulled out a pink pajama top. *They're growing so fast,* she thought. It seemed like just days ago she was swaddling Libby in her baby blanket; now her little girl was asking to have her ears pierced. Mitch, of course, had made his objection clear last night, and Libby had gone to bed in tears. *Sweet child,* Sandy thought as she draped her daughter's shirt over the line and secured it with two wooden clothespins. She pulled Craig's faded T shirt from the basket and pressed it to her chest. Sandy worried about her oldest son most. He had shown no interest in driver's ed, but Mitch would never let him use the car anyway. Besides, Craig rarely left his room, so Sandy supposed her son had no need for a driver's license. *My poor boy,* she thought, *robbed of a normal childhood.* Sandy blamed herself for not taking control of the situation years ago. *Why has it taken me this long?*

She had considered leaving Mitch a number of times, but with no job skills and no money, she saw no other choice but to stay and try to make their home as happy as possible for the children. The price, however, was becoming too high. She lifted Craig's shirt to the clothesline and pinned it on.

After hanging her husband's socks, Sandy hurried back to the laundry room to check the pockets of his police trousers. Sometimes she got lucky and found some loose change. Today she found a gum wrapper and a dime. *Every little bit helps,* she thought, and slid the coin into the pocket of her jumper.

~

As Chief of Police, Kurt Malone knew he could have Mitch's badge for what he was doing to Sandy, if only he could prove it. Kurt lived in a constant state of internal struggle. Sandy was his daughter, and Kurt felt like less of a man for not doing more to protect her. But she was an adult, and Mitch was an outstanding officer in spite of his personal issues, so Kurt knew he had to prove his suspicions beyond a doubt. It didn't help that he couldn't get Sandy to talk about it, though he had never had the courage to come right out and confront her. She made excuses for the way she held her ribs when she got up from the table to make him a cup of coffee, or the way she winced whenever he hugged her during his visits. But because of the lack of evidence, Kurt had no choice but to try to keep things professional with his son-in-law at work.

He had felt the stares and the way certain officers would turn away when he entered the station, the conversations that fell silent when he walked into the break room. He knew what everyone thought; he thought the same thing. But worst of all were the times he was forced to deal with the man face to face.

"Rough night last night, hey Chief?" Mitch said, as Kurt entered the station.

"Yeah, the stakeout was a bust," Kurt mumbled, hoping if he kept walking, he could avoid further conversation with his son-in-law.

"We'll get him," Mitch said, marching over and nudging Kurt in the ribs with his elbow. "No one should victimize women like that."

Kurt shuddered at the hypocrisy of Mitch's words. Turning his back, he walked away from the uncomfortable conversation into the solitude of his office and closed the door. He dropped into his chair and placed his elbows on his desk, resting his forehead on his fingertips. He had wasted an entire night waiting outside an apartment building where a witness had claimed to see a man loitering late at night on multiple occasions. The dates and times coincided with a couple of the attacks, but last night no one had entered or left the building after 10:30, and Kurt was no closer to solving this case. Now all he wanted to do was sleep, but he was on duty and he had to find a way to make it through the day. He picked up the phone and dialed Jane's extension. "Do you have a second to bring me a cup of coffee?"

"Coming right up," Jane said.

She's always so willing to help, Kurt thought. He thanked her and replaced the receiver. He rubbed his neck and turned toward the photos of the victims tacked to his wall.

At sixty five, Kurt had begun to feel the effects of his job in his sore back, his stiff neck. The energy and excitement he had felt as a young officer had died the night his best friends were killed. He should have been more alert for the driver that must have been swerving or showing some other sign of intoxication before slamming head-on into Raymond and Katherine's car. Many nights over the past twenty-five years Kurt lay awake, scouring his mind for images of the car – Had it passed him? Had he missed it? Could he have stopped it? The self-recrimination had become his constant companion.

After that night, Kurt was left counting down the years until retirement; his heart just wasn't in it. But somehow he had still managed to do the job well, eventually earning the position of Chief of Police. He had planned to retire at sixty-two, but that birthday had come and gone, and now here he was, forced to face the man who he suspected was hurting his daughter and trying in vain to catch a serial rapist, when he would rather be home with his wife.

Cathy was a patient woman, but Kurt knew she was growing weary of the sleepless nights too. Even though Bloomfield was typically a safe town, Cathy still worried about him. She lived with the fear that one day she, like so many other police wives, would become a widow. But she believed in the work he was doing, and she had told him many times that he was her hero, whether he caught the rapist or not.

"Kurt," Jane said, setting the coffee cup in front of him. Her face was pale; Kurt felt a knot form in his stomach. "I'm sorry Kurt, but we just received a call from Midwestern Memorial. A dorm supervisor brought a college student in to the E.R. They said she was attacked last night."

"Unbelievable," Kurt mumbled. He turned and studied the spot on the wall where this victim's photo would go. "While I was sitting on my thumbs outside that apartment building."

Jane hesitated, sensitive to the exhaustion evident on Kurt's face. "Kurt?" she said softly. "Do you want to meet with her, or should I send Officer Watson?"

"I'll go," Kurt said, rising to his feet. There was no way in hell he would allow Mitch Watson to collect a statement from a woman who had suffered abuse at the hands of a man.

~

Cathy knocked gently on the door with her free hand, balancing the coffee carrier in the other. When Sandy didn't answer, Cathy knocked harder. A few more minutes passed before her daughter tentatively drew the sidelight curtain to the side and peered out.

"Hi Mom," Sandy said, opening the door and taking the coffee from her mother's hand. "I have coffee here. You didn't have to spend money on it."

"You're welcome," Cathy said, and nudged Sandy playfully. Sandy winced, but her mother didn't notice. "So, what's new?"

Cathy followed her daughter to the kitchen. It had been over two weeks since Cathy had seen her, and she felt the chasm growing wider between them. Sandy had confided in her all her life, but now Cathy could sense there was something her daughter was hiding. The daily visits for recipes had stopped months ago, along with the frantic late night phone calls when one of the children had a fever. A wall had risen, and nothing Cathy said or did could bring it down. She remembered the same feeling when Sandy had first started dating Mitch. But her love for her daughter had never wavered, even when the rest of the town had whispered their judgment of Sandy for "getting herself pregnant" in high school.

"It takes two, you know," Cathy had snapped at the woman in the chair next to her at the salon. The woman's face had flushed beet red when she realized Cathy Malone was sitting next to her.

But Cathy had mostly ignored the comments, focusing instead on supporting her daughter and trying to bring joy into the situation as she rushed to plan the wedding she had always dreamed of planning – her baby girl's big day. She had hoped it would be a few years later, but Cathy had been determined to make the best of it.

Cathy studied her daughter's face, and Sandy shifted her eyes to the coffee cup in her hand. Cathy's heart sank. She had tried every angle she could think of, but there was no reaching her daughter now. She had spent many restless nights in bed, running through their conversations in her mind, but she couldn't put her finger on it. She knew Sandy was less than satisfied with her marriage, but she had four beautiful children, so it couldn't be all bad, could it? Cathy just wished Sandy would talk to her again the way she used to.

"Not much, Mom," Sandy finally said. "Just trying to keep up on the housework." She hoped her mother would take the hint and leave before she began to suspect anything. Sandy was ashamed. Her mother thought the world of her; there was no way she would let her know that she was a failure as a wife and mother. She couldn't let her down. She wouldn't.

"Sandy," Cathy said, "please tell me what's bothering you."

Sandy walked to the sink and began washing the dishes by hand. She couldn't look her mother in the eye when she lied. "Everything's fine, Mom. I'm just tired."

"Well that's what the coffee's for, honey," Cathy said, smiling to Sandy's back, hoping to lighten the mood.

"Thanks Mom," Sandy said.

Cathy watched her daughter scrubbing egg off a pan in the sink. She assessed her plaid jumper and turtleneck – such benign clothes for a girl who had possessed such a keen fashion sense as a teenager. Her heart ached for Sandy; Cathy knew her daughter had aspired to more than washing dishes and running the vacuum. Cathy, herself, had always felt fulfilled as a stay-at-home mom; raising a child and caring for their home had been her biggest dream. But Sandy was different. She had always enjoyed school, and it was generally assumed that she would go on to college and possibly further, until she started dating Mitch Watson her senior year.

Mitch's father had been sent to prison after the accident that claimed the lives of Cathy and Kurt's best friends, and Cathy had never met Mitch's mother; the woman hadn't even bothered to attend her son's wedding.

Mitch spent most of his teenage years hanging out behind the U Stop. Cathy had noticed him there a few times smoking cigarettes with a group of boys she didn't recognize. The first time she had seen her sweet, straight-A daughter with the group, she had been tempted to stop the car and pull her daughter inside by her ponytail. But Cathy knew better than to take a stand with a seventeen-year-old. She had decided if she pretended to like Mitch, Sandy would soon lose interest. Cathy had never forgiven herself for that decision. If only she would have intervened, perhaps she could have prevented the pregnancy. But then she thought of Craig and couldn't imagine life without her darling grandson.

"Mom, did you hear me?"

"I'm sorry honey," Cathy said, raising her eyes to meet her daughter's. "What did you say?"

Sandy turned away again and hung the dish towel over the edge of the sink. "I need to get the vacuuming done." She hoped this wasn't too obvious.

"Oh, of course honey," Cathy said. "I've taken up enough of your time. Please call if you need anything," she said, and let herself out the front door.

Something's wrong, Cathy thought as she backed out of the driveway. *She's growing more distant every time I see her.* Cathy felt as if her heart was sitting in the passenger seat beside her – vulnerable, defenseless. She knew she had to let Sandy live her own life, but she wished she would open up to her like she used to, and share what was bothering her. She felt a faint rush of nausea and took a sip of her coffee. It scalded her tongue. It hadn't had time to cool during her visit with Sandy.

SIX

The icy creek water caressed Anna's skin as it rose higher around her. It numbed her ears, her jaw, her mouth. The absence of feeling soothed her. She took one last breath, sucking red water through her nostrils. The water stung her eyes from behind and hurt like hell, but she knew the end was near. The pain would soon pass. "I'm coming Mom..."

Anna jolted upright. Her lungs instinctively gulped down oxygen.

She picked up her pillow and flung it across the room. "Dammit!" she shouted, and flopped back down onto her bed. She grabbed her hair with both hands and pulled it back hard from her face. "Dammit!"

After all the miserable nightmares over the past twenty-five years, this one had given her hope. It had felt so real; she had been so close – so close to joining her mother, so close to seeing her parents again, so close to love.

"Why?" she shouted. "Why the hell couldn't I have been in that car too?" She tugged hard at the two fistfuls of hair, but the pain at her scalp was nowhere near as intense as the pain in her heart. "Why did you take them and leave me here?" she shouted. "Why?"

Her legs were useless, her eyes nearly swollen shut. She lay on her back staring blankly at the ceiling until reality finally set in. "Dammit" she said, releasing her hair. She had appointments scheduled. She had to get up. She had no desire, none whatsoever, to listen to their crap today, or any day for that matter. Her bed was an umbilical cord tethering her to her dream, to her mother. She didn't want to get up and sever the connection, so she turned onto her side and stared at the red numbers on her alarm clock as the minutes passed by.

Finally, when the red 8:29 changed to 8:30 she scolded herself. "Get over it." She sat up and dropped her legs over the side of the bed and marched to her bathroom.

In the mirror, she saw blood-shot eyes rimmed in red from yet another night of crying in her sleep. "Just great," she said. She applied extra eyeliner in an attempt to mask the damage. There was no time for a shower, so she pulled her hair back in a loose ponytail and dressed. She knew Dr. Patterson would be waiting, watching, hoping to catch her screwing up.

She hurried out the front door.

"Are you in there?" Dr. Patterson called through her closed office door.

"Yes," Anna said. *He knows damn well that I'm in here,* she thought.

"Ok then," he grumbled.

Anna exhaled loudly when the seconds had passed confirming that Dr. Patterson would not bust in to her office this morning. She had neither the time nor the energy to deal with that slime ball. She grimaced as she chugged the bitter coffee she had picked up on her way in; she detested coffee, but she needed the extra jolt today.

After swallowing the thick grounds at the bottom, she threw the paper cup away, tightened her ponytail and checked her teeth in the small mirror she kept in her desk drawer. She rehearsed a smile that felt completely artificial, then let it drop. She didn't have to pretend with James, and for that reason, he was one of the few patients Anna could tolerate. "Good morning, James," she said as she opened her office door.

James looked up from the magazine he was pretending to read and huffed, "Nothing very goddamn good about it if you ask me." He paused, eyeing her suspiciously. "You look like hell."

"Thanks James," Anna said. She smiled then, and this smile felt sincere. *Good old James,* she thought. "Would you like to come in and chat for a while," she asked, knowing he would like nothing more.

"I suppose," he mumbled, groaning as he pushed himself up off the couch in the waiting room. "This damn couch is a piece of shit. Too damn hard for someone my age to get up from." He shuffled into Anna's office and lowered himself into a chair. He looked up at Anna. She saw a brief look of concern in his eyes, then he stiffened. "You get dragged through the damn sewer?"

Anna laughed. "No, James," she said. "I just had a rough night." She stopped at her desk to check herself in the mirror once more before taking her seat in her armchair. "You should've seen how I looked when I first got out of bed," she said. A smile flashed across his face before he reconfigured it back into the scowl he had worn in the waiting room.

James was a lonely man, and his stories sometimes confused Anna. Sadly, she was beginning to suspect dementia. He seemed to get mixed up when he spoke, often confusing his first wife with his current one, but Anna refused to call him out on it. She never questioned him. He seemed to find comfort in his stories; whether they were true or not wasn't all that important.

He had once explained to Anna that he lost his first wife at the age of fifty, then waved off Anna's sympathy. Anna had suggested that talking through his loss might prove therapeutic, but James wouldn't open up about it. Anna had gathered from bits and pieces of their conversations that his current marriage was less than fulfilling. His wife needed more assistance than he could give her, so she lived in a nursing home, and he visited her daily. He told Anna that he sat by her side all day, but Anna worried about how James coped with the lonely nights. Anna understood how it felt to fall asleep alone in an empty house, and she respected James for standing by his wife even though she was ailing. But by the darkening circles under his eyes, Anna could tell it was taking a toll on him.

In the two years she had been treating him, Anna had tried every approach she could think of, hoping to break through with him, but whenever she pushed even a little, James would dig his heels in deeper. Every time she tried to pull information out of him, he seemed to erect a wall around himself, placing Anna on the outside. He would always redirect the conversation to Anna's life and had tricked her on a number of occasions into telling him more than she should have about herself. But today she was prepared.

"We're not here to talk about me, James," she said. So he shifted the conversation back to his latest symptom.

What Anna had originally diagnosed as Obsessive Compulsive Disorder had worsened since she had explained to James what it was. He wore his diagnosis like a badge, and Anna had come to regret ever giving it a name. He had read all he could on the condition and seemed to create new compulsions unique to himself – Checking and rechecking had turned into compulsive hand washing, which had given way to excessive candy eating, then dishwashing, then tooth brushing. Today it appeared that James was exhibiting his latest take on OCD – compulsive cursing.

Anna listened as James cursed and ranted and cursed some more. He was a handsome man for eighty-two, and something about him made Anna want to hug him every time they met. The same fire burned in his smoky grey eyes when he was angry as when he was overjoyed, and his face showed remarkably few wrinkles in spite of his age. He had a thick head of white hair and wore tailored suits to every appointment. He liked Anna; she knew that. And even though she wasn't sure what she was helping him with, she would never give up on him. In her laziness and apathy, she had jumped to a diagnosis, and now she suspected this lonely man was simply creating a reason to see her every week.

After sixty minutes of "shits" and "damns" and "hells" Anna collected her $120 – six crisp $20 bills, and James left, still cursing, with a "date," as he called it, for the same time next week.

She finished up what notes she could make about the session then stood to usher in her next patient. The morning dragged on as Anna allowed the "tick tock, tick tock" to distract her from the grumbling and droning of her next two patients. *How many times can they tell the same stories before they decide to make different choices,* she thought.

When lunchtime finally arrived, Anna was brain dead and famished. She pulled her can of condensed chicken noodle soup from her briefcase and said a quick prayer that she wouldn't run into Dr. Patterson in the break room. *If only I could have a microwave in my office,* she thought.

She opened her office door, stepped into the waiting room and froze.

~

The nurse smiled as James entered Ruth's room. She closed the door quietly as she left. James pulled the plastic chair up beside his wife's bed and touched the hand that lay motionless on top of the floral duvet. He clasped her frail fingers in his shaky hand – a hand that had once possessed the strength of a titan. The hand that, decades earlier, had held the ring steadily as he spoke the words he had rehearsed a hundred times. "You are all there is for me in this world, Angel Eyes. Please marry me." *Does she remember those words,* he thought. *Does she remember all the happy years?* James would do it all over again if he could, but this time he would be a *real* husband.

More and more, Ruth passed her days sleeping. Her hand felt ice cold, like sweet tea in August, and James sensed a slight twitch as he gently stroked her delicate knuckles with his thumb. *Does she feel me,* he wondered, as his mind drifted back in time.

August afternoons in the backyard of their home on Cardinal Lane had been some of James' most cherished moments of married life. Ruth would make a pitcher of sweet tea, and they would sit on lawn chairs, swatting mosquitoes off their arms as they talked for hours until the sun had floated toward the horizon and tucked itself in for the night. Ruth would share her dreams for their daughter, and James would listen, captivated by her angelic eyes as she spoke about their child. Ruth had wrapped her entire existence around her family - a soft blanket, warming and protecting them, giving them strength. In Ruth's presence, James had found his fortitude as a man. When his father died, when he lost his job at the firm, when his sister was diagnosed with cancer, Ruth had held his hand. And when he was so sick with the flu that he couldn't hold his head up, Ruth had held it up for him. As a result, when Ruth's mother died, James had felt the strength and compassion to hold his wife while she cried. Yes, she had made him a stronger man, strong enough to hold her when her heart was in pieces... *but not strong enough,* he thought.

Groaning inwardly, James made himself as comfortable as possible on the sterile plastic chair he inhabited on his daily visits. After a few minutes, his bones would grow accustomed to the brutality of the rigid surface, and after a couple hours, his heart would be so full that he no longer noticed his numb backside. Ruth never spoke, but even while she slept, her presence always rejuvenated him.

Every now and then, there were days when she would open her eyes, and James would hold his breath, praying that today would be the day. But each time, as nighttime crept in, James would leave with the hole in his heart torn wide open again.

He brought Ruth's hand to his lips and kissed it tenderly before lowering it back to the bed. He gazed at the whisper of a body that barely displaced the duvet. Even at eighty-two, confined to bed, Ruth was still the most beautiful woman he had ever seen. He studied the delicate lines on her face, willing her to open her angel eyes and know him again. While he was away, the memory of those eyes had tucked him in every night, greeting him before he opened his own eyes each morning. *I have wasted so much time,* he thought. James could barely stand to look at himself in the mirror every morning after what he had done to his wife, and he intended to spend the last years of his life making up for it, if that was possible.

After Ruth's stroke, James had been sucked into a vortex. He hadn't known how to cope with the pain of losing his wife so young – looking into eyes that showed no sign of recognition, eyes glazed over like the marbles their young daughter had shot under Ruth's feet as she worked in the kitchen. She was all James had ever known, and the first time she looked at him as if he were a stranger, his heart had shut down. When the doctors explained that there would be no improvement, every cell in his body had withered. He didn't want to know life without Ruth; he didn't exist without her. So he had left. His family had never made an attempt to find him; he knew they were just too hurt, too angry.

He had accepted that when he walked out on his wife, he was walking out on his entire family, but he couldn't stop himself. The pain was too intense - a fire he had no choice but to leap out of, for fear of being burned alive.

When he had first walked into the community room at Maple Manor two years ago, his eyes were instantly drawn to Ruth's fragile frame, her ivory face turned toward the window, watching a cardinal as it fluttered from branch to branch on a tree just outside. Cardinals had always been Ruth's favorite, and seeing that she still enjoyed them, James had allowed himself to wonder if the doctors' prognosis might have been wrong after all. As he approached her that first day, she had turned toward him. She gazed at him so lovingly, with the same eyes he had known and loved all his life, the same eyes he had walked away from three decades earlier. Her eyes had shimmered then closed, but James refused to give up. He had seen *something* in them that first day, hadn't he?

Her nurse, Julia, had greeted him and explained that Ruth had suffered a stroke at the age of fifty, and that she had been with Maple Manor since. Of course James knew all this, but that first day he had kept mum, too ashamed to tell Julia who he really was. He had claimed to be a volunteer, James Alexander – a coward hiding behind a name.

Every day he would come and visit with Ruth in the community room for an hour; he needed his wife as he always had. For the first few months, she would sit next to him on a loveseat in the spacious common area, her fragile hands folded in her lap, her eyes glistening as he told her all about the world outside. She never spoke, but her presence gave him the strength to finally tell her nurse the truth.

He had studied the floor as he made his confession, and when he had finished, Julia placed a gentle hand on his shoulder and asked if he would like to stay longer than an hour. James had raised his eyes to meet Julia's and nodded.

He hadn't missed a day in two years. He stayed by Ruth's side, even after she had grown too weak to sit up in the loveseat; James had simply pulled that plastic chair up beside her bed and held onto her hand for dear life.

SEVEN

Taylor Wellington's mother raced around the kitchen tidying up. "Aren't you going to eat more than that?" she nagged, eyeing the toast on Taylor's plate.

"I'm fine, Mom. I'm just not hungry."

Since school had let out for the summer, Taylor had quickly fallen into the habit of sleeping in. Life was more fun at night, plus her mother was typically out shopping or at the spa by this time of day. Not today, though, so Taylor was forced to endure the lecture.

"You look like a twig," her mother said. "Have you looked in the mirror lately?" she asked, wagging a long crimson fingernail at Taylor from across the kitchen.

"Yes Mom," Taylor said, looking down at her dry toast so her mother wouldn't see her roll her eyes. "I look in the mirror every day when I get dressed," she mumbled.

"Do you have an appointment with Dr. Cunningham soon?"

"Yes Mom."

"Well please make sure you don't miss it. And please tell her that your father and I would like to meet with her when we return from Italy."

"Ok Mom." Taylor had no intention of passing that message along. It was fine if her parents wanted to waste their money on therapy, but she didn't need the humiliation of her mother interrogating the shrink about her as if she wasn't in the room. Her mother was convinced that Taylor had an eating disorder; it was as if her mom didn't remember being a teenager – how much pressure there is to look hot. Not that Taylor cared one bit what the loser boys at school thought about her. They were all immature and ignorant. No, Taylor had her eyes on a bigger prize. When her mom whirled out of the kitchen, Taylor picked up her cell phone and pressed "1" then "Send."

"Hey girl!" The sound of Jodi's voice always lifted Taylor's spirits. Not once in all their years of friendship had Jodi nagged or judged or told her what to do.

"We still on?" Taylor asked.

"Hell yeah! I can't wait," Jodi said.

"Ok. I can't talk. She just walked back in." Taylor clicked off her phone and shoved it into her pocket.

"You have the number where we are staying, right dear?"

"Same place as last time. I know the drill, Mom."

"Do you work today?" her mother asked.

"Yes Mom."

"Ok. Please make sure you walk to your car with someone. That rapist is still out there, dear."

"Yes Mom," Taylor said, studying her toast again. *Who's going to attack me at an old folks' home,* she thought.

"Good," her mother said, as she picked up her suitcase and headed for the door. "Taylor, please try to eat while we are gone. Marie is coming by to do the cleaning on Monday, and I have asked her to make a few meals that you can just take from the refrigerator. Until then, there is meatloaf in the freezer and the vegetable crisper is fully stocked."

"Yes Mom."

"Ok then. The driver is waiting. I have to go. Love you," she said and blew Tayor a kiss.

Taylor looked up and flashed what she hoped was a sincere looking smile, and her mother left.

Meatloaf? Really?! Taylor walked to the refrigerator, opened the freezer, retrieved the loaf and tossed it in the trash. The frozen brick hit the bottom with a "thud." *That woman is clueless.*

~

Anna felt the blood return to her cheeks as she sized up the little creature in her waiting room – Alice in Wonderland on the overstuffed couch, her scrawny legs bouncing joyfully, the heels of her pink sneakers patting the leather. The girl smiled as if Anna had been expecting her, as if they had been good friends for years.

Anna stood motionless, taking in the miniscule stranger. It took her a moment to find her voice. "How are the tadpoles?" she finally said.

"Fine," the girl replied, still smiling but adding nothing more.

Anna waited, but the child just stared at her, smiling. "Umm… may I help you?" She scanned the otherwise empty waiting room for the girl's parents.

"Sure," the girl said, her eyes alight with the excitement of a child on the first day of summer vacation.

Anna waited for her to continue…

Nothing.

"*How* may I help you?" Anna tried a different approach.

"I want to see the shrink," the little girl announced.

Anna flinched; she despised that title. "I am the *psychologist,*" she corrected. "Do you have an appointment?"

"Sure," just like before.

It was obvious that the girl had come alone, and in ten years of practice, Anna had never scheduled a single patient during her lunch hour. "What's your name?" Anna asked.

"Sunshine." A simple response, and the smile that danced from cheek to cheek told Anna that this little girl had no intention of confessing her real name.

"Sunshine, huh?"

"Yep."

Anna heard her stomach growl. "Ok, Sunshine, what brings you to my office today?"

"I have an appointment."

"Are you sure?"

"Yes, I'm sure," she said.

"Well, come in then," Anna said, but something in that little girl's smile made Anna fear she would regret that invitation. Sunshine bounded from the couch, her eyes locked on Anna's.

Anna felt small in the child's gaze. She stepped backwards into her office, spellbound, and blindly lowered the can of soup onto her desk. Sunshine entered, looking away just long enough to find the largest of the four chairs – the one that had always, by some unspoken understanding, been reserved for Anna. She skipped over and hopped up into Anna's leather armchair with the same enthusiasm demonstrated when she had dismounted the couch in the waiting room. Once again her eyes found Anna's and locked in.

Uneasiness finally forced Anna to shift her gaze, and she glanced out the window as she took a seat in one of the smaller chairs. "Are your parents planning to join us?" she asked, forcing herself to look at the girl again.

Nothing.

The child's face was placid, yet exuberant all at once, and her smile threatened to infect Anna and spoil her sour mood.

"Is something bothering you?" Anna ventured, mentally vaccinating herself against the girl's cheerfulness.

No response. Only that teasing grin.

Why the hell is she here? Anna thought. *Maybe someone's trying to play a practical joke.* Anna looked around to see if Dr. Patterson had perhaps installed a hidden camera and was laughing behind the closed door of his office. But Dr. Patterson was not one for practical jokes; Dr. Patterson had probably never laughed once in his life. Anna turned back to the child and studied her face. She seemed excited to be there, but she was giving Anna nothing to go on. *She's wasting my time,* Anna thought. She glanced at the hands of her grandfather clock; the minutes of her lunch hour were slipping by. The blood began to simmer in her neck and she felt it rise to her cheeks. Anna found comfort in knowing who she would be seeing each hour of the day and in eating the same condensed chicken noodle soup every day for lunch, at the same time, in her own leather armchair. She needed that structure, and this little game was quickly getting old. "What is it that you need?" Anna tried again, failing to hide her growing frustration.

Still, Sunshine simply smiled.

Anna heard her stomach growl. Maybe it was the mischievous grin or the way this girl stared relentlessly into Anna's eyes. It might have been the way she hopped right up into Anna's chair with complete disregard for social custom. Perhaps Anna's blood sugar was just low, but whatever it was, Anna suddenly felt the urge to pick this little creature up by the scruff of her neck and throw her out the door.

Never mind the sweet blond curls framing her soft freckled cheeks like cotton candy, or her bright blue eyes filled with excitement and mystery not yet extinguished by the harsh realities of life. Anna struggled to ignore the tiny hands folded in such a sophisticated manner in her lap, dirt trapped under her fingernails. No, this "Sunshine" needed to leave immediately. This was Anna's lunch hour, and that was her chair! This girl had no appointment, no parental consent, and no way, Anna was sure, to pay the $120 hourly fee.

Anna dug her fingernails into the arms of the smaller chair. "Will you *please* tell me what it is that you need?" she asked.

"What do you do for people here?"

Finally! Something! "Well, lots of things," Anna said, releasing her grip.

"Ok then, do that for me."

Anna was an experienced psychologist; she could control this situation. Picking up this bony kid and hurling her through the window was out of the question, so Anna's only choice was to see this through. She took a deep breath and continued. "Were you referred to me by your doctor or your school counselor?"

"Sure."

Really?! Anna's cheeks burned now. She sucked in another deep breath, reminding herself why she had gotten into this profession, and exhaled slowly as she counted to ten in her mind. Losing her parents at such a young age, Anna had always longed for someone to talk to when she had worries or big decisions to make. When she felt she would rather stay in bed than face yet another lonely day, all she had needed was a friend. She had pursued her course of study with the goal of becoming that person for others someday – safety in professionalism.

Anna's optimism and idealism had faded over the ensuing decade as she gradually came to realize that she could never "cure" anyone. How do you know when someone is truly better? The same patients returned to her, time and time again, to deal with the same issues they kept bringing into their lives. She had tried every approach she had learned in school and sometimes felt she was making progress, only to have the same patients come back again with the same old problems.

Acknowledging that this girl was about the same age as she had been when her parents were killed, Anna felt the slightest tug of compassion. She took another deep breath, exhaled and then repeated, "Is there something bothering you today?" Perhaps this little "Sunshine" truly did have something on her mind but was afraid to talk about it, though with the gleam in her eyes and nauseatingly sweet smile on her face, Anna doubted this girl had ever suffered a moment in her life.

"Sure."

"Like what?" Anna tried for a cheerful tone.

"Is this where you work all day every day?" the girl asked, releasing her stare long enough to size up the office.

"Sure," Anna responded, enjoying a little payback.

"Kinda boring," Sunshine said, and her eyes returned to Anna's.

Anna winced. She had worked hard over the years to create a welcoming environment, hoping ambience could somehow compensate for what she had gradually begun to fear – her lack of competence as a therapist. This office had become like a second home. Lord knows she had spent many long days and nights here. Yet in decorating the space, it had been important to Anna that she surround herself with the symbols of authority and credibility that generated trust from a patient's perspective – leather furniture, framed diplomas and awards, dark woodwork, expensive pens.

"Window's kinda small and there're no colors in here," Sunshine said. "You don't have kids, do you?"

Anna didn't see the fist, but the blow to her gut stole her oxygen. She counted in her head, *one, two, three, four, ten!* *What is this little monster doing here?* Whatever fantasies Anna had imagined yesterday by the creek vaporized instantly. The girl's childish honesty crept through every cell in Anna's body and boiled up through the veins in her forehead. Where were this girl's parents? Hadn't anyone ever taught her manners? *How dare she ask that question!*

"How old are you?" Sunshine asked.

"Thirty-five." The truth slipped out before Anna could catch it, and her mind grasped frantically at the words, trying to pull them back in. *Damn that mouth of mine!* Anna knew what was coming next.

Sunshine's jaw dropped open; her eyes bulged. "You're *that* old and you don't have kids?!"

"No! No I don't have kids! Are we done now?" *Aren't I the one who's supposed to be asking the questions,* Anna thought, suddenly feeling as if *she* was the child, and Sunshine was the therapist. *Damn her!* The girl's words stung. Anna wanted to dart out of her office and never look back.

Sunshine simply smiled.

As a child, Anna had dreamed of falling in love and marrying her soul mate, having children of her own, throwing dinner parties and pretending not to see her daughter peeking around the corner. She remembered the promises she had made to her mother – that she would always love herself and her family, no matter what, yet here she was, thirty-five and single, with some disrespectful little pain in the ass reminding her of her biggest failure in life. Anna took another deep breath to regain her composure. "No. None yet. How about you? Do you have any sisters or brothers?" She *had* to gain control of this conversation.

"Why not?" The girl asked, her expression innocent and genuinely curious.

"Why not what?" Anna snapped.

"Why don't you have kids?"

"I think our time's up for today," she blurted out, wild-eyed – a possum trapped in a corner, ready to strike out if necessary.

"Sure," the girl said and bounced from the armchair. Anna felt her shoulders drop as Sunshine looked away. She hadn't realized she had been tensing them.

Sunshine skipped over to Anna's desk, glanced down at the pocket of her pink cotton shorts, slid her hand in and pulled out a perfectly flat, round stone. After placing it on the desk, she lifted her eyes to meet Anna's again. "Thank you," she said and skipped out the door.

Anna rose and returned to her own chair. *Sunshine? Some sunshine,* she thought. *More like a dark cloud hanging over my day, reminding me of all the things I haven't accomplished in my life.* Parents could be so irresponsible with their kids. No discipline, no rules. *"We don't want to stifle her creativity,"* Anna could imagine the girl's parents saying. *Kids need rules, dammit! They thrive on rules. They want rules. For instance, let's start with "Don't go wandering around town popping into a professional office building to harass a psychologist on her lunch break!" Or how about respecting authority? How can she ask me such personal questions? Who does she think she is? That kid is probably in the Principal's office every day. I wouldn't be surprised if she's been suspended from school a hundred times if she disrespects her teachers the way she disrespected me.* Inhale… Exhale… *What kind of home does that child come from? She obviously has no guidance, no role models.* Anna certainly knew that feeling. But then how could the child be so cheerful?

Anna leaned her head back against the cool leather and focused on the ceiling. When she was in college, she had talked with a therapist who told her that it is impossible to feel down if you're looking up. Apparently by turning your eyes in an upward direction, your mood improves instantly. Right now, however, it wasn't working.

Something about the way that little girl just pranced into Anna's space with no regard for her schedule, the way she hopped into Anna's chair as if it were her own, the way she insulted Anna's office and questioned her accomplishments. *Damn her!* Anna thought. *And what a foolish nickname, "Sunshine."*

"Focus," Anna told herself. She had already lost half of her lunch hour thanks to that "Sunshine," no point in making matters worse by starving to death. She studied the can of soup on her desk.

The longer she stared, the more she felt like crying… or throwing up. *What is the shelf life of this crap,* she wondered. She picked up the soup for closer inspection. "Best by Feb 2009." *Seven years?* She tossed the can in the wastebasket and let her head fall back against the leather again. Her office was silent, except for the "tick tock, tick tock," counting the seconds, days, years creeping by. Measuring out a wasted life; the lonely life Anna had created.

A firm knock startled her from her self-loathing; she looked up at the door the girl had left wide open. *Dammit,* she thought. *Not Dr. Patterson. Not right now.*

"Can we have a few words?" he asked, brushing lint off the sleeve of his tan tweed sport coat as he entered. Every article of clothing Dr. Patterson owned was the color of mulch.

"Ok." *What choice do I have?* Anna thought.

"I need you to cover for me this weekend. I'm on call but I have plans." Ron admired his manicured fingernails and waited for Anna's predictable reply.

He does this every time he's on call, she thought. But annoying as it was, she really had nothing else to do anyway. "Ok," she said. *Just get out of my office.*

When Dr. Patterson pulled the door shut, Anna heard a little voice inside her head mumble, "Doormat."

"I am NOT a doormat," Anna hissed. "I am a crappy, inefficient excuse for a woman, thank you very much." She closed her eyes and leaned her head back once more. *And a doormat,* she thought.

EIGHT

"Why won't that woman let me get a job at the mall like all the other girls at school?" Taylor grumbled, stirring the stew. Her mother just didn't get it.

It wasn't that Taylor hated her job at Maple Manor, it's just that she was surrounded by old people. There were no hot guys; there was no action. It was boring, that's all. And it was dangerous! They made her chop vegetables, and she had nearly lost a finger on at least three occasions. Well, not a finger exactly, but the chef's knife was hell on her nails. She paid good money for her manicures, and she wasn't sure how much longer she could deal with the carnage.

The scent of beef ambushed her senses and she cringed. She held her breath as she gave the stew one last stir before ladling out individual portions for the residents. After placing a bowl on each tray, she added a cloth napkin and silverware, a side salad, a slice of French bread and a glass of iced tea, and carried a tray to the first resident's room.

Ruth didn't look up when Taylor entered; she didn't expect her to. Taylor's job was to deliver the food, not to interact with the residents. She set the tray down gently on the wheeled table beside the bed and glanced over at the bony old woman. Ruth's eyes were closed, and Taylor could practically see right through her tissue paper eyelids. *God, please don't let me get old,* Taylor thought. *What a miserable existence – spending every day in bed with nothing to look forward to.* No, Taylor decided then and there that she would never grow old; she would do whatever it took to stay young and beautiful forever.

Quietly rolling the table close so that Ruth could reach it when she woke up, Taylor inhaled the familiar disinfectant and stale air. *Why doesn't anyone open the windows in this place,* she thought.

She turned toward Ruth's window and admired the view of the flower garden and a beautiful lilac just outside. She walked over and peered out. Ruth's sad old husband was eating a bagged lunch at the table in the middle of the courtyard; he looked so lonely. *Poor James comes here every day,* Taylor thought. It was pretty cool that he hung out with his wife though, even when the old woman never said a word to him. *He sits in this stuffy room, day after day,* she mused. *He must really love his wife.* Taylor doubted her dad would do that for her mom. They rarely even spoke, but her mom seemed fine with it as long as he allowed her the use of the driver and the credit cards.

Eyeing the lilac, Taylor reached for the lock on the window. She knew she could get fired for it, but just a little crack wouldn't hurt, so she gently eased the bottom pane up about an inch. The sweet perfume wafted through the small gap, and Taylor inhaled deeply. She heard Ruth stir, and her heart jumped. She turned toward the woman in the bed. Ruth's eyes were open slightly, a faint smile on her lips. Taylor pointed with her thumb over her shoulder toward the window.

"Do you want me to leave it like this?" she whispered, though she knew this resident couldn't speak. Of course Ruth didn't answer, but Taylor was sure she saw the woman nod. *Very cool,* Taylor thought. *It's like she's talking to me.* "I'll leave it just like this then, but don't tell on me, ok?" Taylor said, smiling. Ruth closed her eyes again, and Taylor watched her feeble chest slowly rise as if she, too, was breathing in the fresh scent.

~

June, 1998

"James," Christy said, setting his Chinese carry-out on his desk. "Can I get you anything else before I go?"

James looked up from his computer screen and smiled at his secretary as she came around to stand beside him. "No dear. It's late. You need to get home to your boys." Christy laid her hand on his shoulder, careful not to be caught peeking at his computer screen.

"You should go home too, James." James was far too old to be working so many late nights. Christy glanced at his left hand speckled with rust-colored age spots, the weathered gold wedding band dangling from his ring finger, and wondered again about the wife he never mentioned. *How does she feel about her husband working such long hours,* Christy thought. Everyone in the office wondered the same thing, but they respected James too much to mention it. It was generally understood that James preferred to keep his life outside of work private. But every so often, curiosity got the best of Christy. She snuck a glimpse at his computer screen before he minimized the page he had been reading. Christy blushed. "I'm sorry, James. You're right. I should get home."

As she turned off the lamp on her desk, she contemplated the lovely picture she had seen on James' monitor. "Bloomfield," the caption had read. *What a darling place*, she thought, recalling the image of a cobblestone street lined with whimsical shops with overflowing flowerboxes, an ice cream parlor's pink and white striped awning, old-time lamp posts dotting the brick sidewalks. *Like stepping back in time,* Christy thought. She hadn't heard of a Bloomfield in the northeast, and she wondered if James was planning a vacation. *He's long overdue,* she thought. Christy had been his secretary for the last twelve years, but she knew so very little about the man. Talk in the break room had filled her in on the scant details that were known about him, and as far as Christy was aware, he had never taken a vacation or even a personal day since joining the firm twenty eight years earlier.

Christy gathered her purse and sweater then poked her head back inside James' office to tell him she was leaving. She turned back silently when she saw him at his desk, his face buried in his hands, sobbing.

May, 2002

James picked at his turkey sandwich. He had lost weight over the years without his wife's divine cooking. He had never bothered to learn to cook, opting for take-out in the office most nights. He left the joint checking account untouched while he was away, wanting to ensure that the funds were available for Ruth to receive the best care available. He had joined a law practice in Vermont and had poured himself into his work. As a result, he was able to make large deposits into the checking account every month. And he was able to afford take-out.

He set the meat aside, took a bite and chewed slowly, forcing himself to swallow the bland white bread. He thought of Christy and his other kind coworkers back in Vermont. Everyone had admired his work ethic and the fact that he was just as effective at his age as the young attorneys fresh out of law school. No one had pried into his personal life, and for that he was grateful; they seemed to understand that he had secrets he didn't wish to share.

On his last day of work, they had thrown him an extravagant retirement party, each person taking a turn speaking of the kind man who had brought so much success to the firm – "Willing to work from sun up to sun down," "No one more dedicated," "The most honest man I know," "Integrity should be your middle name, James."

If they only knew, he thought. He wrapped the turkey up in the brown paper bag and dropped it in the trashcan by the door.

Ruth was hazy when he shuffled back into her room, but she was awake. James smiled at her. "You haven't eaten a bite," he said as he pulled his plastic chair back up beside her bed. He scooped up a spoonful of beef stew and moved it toward her lips. She closed her eyes, refusing the food. James sighed and set the spoon in the bowl. "Angel Eyes," he said softly, "you have to eat something." Her eyelids twitched almost imperceptibly as she drifted back off to sleep. As always, he took her hand and watched her while she slept. *My dear*

Angel Eyes.

Julia came in and placed her hand on his shoulder. "James," she said quietly, "I know I've said it before, but I'm offering again. Will you please let me bring in a more comfortable chair for you?" James shook his head. He didn't deserve that kind of luxury.

Julia walked over to close the window. "Did you open this?" she asked. James glanced over and noticed that the window had been raised slightly.

"No," he said. Julia lowered it and turned the lock to secure it.

"Strange," she said as she walked out of the room, leaving James alone again with his wife.

~

Anna should have refused payment from her last three patients of the day; their words blurred together even more than usual – a woman named Mary Beth who was struggling with depression, a young couple whose marriage was suffering due to their trouble conceiving a child, and seventeen year old Taylor Wellington and her inability to eat more than a piece of toast at every meal. Anna had been tempted to pull the can of soup from her wastebasket and force-feed it to Taylor as she spoke. She resented that Taylor's parents had more money than Caesar, yet Taylor refused to eat. Anna knew all the facts about Anorexia Nervosa; she had struggled with it herself during her teenage years, but today she felt no sympathy. *Yep, I should have refused payment*, she decided.

Maybe it was time to give up on this "helping" profession. How could she help anyone when she had these thoughts running through her head? How could she help Mary Beth pull herself out of the darkness when she couldn't even do it for herself?

Leaving the days' notes unfinished, Anna retrieved the can of soup from the waste basket and left at five o'clock, hoping to beat the collegiate masses to the grocery store. After grabbing a box of tea bags and a loaf of bread, she approached the customer service counter with the can of condensed chicken noodle soup.

"I'd like to return this."

NINE

Cathy looked up from her book as Kurt came through the front door. She always felt a weight lift off her chest when she heard the latch click – confirmation that her husband was safe. She watched him close the door and hang his keys on the hook. She thought of Sandy, and the nausea returned. She desperately wanted to tell Kurt her concerns about their daughter, but he already had too much on his plate. She took a deep breath to ease the queasy sensation.

"Honey," Kurt said, turning toward her. Cathy noticed the lines on his face had deepened, aging him years in just this one day. She closed her book and laid it by her side.

"What is it, Kurt?" she asked. Her husband had been under so much pressure lately with the attacker evading his efforts at every turn. She knew this was the reason for his recent emotional and physical distance, and she tried to be understanding.

Kurt didn't say more. He hung his hat on the peg next to his keys and walked over to the couch.

Cathy had never seen this look before. He was devastated, distant, and forty years of marriage had taught Cathy that he would never open up with her about his issues at work. Kurt thought he was protecting her from the violent realities of his job, but what he was really doing was driving a wedge between them. Tonight though, Kurt's body language suggested that he intended to eradicate that wedge. He took Cathy's hands in his, lifted her to her feet and folded her into his arms. When he finally pulled back and looked into her eyes, she saw pain; she saw worries he had no intention of sharing with her. When he lowered his lips to hers, she knew she could give him the one thing he needed most – her.

Careful not to wake her, Kurt ran his fingertips gently over the fine lines that formed rays of sunshine at the edges of Cathy's eyes. *This woman grows more beautiful every year,* he thought. Cathy was his rock, his calm place. How could he tell her his suspicions about Mitch and Sandy? It would break her heart. She deserved to know the truth, but he couldn't bring himself to hurt her like that. Cathy and Sandy had always been close, until recently, and Kurt knew Sandy's behavior worried his wife. Kurt was aware of the reason for their daughter's distance, but Cathy wasn't, and the guilt he felt for not sharing it with her consumed him. But what was he supposed to do? Tell his wife that her child was being abused, but that he had no proof? No, he wouldn't put her through that. He would fix this on his own, one way or another.

~

Anna flung her bag of groceries onto the passenger seat and dropped her forehead to the steering wheel. She felt trapped inside her own body; she wanted to crack her chest open and release the little monster that was screeching, trying to claw its way out. She wanted to silence the beast and end the pain. She pressed her palms to her ears, but the noise grew louder. She lifted her head, turned the key in the ignition and backed out of the parking space. As she drove toward her house, the beast grew louder, the thoughts came faster... *"How old are you?"* The child's words pounded in Anna's head, over and over. *"You're that old and you don't have kids?!"*

Anna slammed the brake pedal to the floor, turned her car around and headed toward town. There was no way she could go home and face the silence; the thoughts would eat her alive. She needed noise; she needed distraction. She pulled up in front of Riley's and peered through the window into the crowded bar.

Her college weeks had been punctuated by Friday nights at the local hangout where she would spend the evenings with a few other students, either to celebrate or commiserate, depending on how their classes were going at the time. The group changed from one semester to the next, and Anna had not made an attempt to stay in touch with any of her classmates. But the Friday nights at Riley's had been the highlight of her college years. Thelma, their usual waitress, had chatted with the students and occasionally joined them for a shot or two. Anna wondered if Thelma still worked at Riley's. *She'd have to be about ninety by now*, she thought, as she stepped inside Riley's for the first time in years.

The place looked pretty much the same as Anna remembered – the same tacky flashing neon sign above the door, the same dark wood paneling, the same smoke scarred ceiling, though the wood floors were a little more scuffed than she remembered. The smoky haze on the windows suggested that no one had washed them since the last time Anna had been there, since smoking had been banned in the bars in Bloomfield for a decade. The fashions had changed, but the college students still clustered around tables chugging pints and toasting their achievements with shots.

She found an empty booth in the corner by the window, allowing her to face away from the crowd. She hadn't wanted to be alone in her house, but she did want to be left alone at the bar.

A tall blonde waitress approached her table. *Definitely not Thelma*, Anna thought, as the perky young woman greeted her. Anna ordered a pale ale and inhaled the stale air. Cigarette smoke had permeated every surface in the bar, rendering itself immortal. Even though her parents never smoked, the parties they attended had been smoker friendly – it had been the 70's after all. Anna marveled at how certain smells could take her back in time, and for a moment, the beast was silenced. The clink of a glass on the table startled her, and she accepted the bottle from the waitress, pushing the glass aside.

~

"What a slut," Ron growled, as he watched Anna enter the bar. She usually went straight home after leaving the office. *What the hell is she doing here,* he thought. *What kind of woman goes to a bar like Riley's alone?* He was pleased, though, when Anna chose one of the booths in the front of the bar by the window – he could keep a close eye on her. He pulled out a smoke and reclined the driver's seat, then lit the cigarette and took a long drag. *She looks miserable,* he mused, blowing the smoke out in rings. "Serves her right."

He absently rubbed the scars on his forearm through his sleeve, and his mind shifted back to the foster home, the parties, the burning cigarettes. *"Someone needs to teach this kid some manners."* The man's voice was still fresh in Ron's mind, even after all these years. He pressed his hand to his chest where more burn marks mapped out his childhood, then forced his gaze back toward the bar.

A potbellied redneck in a flannel shirt approached Anna's table, and Ron sat up in his seat to get a better view. He took another drag. A slow smile spread across his face, smoke slithering out between his teeth, when he saw the man walk away from Anna's table, rejected. "I know the feeling, you pathetic loser," he said. "The bitch is impossible to please."

~

"So, what's a girl like you doing in a place like this?"

Anna froze, her beer bottle suspended an inch from her lips. *Oh my God,* she thought. *Please tell me that corny pick up line was not directed at me.*

"Are you meeting someone?"

Anna rolled her eyes, set her bottle on the table and slowly pivoted her body to size up the sleaze ball who dared to interrupt her pitiful reverie - a short, balding forty-something man in jeans a couple sizes too small, a plaid flannel shirt that looked like he had owned it since high school, perhaps even worn it every day since, and a gut that virtually screamed "I LOVE BEER!" *Yep, that's about right,* Anna thought. *Add insult to injury.* "I came here to be alone," she said, returning her attention to her pale ale.

"If you wanted to be alone," he said, "why did you come to a public place?"

"Just go away," she said, watching a drop of condensation trickle down her beer bottle. She closed her eyes and willed him away with her mind and heard him mumble "bitch" as he lumbered off.

She opened her eyes and downed the beer. That first beer mollified the beast, so she ordered another. As she brought the second bottle to her lips, a gentler voice in her head implored her to eat, but she ignored it and finished the second beer even faster than the first. She smiled as her mind slowly fell silent. She felt her shoulders relax and flagged down the waitress for another beer.

The waitress eyed her and hesitated slightly as she set the third beer on the table. Anna turned away and lifted the bottle.

"Eat."

Anna slammed the bottle to the table. *Dammit,* she thought. *Now that little brat is inside my head too!* Anna waved to the waitress to signal for her check. She glanced over at the short, bald, beer-gut guy. He was still glaring at her. She paused. Looking at him again, she realized that he actually wasn't half bad, in a rough guy sort of way. Maybe she had been too quick to judge.

When he saw that she had made eye-contact, he smirked and walked back over to her table, stopping first at the bar to buy her another pale ale. "Can we try again?" he said, placing the bottle in front of her. "I think we got off to a bad start. My name is Tommy, and you are?"

"Anna," she replied, gesturing for him to have a seat across the table from her. He might not have been her ideal man, but it *would* be nice to have someone to talk to – someone who wasn't her boss, a patient, or an irritating little girl. "So what do you do for a living?"

"I'm a mechanic," he said. "How about you?"

"I'm in sales," she lied. Anna was not in the mood to discuss work or to get into a counseling session with this guy, which is what always seemed to happen when she told people what she did for a living. Instantly they would want her opinion on a dream or a symptom or a family member who they thought needed help.

When the waitress brought her check, Tommy slid it off the table. "I'll get that."

"You don't have to do that," Anna said, though she did appreciate the chivalrous gesture. *Maybe all men aren't slime after all,* she thought.

The conversation flowed as easily as the alcohol; once she opened the dam, it came pouring out. She confessed her true profession, but Tommy didn't press. Instead he ordered two shots of whiskey, saying, "Here's to new friends and a great night."

The first shot burned Anna's throat, but after two more, she couldn't feel it anymore. In fact, she couldn't feel anything, not the clawing of the beast, not the cold, not the loneliness… nothing. And she liked it.

~

"A total slut," Ron mumbled, lighting another cigarette. He didn't bother to roll down the window; he enjoyed inhaling the smoke over and over. He thought back to the times he had asked Anna out. He was doing her a favor. She was young and new to the profession, and he had given her a job, for God's sake. And how did she repay him? By turning him down, time and time again – rejecting him. *Just like you did, Mother,* he thought, feeling his eyes begin to burn with rage or tears or both. But now he knew why; the tramp would rather pick up rednecks at a bar than date a distinguished professional like him. *I'm not good enough for either of you bitches, am I,* he thought. *Well, have at it then.*

He started his car, took one last drag of his cigarette and crushed it in the ashtray, then glanced back into the bar. The redneck had moved over beside Anna and had his arm wrapped around her waist. "Slut," Ron grumbled. He cut the engine and lit another cigarette, settling in to watch.

~

James opened the top drawer of his dresser and retrieved the pale pink hat box. His shaky fingertips attempted to smooth the tattered white bow on top. He closed his eyes, lifted the box to his face and inhaled slowly, searching for Ruth's scent. Her scent had been potent when he took the box from her closet three decades earlier, the only item of hers he had taken when he walked out. He had slept with the box on the pillow next to him every night while he was away.

Her scent was gone now.

Walking over to sit on the bed, he allowed the memories to return like old friends. He took the lid off the box and lifted the photograph carefully, as if it were a newborn child. Though the image had faded over the years, her eyes were still unmistakable. "Angel eyes," he had blurted out the first time he had mustered the courage to speak to her. Ruth had laughed, nervous and uncomfortable with the compliment, but James had meant it. It was the first thought that had come to his mind when he looked into her eyes that night at the high school dance.

"Would you like to dance?" he had asked, straightening his bowtie, attempting to appear confident. She smiled at the ground and he led her to the dance floor. A year later, just one week after graduation, they were married. The first time they kissed, when the minister announced their union, James had felt like a child twirling around and around. When their lips parted and Ruth smiled at him, he felt so dizzy he could barely remain standing.

He touched the photograph tenderly, as he had so many times over the years – the only picture he had from their perfect wedding day. James had taken it with him when he left, safe in Ruth's precious hat box.

After gently laying the picture on the bed beside him, he lifted the first letter from the box, the letter dated April 1, 1970 –

Dear Angel Eyes,

The doctors say there is no chance you will improve, so I suppose you will never read this letter. But I need to tell you why I am doing this. You are the love of my life, Ruth. I know you will be well cared for at Maple Manor, but I couldn't watch as they transported you from the hospital today. I'm so sorry I walked out of your room. I should have ridden alongside you to the nursing home. I should have been there for you. I should have. After all you have done for me.

Oh Ruth, everywhere I turn in this house I see you. Every time I breathe I smell you. I don't know how to live without you. I don't know who I am without you.

I don't know where I'm going. It makes no difference where I end up because you won't be with me. I just can't stay and face our home, our town, our memories, without you. I hope someday you will forgive me. I love you. That will never change.

Yours always,

James

He never mailed that letter or any of the letters he had written to her every week from his one bedroom apartment in Vermont. Every Sunday night he would sit at his small kitchen table with a cup of tea and the pen Ruth had given him when he passed the bar exam so long ago – so many letters, but that pen had never run out of ink. Most of the time he would write about his days at the law firm, sharing stories he would have told her over dinner, under different circumstances. He had kept his side of the conversation alive on yellow 4"x6" stationary, conjuring up her side in his mind. With those letters, James had created the reality he longed for.

Sometimes he would close his eyes and imagine her soft hand on his, as she spoke of the lilies opening or the pileated woodpecker's daily visit. With his eyes closed, he had witnessed her hair graying more and more each year, the fine lines on her face deepening. She had retained her grace and beauty as he celebrated each of her birthdays with his eyes closed at that table. In his mind, he had slowly grown old with his wife. And in his mind she had known him again – it was the only way he had been able to go on.

~

Taylor flipped through the channels on the 70" flat screen TV in the home theatre, a windowless room in the basement with stadium seating, cherry wood paneling and surround sound speakers mounted on all four walls – the perfect place to pass the hours engrossed in someone else's life. *American Pie,* "Saw it," she said. *Legally Blonde,* "Cute, but saw it." She couldn't find anything that looked good, even on HBO. She clicked off the remote and wandered upstairs to the kitchen. She knew she should feel hungry, but the hunger pangs had disappeared months ago, along with her period. She opened the refrigerator and pulled out the vegetable crisper, then closed it again.

She dialed Jodi, but hung up when voicemail picked up. She dropped her phone on the counter and made her way through the French doors to the stone patio and stopped at the edge of the pool. The water glistened, a million slivers of moonlight shimmering on tiny ripples. Taylor undressed under the stars. She didn't bother with a swimsuit; no one could see her through the thick wall of arborvitae that encircled the pool. She ran her hands down her sides and noticed a soft spot just behind her hip bones. Sighing, she dove in and began to swim laps. She had already completed her workout for the day, but a little more couldn't hurt.

After twenty-five laps, she pulled herself from the pool and felt the soft spot again. *Still there.* She rubbed at the spot as she made her way to the pool house.

Taking a thick white towel from a shelf, she dried off, wrapped the towel around her body and walked back through the French doors. She allowed herself a quick glance over in the general direction of the answering machine – no blinking light. *Of course they wouldn't call,* she thought. Her parents were far too busy touring Italy to take time out to check on her. Taylor tried not to let it bother her. What did she care? They were old and obtuse anyway. She climbed the sweeping staircase to her room and slid into bed, relishing the feeling of the cool satin sheets against her skin. *When did Mom buy these,* Taylor thought, shaking her head. *All that woman does is shop. Shopping and travel, what a life.* No time for talks about Taylor's hopes and dreams; no time to answer her questions about dating or sex. "I don't need that woman," she said as she turned out the light. Taylor had so many questions, some Jodi could answer, some she couldn't.

Jodi had been Taylor's best friend since they were five. Her family lived directly across the street in an enormous Victorian mansion, and as young children they had spent many nights exploring the nooks and crannies of Jodi's home – the secret rooms behind bookcases, the brick tunnels beneath the house.

Growing up, Taylor had spent more nights in Jodi's home than her own, but lately Jodi's drinking had begun to worry Taylor. She didn't mention it, for fear of alienating the only true friend she had. But more and more it seemed like that was all Jodi wanted to do, and Taylor missed the closeness they had always shared. She wanted to sit and laugh and talk about boys, but Jodi just wanted to sneak vodka from her parents' liquor cabinet. Taylor knew she had to choose – either walk away from the friendship, hollow as it had become, or join her. At least it was more fun than sitting around this big empty house alone.

Taylor climbed out of bed and padded over to her window. Through the large bay window at the front of Jodi's house, Taylor could make out the colorful flickering of the television. The glow from Jodi's bedroom suggested that she was awake, and Taylor considered calling her again. Instead, she turned away from the window, crawled back into bed and allowed the silence to bore her to sleep.

TEN

Anna stretched her arms out wide as the fog in her head began to lift. A dull ache tiptoed up from the base of her skull, slowly at first, but soon the intensity of the pain paralyzed her. She tried to inhale, but an immense weight crushed her abdomen. She forced her left eye open, then her right. She tilted her head slightly, amplifying the pain in her temples, and discovered the source of the weight. *Oh God!*

Anna had once heard that a coyote would chew off its own leg if it was caught in a trap, and at this moment, she considered chewing herself in half at the torso. She cringed as she carefully pushed the thick leg off of her mid-section and laid it beside her body. She slipped out of bed like a ninja – a ninja with a killer headache, but stealthy nonetheless.

She quietly gathered her clothes from their various locations around the room, then searched frantically for her panties. *Dammit*, she thought. *They must be under the sheets!* Swallowing the groan that threatened to erupt from her chest, she decided to leave them and get out. She crept to the living room and dressed quickly by the front door.

As she approached her car in the driveway, the realization struck her that she had zero memory of driving to Tommy's house the night before. *Totally irresponsible,* she thought. Her parents had been killed by a drunk driver, and Anna cursed herself for making such a reckless decision. Not that she had any recollection of making the decision, but that was no excuse. "I deserve every second of this hangover," she muttered, then stumbled over to the edge of the driveway and threw up. *Serves me right,* she thought, wiping her mouth with the back of her hand before lowering her aching body into her car.

Fortunately she knew every inch of Bloomfield, so she found her way home quickly. She left the bag of groceries in her car and trudged into her house, dragged her body up the stairs and collapsed onto her bed. Pulling her covers up tight around her neck, she cried. She cried for her mom and dad. She cried for herself and her stupid choices. She even cried for the pathetic creep who had to get women drunk at a bar to get laid. And then it occurred to her – she was no different than Tommy.

~

James' hands shook as he turned left onto Cardinal Lane. He had risen early with one thought – *I have to face the memories.* But as he pulled his car over beside the curb, he suddenly doubted whether he was strong enough. He hadn't driven by the house since his return, unable to lay eyes on the front door he had walked out of so long ago. "You have to do this," he told himself, then willed his trembling hand to pull the lever on the car door. He climbed out and looked around.

It felt as if he had been standing on this sidewalk just days ago, holding his wife's hand as they enjoyed the colorful display of Christmas lights that illuminated the Thompsons' house every year. "Such an extravagant display," Ruth had said, noting that the lights flooded not only the Thompsons' property, but the houses on either side as well. James sighed as he turned away from the Thompsons' and began his journey.

He plodded along with his head ducked, hoping the neighbors wouldn't recognize him. He wasn't sure which of their old friends still lived on Cardinal Lane, but he couldn't bear to face any of them.

He glanced over his shoulder when he passed the Henricks' house and his gaze fell upon the old brass knocker on the front door. He pictured his daughter's face painted white, beaming that Halloween night so long ago when she was finally tall enough to reach it. Standing on her tiptoes, her fingers had just barely grazed the bottom of the knocker, but she was proud nonetheless. Joan Henrick had opened the door to greet them and filled his daughter's bucket to the top with bubblegum and chocolates, bringing priceless delight to an eight year old girl.

James smiled as he passed the Stevens' house, recalling the evenings he and Ruth had enjoyed with the friendly couple on their back patio, drinking wine and playing cards well into the night. *I wonder where Bill and Phyllis are now,* he thought, then brushed away the happy times and continued on his mission.

When he reached the end of the brick walkway at 6211 Cardinal Lane, he stopped and turned slowly, surveying the two rows of vibrant daylilies edging the path up to the house. He pictured Ruth on her knees, her hands caked with dirt as she planted the bulbs one by one. He chuckled as he recalled his wife's refusal to wear gardening gloves. *Such a stubborn woman,* he thought. *Such a beautiful, stubborn woman.*

His gaze meandered up the walkway, retracing the steps he had taken every afternoon when he arrived home from work. When he finally allowed himself to look at the house, he felt his legs go weak. He saw her there, standing in the open doorway in her floral apron, her flaxen hair swept up into a loose knot, wearing a smile that lit up his world.

"Welcome home, dear," Ruth said as he approached, her angel eyes sparkling. He stepped up onto the porch and kissed her cheek, and she wrapped her arms around his neck. Pulling back to study her soft features, James knew he was the luckiest man alive. Taking his hand tenderly, she led him into the house where chili and cornbread awaited him.

"May I help you, sir?"

James stepped back abruptly. "Oh my," he said. "I'm sorry to have bothered you." He staggered off the porch toward the sidewalk.

"Are you ok?" the young woman called after him.

"Yes. I'm fine," he said. *No. I'm not,* he thought.

"Good day," the receptionist said, as James signed in at the reception desk. "Is it?" he mumbled, shuffling toward Ruth's wing.

Ruth was waiting for him in the community room when he arrived; he was surprised to see her out of bed. She looked up at him, and James was sure he saw the slightest hint of a smile pass over her face. "How are you?" he said, lowering himself onto the love seat beside her.

Her angel eyes watched every movement of his lips as he told her about his walk through their old neighborhood, and how their home appeared to have been lovingly maintained. He thought he heard a sigh escape her lips as he related his memory of their daughter on Halloween. Ruth had shared a special bond with their daughter; James hadn't understood things like dolls and cooking, and during those days, that's what little girls loved. These days, girls played baseball and soccer and climbed trees. He smiled as he remembered his three year old granddaughter zooming toy cars across the tile kitchen floor under Ruth's feet as she cooked. Ruth would pull out the wooden spoon and tell her to "scat." She had tried to look stern when she reprimanded her granddaughter, but her smile always betrayed her.

James continued his story, reminiscing about the Christmas lights at the Thompsons' and sharing with Ruth all the things that had changed in the neighborhood. He omitted the ending though. He still couldn't make sense of what had happened on their old front porch. *That young woman must have thought I'd gone mad*, he thought. He shook his head then lifted Ruth's hand to his lips.

Sharing the memories with his wife brought him great joy, and the small signs that perhaps she remembered – the soft sigh, the flicker of light in her eyes, the hint of a smile… those gave him hope.

ELEVEN

July, 1984

Sandy giggled when she caught her friend's bouncing reflection in the mirror. "You're definitely no Madonna," Sandy said, pulling her lower right eyelid down, painting on the liquid eyeliner.

"I know," Megan said, grooving her hips to the music. "I'm a much better dancer." Sandy rolled her eyes at her friend in the mirror then painted the lower lid of her left eye. She assessed her reflection one last time then turned toward Megan.

"Do you think he'll like this?" she asked, motioning toward her black and blue paisley mini skirt. Megan teetered as she halted her moves long enough to look Sandy over.

"He'll love it."

Sandy stepped out of Megan's Chevette and glanced around nonchalantly, attempting to make it appear as if the two of them just happened to be stopping by the U Stop on a random Friday night. Two boys skateboarded past the girls, hitting kickflips and ollies.

Where's Mitch, Sandy thought. She tried to look disinterested as she scanned the parking lot. She spotted him smoking a cigarette over in the shadows with a thin bleach-blonde draped around him. *There's no way I compete with a girl like that,* Sandy thought. But Mitch's black leather jacket, dirty brown hair and dark eyes stirred something inside her that she couldn't identify, something she couldn't ignore.

Mitch glanced up and noticed Sandy trying desperately to look like a "bad girl." *Poser,* he thought, then he re-evaluated his assessment. *I could have some fun with that one – A cop's daughter... I'd love to see the look on her daddy's face if he saw my arm around his precious little angel.* The blonde girl whispered something in his ear, but Mitch didn't hear her; he had a goal and he deserted the waif mid-sentence. He flicked his cigarette butt onto the concrete and sauntered over toward Sandy. It wouldn't be cool to start a conversation with her. No, *she* needed to make the first move, so he lit another cigarette and leaned against the fence in front of the Chevette.

"He's staring at you," Megan whispered, nudging Sandy in the ribs. "Go talk to him."

"What do I say?" Sandy said. Adrenaline raced through her veins and her legs felt like noodles. Megan shoved her toward Mitch, and Sandy tripped over her shiny new Mary Janes, throwing her hand onto the hood of the Chevette to break her fall.

"What's up?" Mitch asked, as Sandy straightened her hair and pulled her skirt up a little higher.

"Um…" she said. "I'm just… um… hanging out." *Darn it,* she thought. *That was dumb.* Mitch took a drag of his cigarette and allowed his eyes to wander from her face to her chest then down her legs before blowing the smoke out slowly.

"That's cool," he said.

An hour later they were in the passenger seat of his buddy's rusty VW bug, the buckle of the seatbelt bruising Sandy's lower back as Mitch fumbled with the zipper on his jeans and opened the condom wrapper with his teeth. "You're not going to make me waste this, are you?" he said.

"No," Sandy said, feigning confidence. This wasn't how she had imagined it would be, but what did she know? She was a virgin.

May, 2002

After dropping the children off at school, Sandy returned home and poured herself a cup of coffee, then retrieved the classifieds from behind the flour and took a seat at the table. She scanned the Help Wanted section and circled a few postings. "Retail Sales Clerk," "Receptionist," "Waitress." She rubbed her eyes and sighed. Mitch had firmly objected to her request to look for a job, and Sandy had the bruises to prove it, but she had to speed things up somehow. A couple dollars from his trousers here and there was not going to cut it. *How can I do this without him finding out,* she thought. *Dear Lord, if he ever discovered me going against his orders...* Sandy snapped her fingers to stop the thought in its tracks; she would not let her mind go there.

A few months ago, Sandy had asked Mitch what he thought about her taking some college courses. She deeply regretted never having earned her college degree, but becoming pregnant her senior year of high school had made those aspirations irrelevant. But since all four of her children were in school now, Sandy had the time. "What's the point?" Mitch had said, not bothering to look up from his newspaper. "No matter what you do, you'll fail. That's what you do." And with that, Sandy had given up on the dream she had held since she was eight years old.

Sandy's second grade teacher, Mrs. Holland, had an upright piano in the classroom, and when the kids needed a break or became rambunctious, Mrs. Holland would play. She had encouraged the children to sing along, as her fingers danced across the keys. Sandy was captivated.

She dove head-first into learning to play, taking advantage of every free moment to sneak down to the Willhelm Hotel to the grand piano in the lobby. She had continued to play there at least once a week throughout her teenage years and even after she was married. After Craig was born, she would take him with her in his car seat; he would sleep while Sandy's heart sang along with her fingers. The guests changed nightly, and the anonymity suited her. But after Todd was born, Sandy was forced to pack the Wilhelm away in her mind, leaving a gaping hole in her heart. She had filled the void by doting on her children. They were her life and they came first. She knew they deserved a better life. She was well aware of the price they would pay for growing up in this home, but at least Mitch had never laid a hand on them.

Mitch generally ignored the children, except to correct them when they forgot to close the toilet lid or left the toothpaste on the counter. "Mindless brats," he would call them. Sandy didn't mind that Mitch never joined them for dinner. She could only imagine his reaction if he witnessed the many times sweet Libby had spilled her milk over the years. Libby was Sandy's accident-prone child, her head in the clouds, always daydreaming, high on life and far too busy to be bothered with trivial things like checking to make sure her glass was on the table before releasing her grip. Sandy delighted in sitting down and relaxing with her children instead of racing around, placating her husband, making sure his chair was pulled out, his food just the right temperature.

"Cosmetics Consultant," Sandy read. That one was out. Sandy didn't even own makeup. Mitch wouldn't allow it. She rubbed her cheek as she recalled their first wedding anniversary. She had worn mascara that night, hoping Mitch would find her attractive like he had before they were married. "You look like a whore," he had said, and dug through her drawer in the bathroom until he found the tube. He stuffed it in his pocket, then grabbed Sandy's face, bruising her cheeks between his thumb and fingertips as he enunciated each word through clenched teeth, "Not. In. My. House." He had stood over her while she smeared cold cream over her eyes and her tears, making sure she got every last bit off. Then he had taken her to Marcy's Diner to celebrate, letting her order for herself for the first and last time.

On their second wedding anniversary, he had casually mentioned that they would not be going anywhere for dinner. When she had asked him why, he replied as if the answer was obvious and Sandy was an idiot for not knowing, "Because then I would have to pretend I was happy I married you." Sandy had gone to bed alone, grateful that Mitch had gone out to the bar. She knew there was no way she could fake it that night. But when he returned home plastered, reeking of smoke and whiskey, he had demanded sex, slurring, "If you don't give it to me, I'll find someone who will." Not that he had ever once actually given her the option of denying him. Todd was conceived that night.

Sandy folded the classifieds and tucked them back behind the flour; she was careful not to leave the evidence out. Mitch had made his feelings clear about her working, but she *would* find a way to get her children out of this situation.

TWELVE

Anna stared into the mirror. Her bloodshot eyes glared back at her. Every time she looked at her reflection, she saw all the things she wasn't – She wasn't a wife. She wasn't a mother. She wasn't *her* mother. *And I never will be,* she thought. Her mother would have never driven drunk; her mother would never have gone home with a random guy from a bar. She patted the dark puffy circles with her fingertips; there was no time for the frozen spoon trick she had learned in college, so she applied a little extra concealer and left for work.

She suffered through her morning appointments, swallowing two ibuprofen between each one. Her head was still pounding as lunchtime arrived, so she decided to break tradition and go out for lunch, hoping a little fresh air might help with the hangover.

As she locked her office door, she felt the chill again. *It's not just my imagination,* she thought, realizing now that she was, indeed, being followed. For once she wished Dr. Patterson would appear. Her hands tingled as she slowly reached in her purse for her pepper spray then whipped around.

There she was, just like before, smile and all. Feet dangling, patting the leather couch happily, eyes fixed on Anna's.

Anna placed her hand on the back of the closest chair and bent over to allow the blood to return to her head. She sucked in a deep breath and glared at the child. "You nearly gave me a heart attack!"

Sunshine simply smiled.

"You really shouldn't sneak up on people like that," Anna said. *Damn her!*

"Where ya goin'?" Sunshine asked, oblivious to Anna's irritation.

Anna's mind raced back to the previous night and the little voice that had implored her to eat. *Why didn't I listen,* she thought. "I was just going out for some lunch," she said. "Why are you here?"

"I have an appointment."

"Are you sure?"

"Yep."

Pulse pounding in her temples, Anna rubbed her forehead and sighed. "Ok then, let me unlock the door."

"No," Sunshine said. "It's too stuffy in there. I'll come with you to lunch."

Damn her! She had insulted Anna's office and barged into her day yet again, all while wearing that stupid smile. "Great," Anna muttered, knowing the girl wouldn't pick up on the sarcasm in her voice. Sunshine bounced off the couch and skipped out the door.

Anna clicked her keyfob and shouted to the girl as she opened her car door; the girl skipped on. Anna rolled her eyes, dropped her keys in her purse and trudged along in the direction the girl had gone.

Sunshine stopped, spun around and waited for Anna to catch up.

"Are you hungry?" Anna asked as she reached her. Wandering around town all alone, it wouldn't have surprised Anna if no one cooked for the girl at home, though she looked healthy enough.

"Sure," she replied, and skipped on.

Anna's head throbbed as she attempted to keep up with the little girl who merrily made her way toward town. *Dammit,* Anna thought. *I'm never drinking again.*

Sunshine stopped every fifty feet or so to allow Anna to catch up, and then skipped on again, over and over.

"Hey, slow down," Anna called to her. "Why are you skipping?"

Sunshine stopped abruptly and turned to Anna. "Why aren't you?"

Anna and Sunshine ate in silence. Anna had opted for a salad and the soup of the day, which turned out to be chicken noodle. *Go figure,* Anna mused. Sunshine seemed enthralled with her French fries and chocolate milkshake. She inched closer to Anna's side.

Anna watched as the girl dipped her fries into her milkshake one by one before popping them into her mouth. Anna had loved French fries and milkshakes as a child. A couple times a month her father would take her out to her favorite fast food restaurant and let her order the two unhealthy treats, but he had made her promise not to tell her mother. It was their little secret.

As if reading Anna's mind, Sunshine looked up at her and held out a chocolate-drenched fry. Anna laughed and took the French fry from the girl. She took a bite and closed her eyes, allowing the hot and cold, the sweet and salty to battle on her tongue before she chewed and swallowed. *Even better than I remember,* she thought. Opening her eyes, she noticed a slow, slightly sinister smile spreading across Sunshine's face. Anna felt her pulse quicken. Suddenly, the girl reached for the plastic box of sugar packets, raised it above her head and dumped the contents onto the table. Anna whipped her head around and scanned the restaurant, praying that no one had seen the child's antics, worried that they were about to be escorted out the door. No one seemed to notice. *Thank God,* she thought. *What the hell was I thinking bringing her here?*

Anna turned back toward the girl nervously, convinced she had just witnessed the first stage of a meltdown. Soon the child would be thrashing around in the booth wailing, sending the dishes flying off the table. But when Anna looked down at her, Sunshine was humming contentedly, placing four sugar packets on their edges, balancing them like a house of cards. She carefully placed one sugar packet and then another diagonally across the corners of the four walls she had constructed, then placed two more across the middle. She turned her bright blue eyes up to Anna. "Your turn."

"What?" Anna said.

"You build the second story."

Has she completely lost her mind? What kind of psychologist builds houses out of sugar packets in a restaurant? What if one of my patients is here? What if someone sees me? Anna's mind was racing. This broke all the rules of table etiquette.

"What?" Sunshine said. "Are you chicken? You afraid you'll topple it?"

A challenge, huh? "Of course I'm not afraid," Anna said, shoving her chin into the air. "Push the pile my way."

Anna counted out eight sugar packets and balanced four of them on their edges on top of the first story Sunshine had built. She placed the fifth sugar packet diagonally across the top, then picked up the next one and carefully lowered it across the opposite corner. She released a slow breath when she let go; they all stayed in place. She pumped her fist in the air and laughed out loud. Sunshine bounced up and down in the booth clapping.

"And now for my next trick," Anna said, taking a little bow before picking up the seventh packet and confidently lowering it into place. It held.

As she reached for the last packet, she felt him. The warmth of his gaze embraced her, and her hand trembled as she laid the eighth sugar packet flat across the top, completing the house.

"I did it Daddy!" she said, beaming as she raised her eyes to meet her father's. But he was gone, and Sunshine was no longer at her side. "Damn her," Anna hissed.

She fumbled through her wallet, pulled out a twenty, slid it onto the table then staggered out of the restaurant in a daze. Her hands were still trembling. He had seemed so real. She had felt his presence as if he were sitting right across the table from her, watching her with pride as she succeeded in completing the structure. *Why didn't I stop building that stupid house and look up to see him, reach over to touch him?* Now he was gone… again.

She heard quick footfalls behind her and spun around to see Sunshine skipping toward her, the child's hand raised for a high-five. Anna ignored her, and Sunshine went on her way, laughing and skipping. *Go on,* Anna thought. She wanted as much distance between herself and that little girl as possible.

Sunshine shifted from foot to foot as she waited by Anna's office door. Anna groaned when she saw her. She reluctantly unlocked the door and pushed it open. The girl skipped in, pulled another smooth round stone from her pocket and placed it on Anna's desk. "Thank you," she said and skipped back out the door.

Anna picked up the stone and lowered herself into her armchair. She rubbed her thumb across the flawless surface and sighed. Maybe this little Sunshine wasn't as bad as she had originally thought. Anna turned the stone over in her hand and replayed her lunch with Sunshine in her mind. She had reminded Anna how to build sugar packet houses, something Anna's father had taught her as young child. Every moment had been a game to him, and a delay in food service was just another opportunity for fun. Anna felt her face relax into a smile at the memories.

Sunshine had also made her laugh. Laughing had felt totally foreign, yet completely natural at that table with the girl. Anna had spent so many years dwelling on her loss, that any joy had been buried beneath her misery. Nothing had seemed funny to her in a long time. Nothing had seemed remotely interesting until this quirky little girl skipped into her life.

~

Ron Patterson tipped his keyboard up and slid a photograph out from under it. He held it up and examined the image of the first woman who had rejected him. His mother's blue eyes seemed to burn into his soul. He heard Anna open her office door then close it again. He rubbed his temples. Trying to keep tabs on this woman was wearing him out.

After watching the action at the redneck's house last night, Ron had passed the remaining hours until morning tossing and turning in bed. He had pulled his covers up over his face and buried his head under his pillow, but the voice was lodged deep inside his mind; there was no way to silence it.

"Get back here you little brat! It's no wonder your mother didn't want you.

Someone needs to teach you some manners!"

Ron dropped the photograph onto his desk. "It was your fault, Mother," he said. He lit a cigarette then leaned onto his elbows, hunching over the photo. "It was all your fault."

He pulled up his left cuff and examined the scars on his wrist. "If it's the last thing I do," he growled, taking a long drag and blowing it out slowly, "I will make you pay."

THIRTEEN

After escorting her last appointment through the waiting room, Anna returned to her office, closed the door and sat down at her desk. She ran her fingers over Sunshine's stones again. She couldn't help but feel touched. *What does she need from me,* she wondered. There were dozens of psychologists in Bloomfield. *Why me,* Anna thought. She slipped the two stones into her purse and decided that if Sunshine returned, she would make more of an effort to discover the girl's identity and the issues she had come to resolve.

Darkness had settled in by the time Anna completed her notes and straightened up her desk. She felt uneasy walking to her car alone after dark. Growing up in this small college town, she had always felt safe, day or night. Recently, however, the attacks around campus had prompted her to purchase pepper spray, and she gripped it tightly whenever she walked alone at night. Her car sat only thirty feet from the front door of the office building, but Anna wasn't taking any chances.

During the day, Bloomfield was a postcard of friendly faces, old Tudor and Victorian homes, flowers blooming year-round seemingly unfazed by the changing seasons. The smell of fried food in the air called up memories of many hung over days during college when the only thing that soothed the stomach was fried cheese and onion rings. But since the attacks, sunset brought empty streets and jumpy women with pepper spray.

Pulling into her driveway, Anna said a quick "thank you" to the new porch light she recently had installed. She had set it on a timer for five o'clock, even though the sun was still out at that hour. Not only did the porch light provide a feeling of security, it also gave an air of elegance to the otherwise neglected Victorian home.

Anna's parents had purchased this home the year she was born. Her mother had insisted on having a grand front porch with a porch swing where she and Anna could sit together while Anna's father worked long hours at the university.

Anna paused before entering the house, trying to picture herself swinging with her mother, chatting away the days. Her mother would make up stories starring Anna as the main character – Anna summited mountains; Anna danced with angels in the clouds; Anna slid down rainbows.

She unlocked the door, set her briefcase down and walked into the living room. She surveyed the space she used so rarely now and felt the silence permeate her soul. *I won't be sliding down rainbows any time soon,* she thought. Rubbing her arms for warmth, she fell limp into her father's chair in front of the fireplace. A fire was exactly what Anna needed to warm her house and her heart. She wished she had paid more attention when he had shown her how to build them, but she had assumed he would always be there to do it for her. Always…

Anna sighed. She had felt him today; she had been so sure he was there with her in the restaurant, but he wasn't. She knew that now.

Fighting back tears, she closed her eyes, trying to bring herself back to the nights with her father, sitting on his lap in this chair devouring books in front of the fire. She hadn't known she was learning as they took turns reading one line at a time, and her father had gradually read less and less of each book until Anna was reading entire books on her own. The first time she realized what she had done, she had looked up at her father with wide eyes, and he grinned. "Baby, you've been reading them on your own for months." He hugged her tightly and whispered in her ear how proud he was, and how lucky he was to be her father. They had sat watching the fire dance in the fireplace until Anna faded off to sleep.

After her parents were killed, her aunt moved in, and the warm nighttime fires were snuffed out. Anna spent the next eight years reading alone in her bedroom, the same room she still slept in. She had left the pink floral wallpaper her mother had applied, as well as the matching comforter and pillow shams. The pink music box, the last birthday gift her mother had given her, still sat on Anna's white dresser, a tiny ballerina on top, frozen in time.

~

Taylor slid the fake ID from her pocket and handed it to the man behind the counter. Ignoring the ID, he looked Taylor over approvingly, and she shuddered. He was old enough to be her dad, and she knew he wasn't looking at her to determine her age. With her ash blonde hair, trim body and impossibly full breasts, Taylor was used to the stares. She enjoyed the attention from the college boys who never questioned her age, but this old man's gaze made her feel dirty. She handed him a twenty and turned to leave, not waiting for change.

Vodka in hand, Taylor approached her giggling friend who waited in the shadows outside the liquor store.

"You are a master!" Jodi said. She took the bottle and stuffed it into her bag as they strolled toward campus.

A pudgy college boy was reading over the guest list when the girls entered the frat house. He looked up at Taylor and waved the girls in, not bothering to check the list. Taylor knew her looks had some advantages.

The house was packed wall to wall with college kids throwing back beer, couples making out on ratty couches and a drunk girl teetering as she attempted to dance on a coffee table. Taylor shouted over the music, "Which way should we go?"

"You lead," Jodi said, cupping her hand in Taylor's.

The two girls snaked their way through the crowd and walked out the back door onto the patio. They took a seat by the fire pit. Jodi opened the bottle of vodka then pulled two shot glasses out of her bag and filled them both to the top. "Here's to a great night," she said. They clinked glasses and swallowed the shots.

Jodi wiped her lips on her sleeve. "Did you see the way the guy at the door looked at you?" she said.

"Not my type," Taylor said, rolling her eyes.

"What?" Jodi said. "Are you waiting for Craig Watson?"

Taylor burst out laughing. "What is it with that kid?" she asked. "Have you ever noticed how he wears the same shirt almost every day? And his sneakers! They look like they're about to fall apart!"

Jodi nodded. "I've seen the way he looks at you though," she said. Taylor glared at her. "What?" Jodi said. "I think the two of you would make a cute couple."

Taylor reached over and slapped her friend on the shoulder. "Shut up! He's a total loser!" she said. "Plus, I like my guys a little older *and* taller."

Jodi poured them both another shot. "Here's to that," she said. The two girls clinked glasses, then threw their heads back and swallowed.

"Now *that* guy…" Taylor motioned with her chin toward the doorway. A tall, brawny kid stood leaning against the doorjamb; his dark brown eyes had already found Taylor. Jodi's gaze followed the direction of Taylor's gesture.

"Him?"

Taylor grinned. "He's the one."

Jodi smiled and nodded her approval. "You've got a good eye, my friend."

The girls rose, but Taylor had to sit back down for a moment to regain her balance. "Let's go back inside," she said, standing more steadily this time.

Jodi stuffed the bottle and shot glasses back in her bag and followed her friend into the house. She wrapped her arm around Taylor's shoulder, leaning toward her ear so Taylor could hear her over the music. "Are you going to talk to him?"

"Maybe," Taylor said with a wink. Taylor knew he had noticed her, and she was sure it wouldn't be long before he approached her.

The girls wound their way through the crowd to the makeshift dance floor in the living room. The beer-stained couches had been pushed back toward the walls, leaving a large open space for the DJ.

Grabbing Taylor's hips, Jodi pulled her body close as they moved to the music. They knew that frat boys couldn't resist two girls dancing provocatively together. Every college boy's fantasy was to have two girls at once, and Jodi and Taylor were good at what they did.

As the music came to a stop, Taylor felt a tap on her shoulder. She turned and met the dark brown eyes. "I'm Brian."

"Nice to meet you, Brian," she said, omitting her own name.

"Are you a student here? I haven't seen you around before."

"I take classes part-time," Taylor said, giving her well-rehearsed response to the predictable question. Brian nodded absently. Taylor knew the boys she met at these parties weren't really interested in her life story, and that was fine with her.

"You want a drink?" Brian asked.

"Sure," she said, following him to the bar. "I'll have a shot."

"Have you ever had a depth charge?" he said.

"No, but I'll try it."

Brian grabbed a Red Bull, popped the tab and divided its contents between two pint glasses. Next, he filled two shot glasses with a type of alcohol Taylor didn't recognize and handed one to her. "On the count of three, drop the shot glass into the Red Bull and chug it," he said. Taylor nodded. "One, two, three, go!" Brian dropped the shot glass in, threw his head back and swallowed every drop. Taylor copied him, but struggled to empty the glass without taking a break. After stopping for a breath, she downed the rest and set the glass firmly down on the bar.

"Let's dance," Brian said, placing his hand against her back, pushing her toward the dance floor.

As they moved to Shakira's voice, Brian pulled her close. The buzz was intense, and the rush she felt from the Red Bull made her feel powerful. She ran her hands through his hair and felt electricity shoot through every inch of her body. Taylor loved *this* kind of attention – not the fifty year old dirty guy kind.

When the song ended, Brian spoke. "Where do you live?" he asked, his face close enough that he didn't have to shout over the crowd.

"Jefferson Avenue," Taylor replied without thinking.

Brian took a step back. "Jefferson Avenue? I didn't realize there was student housing on Jefferson."

Crap! Taylor thought. *Think fast!*

Jefferson Avenue boasted the largest, most glamorous homes in Bloomfield. If your first name wasn't "Doctor," you did not live on Jefferson Avenue. College students most definitely did not live on Jefferson Avenue.

The DJ announced the next song, buying Taylor a few seconds.

"Uh, well, I'm a local, so my parents wouldn't spring for student housing. They made me live at home while I take classes."

Brian nodded and pulled her mouth to his, rescuing her from the lies she was frantically concocting.

She loved making out with college boys – they were experienced kissers, unlike the dorks at her school. She knew Brian would expect more, but Taylor was a talented escape artist. She would enjoy the dance and the kissing, and then she would excuse herself to use the bathroom and slip out the back door. That was her routine, and it worked every time.

Feeling the dizziness return, Taylor realized her time was limited. *That was a serious shot,* she thought, especially since she hadn't eaten anything all day. Taylor had known she would be drinking with Jodi tonight, so she had reserved her calories for the alcohol. She hadn't anticipated the sugary energy drink though. She made a mental note to add half an hour to her workout in the morning.

Brian's hands moved down her back. He clutched her and pulled her body tight against his. The zipper of his jeans bruised her pelvic bone, making her well aware of his erection. She winced, wondering why guys thought this was a turn-on for girls.

When the song ended, Taylor made her typical escape, telling Brian that she was going to the restroom, but she couldn't sneak out until she found her friend. She had to move quickly.

She checked for Jodi in the bathroom, then glanced over to where she had left Brian; his eyes were glued to a tall blonde who was moving to the music as she touched every inch of her own body. *Good,* Taylor thought. *He's distracted.* She darted up the stairs, and the dizziness intensified. *Jodi, where are you?* Taylor was beginning to panic.

She checked the first bedroom, then quickly made her way down the hall to the next door. She opened it quietly. Peeking through the crack, she saw her friend.

Jodi was limp on her back on the bed, a heavy red-headed boy hovering over her, kissing her neck while fumbling with the top button of her jeans. Taylor and Jodi had an agreement that they would never let the other one "go all the way" at one of these parties. They had made a pact to save themselves for marriage. Jodi was far too wasted for just two shots. *How much did she have before we left,* Taylor thought.

"Jodi!" she shouted, throwing the door open. The boy's head jerked up. "Let's go."

She marched in, hoisted her friend off the bed, wrapped her arm around her waist and guided her down the stairs. Taylor struggled to support Jodi's weight as they stumbled toward the front door. She spotted Brian on the dance floor, wrapped like an octopus around the tall blonde. *Thank God,* she thought; she didn't want a confrontation.

Once outside, she lowered Jodi onto the curb. She held her friend's hair back as her body heaved, over and over, emptying its contents into the street. Jodi looked up, her eyes bloodshot from the alcohol and the pressure of vomiting. "I'm never drinking again," Jodi slurred.

Taylor rolled her eyes. *I've heard that before.*

FOURTEEN

"Another call came in last night," Jane said, as Kurt walked through the double doors.

"Son of a bitch," he said. "Who was it this time?" Jane followed him into his office. He glanced up at the photos of the first four victims. *Innocent girls,* he thought.

"Another college student," she said. "He grabbed her as she was walking home from Riley's."

"What the hell was she doing walking alone at night?" he asked himself, but Jane responded.

"I have no idea."

Kurt couldn't believe that these college girls still insisted on walking alone in the dark with this maniac on the loose. He had ordered his officers to hang flyers around town, and the news was covering every detail of the case. The *Bloomfield Times* typically featured mundane stories about the university's sports teams, restaurant reviews and gardening tips, so the reporters were devouring this case like ravenous hyenas. It made Kurt sick the way these vampires were preying on the victims, asking them hurtful questions, forcing them to relive their trauma, sucking their blood just to get a good story.

"Where is she now?" he asked.

"Midwestern Memorial. Apparently he beat her up pretty bad."

"Thank you, Jane," Kurt said and marched out the door.

~

Cathy had two hours to prepare for the nine o'clock showing. She paced from room to room tidying up, dusting, tidying up some more. Her real estate agent had tried to convince her to leave during the showings, but Cathy wanted to make sure she approved of any potential buyer. This wasn't just *any* house, after all. She wandered from the living room to the family room to the dining room and back again. She tried to see the house from the perspective of a buyer, but everywhere she looked she saw memories no one else would ever see.

As she walked back into the dining room, her gaze fell upon the faint purple stain on the beige carpet. Her Realtor had mentioned the stain – "an eyesore," he had called it. Cathy had meant to have the aging carpet replaced many times over the years, but that stain was just too precious. *Maybe we could take the carpet with us to our new house,* Cathy thought. She pulled out a chair and sat down at the table, smiling as she remembered that day.

June, 1972

"Mommy!"

Cathy chuckled as her daughter sprinted into her bedroom.

"Mommy, we have a guest," Sandy said, breathless. "He's come for tea."

Cathy followed, attempting to keep up as the five-year-old bounded down the stairs. Sandy waited for her mother on the bottom step then pulled her by the hand into the dining room, scooting out her chair and gesturing for her to sit. She stood on her tiptoes to reach her mother's ear. "Mr. Wiggles was lonely," she whispered, shifting her eyes toward the stuffed bear at the head of the table.

"Oh, I see," Cathy whispered. She turned to the bear and smiled. "How are you today, Mr. Wiggles?"

"You two chat. I'll be right back," Sandy said and galloped off into the kitchen. She returned with a plate of chocolate chip cookies, set the plate between her two guests and hurried back into the kitchen. Cathy spread the cloth napkin across her lap as she waited. *Such a good little hostess,* she thought.

"And now for the tea," Sandy said, as she entered the dining room balancing three porcelain teacups on her mother's silver tray. She walked carefully toward the table, gripping the heavy tray tightly. Her little chest relaxed as she set the tray down then looked up at her mother, her big brown eyes glowing with pride. "Your tea," she said, setting the first teacup in front of Mr. Wiggles. "And for you," she said, handing the second cup to her mother.

"Why thank you," Cathy said, reaching for a cookie. "Will you be joining us?"

"Oh yes," Sandy said and pulled out her own chair and hopped up. As she leaned over to reach for the third teacup, her arm grazed Mr. Wiggles' cup, tipping it. Red grape juice poured across the damask tablecloth, trickling over the edge of the table and onto the floor before Cathy could contain it.

"Oh no!" Sandy wailed. "Look what I did!" She raced out of the dining room and up the stairs to her bedroom. Cathy chased after her daughter, leaving the stain to set.

"It's only carpet," Cathy said, rubbing her daughter's back. Sandy howled into her pillow and Cathy lifted her into her arms, cradling her in her lap. "It's only carpet," she repeated. Sandy looked up at her mother with tear soaked eyes, and Cathy kissed her daughter's hair. "Mr. Wiggles wanted to thank you for the lovely tea party," Cathy said, pulling the bear from behind her back. Sandy wiped her nose with the palm of her hand and giggled, grabbing Mr. Wiggles and pressing him to her cheek.

How can I sell this house, Cathy thought. She raised her eyes from the stain and admired the family photo on the wall – an image of herself with her arms wrapped around the two people she loved most in the world. *So many memories.*

But a five bedroom house was much more than she and Kurt needed at their age. As a young married couple, they had purchased the home with the dream of filling each of the bedrooms with children. As it turned out, it just wasn't meant to be. Cathy had been blessed with one perfect child, and she had never regretted not conceiving more. But now, as she peered out the window, watching a stranger in a suit escort a young couple to her doorstep, she wasn't sure how she was supposed to let go of forty years of memories.

~

James took a sip of his English breakfast tea, then pressed his eyes shut and chose a letter at random.

May 10, 1975
Dear Angel Eyes,

I saw a cardinal on my walk this morning. She was sitting on a fencepost watching me, and I stopped and had a little chat with her. She listened patiently as I told her all about you – how much you love cardinals, how lovely you are when you smile, what a wonderful mother you are. I'm glad no one passed by or I might have been hauled off to the looney bin.

Oh Ruth, I miss you. I want so badly to see your eyes again, to hold you in my arms. I hope in time I can find the strength to do the right thing and come back to you. I promised to love you "in sickness and in health" and yet I have abandoned you. I have failed you. I would ask your forgiveness, but I don't deserve it.

I love you Angel Eyes.
Yours always,
James

He considered bringing the letters with him to Maple Manor. *Ruth should hear them,* he thought, but he didn't want to hurt her all over again. Sighing, he carefully folded the letter and placed it back in the hat box, then rose from the lonely bed and dressed. *Maybe tomorrow,* he thought. *Today we will focus on the happy times.*

His heart sank at the sight of the empty loveseat in the community room. After finding Ruth out of bed on his last visit, James had allowed himself to hope that her condition was improving – that she was beginning to anticipate his arrival. But when he entered her room, he saw her frail body tucked in beneath the comforter, the rise and fall of her chest barely detectable, her ivory eyelids closed but flittering. The scent of lilac caught James' attention, and he looked toward her open window. The aroma was lovely; Ruth deserved some beauty in her life. *I wonder who has been doing such a caring thing for my wife.* The thought warmed his heart.

He pulled the plastic chair up next to Ruth's bed and took her hand in his, gently tracing his thumb over her thin blue veins. She opened her eyes and turned her face toward his, but the sparkle he had noticed during his last visit had been replaced by the familiar blank stare. He swallowed the lump in his throat and spoke. "Good morning, Angel Eyes."

Ruth stared back at him.

"How are you feeling?"

Nothing.

"It's a beautiful morning. Did you notice the scent of the lilac bush outside your window?" He searched her eyes...

Nothing.

He sighed and turned to look at the lilac. "I have an idea," he said, turning back to his wife. "Let's see if Julia will let me take you for a spin in the wheelchair. We could snip some of that lilac to place in a vase right here next to your bed." He patted the top of the nightstand, but her gaze did not follow his hand. "I'll be right back."

He tracked Julia down at the nurses' station. She reluctantly agreed to his idea, and James returned to Ruth's room pushing a wheelchair. He lifted her from the bed and lowered her into the chair, struggling in spite of her slight weight. He had been a much stronger man when he had carried her through the threshold of their first home so many years ago.

"Here we are, Angel Eyes," he had said that day. Ruth had taken his face between her hands as he gently lowered her onto their new bed.

"You amaze me," she had whispered, and James had felt ten feet tall. He had always been so much more in Ruth's eyes.

But now those eyes seemed to see nothing.

Maybe the birds will cheer her up, he thought, letting the wheelchair come to a rest beside a wrought iron bench overlooking the courtyard. After setting the brake as Julia had instructed, he walked over and snapped off a cluster of lilac blossoms, then lowered himself onto the bench by her side.

"Look, Angel Eyes," he said, pointing to the maple tree at the center of the courtyard. A pair of mourning doves rested on a branch and seemed to be watching them. Ruth didn't look up. James took her hand and lifted it to his lips, a gesture that sometimes made her look at him. Her head remained tilted down, her eyes staring at her lap.

With a sigh, James turned back to the doves. *You would never abandon one another*, he thought. Then he took a deep breath and spoke the words he had not been able to speak since his return. "I'm so sorry, Ruth."

He kissed her hand again, laid it gently back down in her lap and stood to push her back inside. As he turned the wheelchair toward the door, a dove swooped just above Ruth's head, startling him. He looked back toward the maple tree with a sick feeling in his stomach; only one dove remained.

FIFTEEN

The icy water burned her lungs, but the pain would be worth it in the end, if she could just hold on...

Warm fingers wrapped around her hand and pulled. She tried to jerk her hand back, kicking as she struggled to stay underwater. The fingers gripped tighter; her eyelids flew open. Through the red water, Anna saw the dark blur of a silhouette.

Mom!

She sat up, fracturing the water's surface, and frantically wiped the red film from her eyes, her heart racing, desperate to see her mother's face. But as the countenance came into focus, Anna saw the girl.

Red tears poured down Anna's cheeks. She snatched her hand away and turned her head, glaring at the water – anywhere but at that girl. Sunshine stood above her, lowered her hand to Anna's head and stroked her hair as if she was petting a kitten. She reached for Anna's hand again and tugged gently. Anna tried to pull her hand away, but Sunshine held on tight.

Anna slowly rose and stared at the girl, frozen in the child's gaze. A buzzer broke through the trance. Sunshine smiled and whispered, "Time's up for today."

Pushing the damp hair out of her face, Anna sat up and threw her legs over the side of the bed. She dropped her palm on the alarm clock to silence it. *Do I really have to do this all over again,* she thought, dragging herself to the shower.

As she pulled into the parking lot, she spotted Sunshine twirling by the front door, her arms outstretched, spinning round and round. *Dammit,* Anna thought. *I can't deal with her today.* Facing up toward the sun with a wide smile, Sunshine didn't see Anna's car. *Thank God.* Anna attempted to drive on through the parking lot without the girl noticing.

No such luck. A mid-spin wave of a tiny hand brought the blood flowing to Anna's cheeks. She pulled into the closest parking space, rubbed her cheeks to hide her guilt and tried her best to look happy to see the girl.

"Whatcha doin?" Sunshine sang, wobbling dizzily toward Anna.

"I was coming in to catch up on some work," Anna said, hoping Sunshine would take the hint.

"Cool."

"And you?" *Is there any chance she'll say she just happened to be playing in the parking lot and will soon be on her way?*

"I have an appointment."

"On Saturday?" This little routine was becoming irritating, yet Anna felt a reluctant smile cross her face.

"Yep."

"Ok then, come on in."

"Nope. Too stuffy. Let's go for a walk."

I should've known she'd say that, Anna thought. She looked around, suddenly feeling foolish for just now noticing the spectacular day. The temperature was in the low 70's, not a cloud in the sky. *I guess I need to remove the blinders once in a while,* she thought. "Where would you like to go?"

"Main Street," Sunshine answered definitively.

What an odd suggestion, Anna thought. She had expected something like the park or the school playground, but Main Street? "Umm... Ok," she said, but the girl had already skipped off.

This time Sunshine didn't stop and turn to wait for Anna to catch up, so Anna jogged after her, knowing full well that she would pay a hefty price in sore knees. *Thank God I wore my sneakers,* she thought as she struggled to keep pace. When the girl finally paused at the corner of Main and Lincoln, Anna whispered a quiet "thank you" and made her way to her side. She bent over and placed her hands on her knees to catch her breath. When she stood upright again, Sunshine was gone.

Damn her! She had done it again. *She dragged me all the way downtown and then disappeared again,* Anna thought.

With her fists in tight balls at her side, Anna turned and headed back toward the office. A soft giggle danced in her direction, and she turned and looked toward the corner of Adams and Main. Sunshine was sitting on the curb, her eyes filled with joy, and maybe a little pity at Anna's lack of physical endurance. *She's laughing at me!*

Anna stomped the whole block over to the child, grumbling under her breath about annoying little girls. "So..." She gasped for air... "why do they... call you... Sunshine?" Anna asked, relieved to finally lower her body onto the curb.

Sunshine twirled a red and white striped straw in her fingers; Anna cringed. *That thing must be covered in germs,* she thought.

"Who?" the girl said, popping the end of the straw into her mouth, taking it between her upper and lower teeth and chewing the tip.

"Whoever it is that calls you Sunshine," Anna said, snatching the straw from the girl's jaws.

Sunshine seemed unfazed as she turned away; a sheet of newspaper in the street had caught her eye, and Anna knew this conversation was over. Sunshine stood and skipped over to retrieve the sheet, grinning from ear to ear as if Santa himself had hand-delivered it.

"Can you believe people litter like that?" Anna huffed. She had no tolerance for littering. "Probably one of those entitled college students whose parents spring for full tuition, room and board, plus a subscription to the local newspaper," which Anna was certain the spoiled brats never read. *Damn kids.*

When she realized that the girl was paying no attention to her ranting, Anna looked up and met the child's sparkling gaze – a ray of sunshine in spite of the nasty thoughts Anna had been spewing, complete with a newspaper sailor's hat perched on her head.

"What are you doing? That thing is filthy!" Anna had a thought to take the girl home and disinfect her from head to toe. *First the straw, now this?! What's next, dried-up chewing gum?* Anna shuddered.

With no regard for Anna's comment, Sunshine lifted the hat, reached over and set it on Anna's head. Anna swiped it off, then stood and marched over to the nearest trashcan.

"What'd you do that for?" Sunshine asked.

"It was a piece of trash!"

Sunshine shrugged. "Depends on how you look at it, I guess. To me it was a hat. Come on," she said, perking right back up as she skipped away, singing in a voice far too big for her diminutive body. Anna scanned the sidewalks. No one seemed to notice. Sometimes it was good that the whole world was so self-absorbed.

She collapsed back down onto the curb, unwilling and unable to follow along any further. She watched the girl skip the length of Main Street and vanish around the corner, not once turning back to see if Anna was following her. Anna remained seated, watching people pass by on the sidewalk – a young boy being pulled along by his dog; a college kid on a mountain bike that probably cost more than Anna's car; a couple, hand in hand, deep in conversation sipping coffee. The familiar feeling of loneliness crept like smog through her chest, and Anna found herself wishing she had followed the girl. She waited on the curb for hours, but Sunshine didn't return.

Anna felt the tears prick the back of her eyes. Over the years, she had grown accustomed to the loneliness and the misery it brought. But since this "Sunshine" had shown up, Anna was raw. Now, the pain seared her every time Sunshine left. She took a deep breath, stood and trudged head down back to her office.

She glanced up as she approached the office building. *Where the hell did that come from?* She wandered over to a stunning Southern Catalpa at the edge of the parking lot. Clusters of tiny white flowers blanketed the tree like snowflakes shimmering in spite of the 70 degree day. She closed her eyes and inhaled deeply. The smell of early summer spiraled around her and wisped into her lungs – a hint of light invading the darkness inside. Anna surrendered, and the light grew, warming every cell in her body. Her mind witnessed a battle between darkness and light – the light blazing; the darkness withering.

When she finally opened her eyes, the sky glowed pink with the remaining traces of the sun. Anna lowered herself to the ground. She rested the back of her head against the warm, smooth bark and stared up through the heart-shaped leaves, feeling her whole body relax. The flowers blended into a hazy mist as she allowed her sight to blur. She felt her eyes drying out, but fought the urge to blink, fearing the beauty would vanish if she did.

And then she saw her – spinning weightlessly, her golden hair gliding on the breeze as she floated to the ground, humming the most beautiful song Anna had ever heard. She kneeled before Anna and smiled, her brilliant blue eyes transferring a little piece of heaven, burning into Anna's soul. "Mom," Anna whispered, but with that one word, she was gone. And the darkness returned.

SIXTEEN

Anna groaned as she pulled into her driveway with less than an hour to prepare for her date with some goofy guy she had met at a conference last month. She would much rather crawl into her bed and hide under the covers, reliving her moment under the tree with her mother.

Why didn't I just say no when he called, she thought, dropping her purse on the floor by the door. But Anna had never been good at saying no. Her usual M.O. was to humor men by saying yes while she gathered the courage to let them down later on. Or more likely, as was usually the case, one date with her would be enough to ensure that the men would not call again.

A few months before her mortifying night with Tommy, there had been Joe. She had felt his eyes on her backside, burning through her jeans as she waited in line at the grocery store. She knew what he wanted the minute he initiated small talk, yet when he asked if they could "get together sometime," she found herself saying yes. She didn't even find him attractive – another redneck with a midsection surrounded by an inner tube of blubber from too many nights crushing beer cans on his forehead.

She had agreed to meet Joe at The Cave; his suggestion of that particular bar should have been Anna's first clue. The Cave was a dingy hole-in-the-wall that she had never once set foot in, for fear of catching something contagious just by walking through the door. She had heard too many tales of cockroaches in the popcorn and mice scurrying under barstools.

She had walked into The Cave that night wishing she could levitate so her shoes wouldn't have to make contact with the sticky floor. Joe was 20 minutes late and his breath reeked of cheap beer when he arrived. Within ten minutes, his hand was on her knee. Five minutes later it was creeping up her thigh. When she politely removed it, he excused himself to go to the restroom and never returned. Anna had been stuck with the bill.

Then there were the times when she would get drunk and end up in their bed, like the night with Tommy, and she would hate herself for weeks afterward. No, dating was not for Anna.

Why do I do this to myself, she thought as she touched up her make-up in the mirror. In spite of being thin, she had never thought of herself as particularly attractive. She was average height with lackluster blonde hair that curled up at the ends, and no matter how much she worked with it, it never lay quite right. But she had often received complements on her eyes. She would search them in the mirror but could never see what all the fuss was about. To Anna they were just average eyes. She stood back and took one last look in the mirror. *Yep. Average. That's me.*

A rush of anxiety and the usual nausea bubbled up in her stomach when she heard the doorbell. *His name is Dan,* she reminded herself as she turned the doorknob and forced a smile.

"Hi," he blurted out, shoving a bouquet of white carnations toward her.

Carnations? Really? Anna greeted him without making eye contact for fear that she might puke down the front of his turquoise and burgundy 80's style Cosby sweater. *Is this his first date in decades,* she thought. *His first date ever?* She accepted the flowers and placed them in the vase on the table beside the door. Men were so predictable that Anna always filled a vase with water before a date arrived. *But carnations?!*

"Ready?" he asked, seemingly unfazed by Anna's presumptuousness in having a vase ready and waiting.

"Ok," she responded, gawking at the sweater in disbelief. He walked a few paces in front of her, and her eyes wandered from the burgundy neckline down a turquoise stripe to the mustard-yellow cuff.

In the driveway, Anna spotted his charcoal Land Cruiser. She considered the sweater then looked again at the Cruiser. *Great taste in vehicles, clueless with fashion,* she thought.

Dan opened the passenger side door for her, and she rolled her eyes as she climbed up into the SUV, thinking to herself how this chivalry would end after another date or two. *If there even is another date,* she thought. He shut her door carefully and walked around to the driver's side.

"I couldn't get reservations for another hour," he said as he pulled out into the street. "Would you like to have a drink beforehand?"

Sure, Anna thought, *get me drunk so you can make a sad attempt at some action later.*

Dan looked over at her and smiled as if he had read her mind, and she felt the blood rise to her cheeks. "That's fine," she said, and he focused back on the road.

~

Who the hell is this jackass, Ron thought, watching some fashion-challenged dork open the passenger side door of a beastly mountain man truck for Anna. *Where did he come from?* Had the little tramp snuck out on one of the nights he hadn't followed her? No, this just would not do. Ron would have to rearrange his schedule to make sure this didn't happen again.

His eyes explored her legs as she climbed into the SUV. He imagined those thin, inviting limbs wrapped around his waist... He shook his head to release the fantasy. *This woman has terrible taste in men,* he thought, assessing Anna's date. *What the hell is he wearing?* At least she seemed bored. That was a good thing.

He followed the truck into town, making sure to keep his distance. When it came to a stop in front of The Gateway Restaurant, Ron parallel parked a block away and lit a cigarette. *I won't let her out of my sight again,* he thought, watching the dork escort her toward the door. When Anna glanced in Ron's direction, he felt his cheeks go numb. Even from a block away, her blue eyes and blank expression felt like home, and he suddenly felt himself being sucked back in time.

"Good night, Ronny," his mother whispered, her gaze flitting around the perimeter of his bedroom.

"Mommy, are you ok?" he asked, reaching up and grasping her face between his chubby palms, turning her head, forcing her eyes to meet his.

"I'm fine," she said, brushing his hands away before standing and walking out of his sight for the last time.

Ron shook his head. *I won't let her out of my sight again.*

~

Dan greeted the hostess by first name and escorted Anna to the bar. The bartender wiped the gleaming wood down with a damp towel, looked up at them and extended his hand. "Good to see you, Dan," he said, nodding to Anna as the two men shook hands. A man at a table across the room gave Dan a slight wave.

"Do you know everyone here?" Anna asked, searching his eyes for confirmation that this Dan guy was indeed a bar fly. A ritzy bar fly perhaps, but a regular nonetheless.

"Not everyone," he said with a chuckle.

He pulled out a barstool for her, and she took a seat on the stool next to it. He hesitated, then sat down on the stool he had pulled out for her.

As Dan spoke with the bartender, Anna took the opportunity to really get a good look at her date. She had to admit, in spite of the sweater, he was actually much better looking than she remembered from their brief conversation at the conference. *Now those are truly bright blue eyes,* she mused. *Much brighter than my average eyes.* His dark brown hair contradicted his lack of fashion sense – unevenly cropped and messy, as if some hot woman had just had her way with him. Instead of making Anna feel inadequate though, the thought warmed her just a little. His face was thin, his cheekbones defined, and he turned to her and grinned as if he knew she was sizing him up. His stunning smile curved up just a little on one side, and sucked the air right out of her lungs. *Dammit,* she thought. *I'm in trouble.*

"What would you like?" he asked.

"Uh, a beer would be great," she said, trying to regain her composure.

"Two pale ales, Jeff," he said.

"Thanks," Anna said as the bartender set a bottle on the bar in front of her. *The man has good taste in cars* and *beer,* she thought.

"Would you like a glass?" the bartender asked.

"No, the bottle is fine," she said.

Dan smiled and shook his head at the bartender, indicating that neither of them would need a glass. *Just like me,* he thought, eyeing her. *Straight from the bottle. My kind of girl.* It also didn't hurt that she was gorgeous... but then she always had been.

He stared at Anna, completely at ease. Anna, however, had no idea what to say; her gaze shifted from her beer bottle to the shelves of liquor behind the bar, then back to her beer bottle. She wasn't prepared to find him attractive.

When he asked her about her work, she inwardly rolled her eyes, figuring it would be a very long night of shop talk – the reason she never dated psychologists. *At least the beer is good,* she thought. *And the eye candy is a bonus.*

As she swallowed the last of her beer, she felt herself begin to relax. The hostess approached to announce that their table was ready. Anna stood and felt the ground shift a little. Dan placed his hand at the small of her back as they followed the hostess to their table. Anna paused to allow him to pull out her chair. He smiled. She blushed.

He asked her a few questions, but she had trouble giving sensible responses. Every time he smiled at her, her mind went blank. He seemed to sense her uneasiness, so he stopped pressing. "I enjoyed talking with you at the conference," he said, rescuing her.

111

Honestly, Anna barely remembered talking to him at the conference. *How did I not notice this man,* she thought.

A stunning waitress appeared and the young woman's eyes lingered on Dan for a few seconds before she spoke. Anna felt her jaw tighten.

"A bottle of Merlot to accompany your dinner, Sir?" the waitress said, not bothering to acknowledge Anna. "It's on the house." Dan looked across the table at Anna.

"Do you like Merlot?" he asked.

Anna shook her head.

"Thank you," Dan said to the waitress, "but we're fine with the pale ales." After giving Dan one last lengthy appraisal, the waitress sauntered off. Dan continued as if they hadn't been interrupted. He told Anna a little about his own practice and about the years he spent in Colorado.

"It was so different from Bloomfield. Almost other-worldly," he said, turning his gaze toward the ceiling. "The mountain air was so crisp, the skies impossibly blue, and the snow..." he suddenly seemed lost in his memories. "Sometimes it snowed so much, you didn't know if it was ever going to stop." He returned his attention to Anna and smiled. "I'll take you out there someday."

Anna's head began to spin – not from the beer, but from the realization that this beautiful man was talking about making plans beyond this first date.

"You know," he said, interrupting her thoughts. "I didn't mention it at the conference. I probably should have." He took a sip of his beer before continuing. "I grew up in Bloomfield too."

Anna straightened in her chair. "You did?" She wracked her brain but couldn't recall a single guy as hot as Dan in school. *Dan Everett,* she thought. *Dan Everett... Why doesn't that ring a bell?* Of course Anna had lived in her own world in those days, so she wasn't surprised that she didn't remember him. "Did I know you back then?" She felt ridiculous asking.

"No," he said. "But I remember you."

"You do? How..." Anna's words trailed off. She stared at him, dumbstruck.

"I remember you," he said, setting his beer bottle on the table and looking directly into her eyes, "because you're impossible to forget."

Damn him! Anna flagged the waitress down and ordered another beer. From that point on, everything else was a blur.

~

Sandy opened The *Bloomfield Times* to the article she had noticed earlier:

"Nursing Home Seeking Volunteers to Entertain Residents: Maple Manor, Bloomfield's most distinguished convalescent care facility, has implemented a program to involve community members in the daily lives of its residents. Volunteers are invited to play piano, lead songs, provide arts and crafts or other forms of entertainment for the residents."

Sandy's heart skipped; what she wouldn't give to play again. She had asked Mitch about buying a piano after Todd was born, but he had refused. He had insisted that she didn't have time for "such a stupid thing" – she had a house to keep up and a family to take care of. Sandy had argued that she could play after the housework was done, while Craig and Todd napped. Sandy had learned that day to never argue with Mitch.

She carefully folded the newspaper and left it on the table just the way Mitch liked it, so he could read it when he got home from work. She said a silent prayer that he wouldn't notice the missing classifieds. She wiped down the counters one last time, checked the refrigerator to make sure everything was ready for her to make his breakfast in the morning, then turned off the light and padded barefoot up the stairs to check on her sleeping children.

After kissing each of them goodnight, Sandy retired to her bedroom. She fluffed Mitch's pillow out of habit, then crawled into bed, curling herself onto her side with her back to the empty space beside her. She thought of her mother, and how she had tried to put on a happy face when Sandy's father worked nights. Her mother had read Sandy an extra book on those nights, delaying the inevitable lonely bedtime, Sandy now realized. But Sandy preferred the empty bed. Mitch was nowhere near the man her father was.

She closed her eyes and tried to force herself to sleep, but her mind kept bouncing back to the article in The *Bloomfield Times*. Could she get away with it? Could she sneak away and play at Maple Manor without Mitch finding out? She needed the music – the feeling of the cool keys under her fingers, the freedom from her constant worries. She rolled over and touched Mitch's pillow. *Freedom from you,* she thought, allowing herself to hope.

SEVENTEEN

Anna opened her eyes, bolted upright and jumped to her feet. *Dammit! I did it again,* she thought. But after frantically surveying the room, she realized that she was alone – and fully dressed. She quickly made the bed then crept down the stairs. Dan was wrapped in an afghan on the couch.

Anna tiptoed out the front door, closing it softly; she didn't want to wake him. She knew he would feel obligated to kiss her and ask for another date and say a bunch of crap he didn't mean, and she refused to put either of them through that. She stopped on the front porch for a moment to slow her thundering heart and felt the heat of his stare on her back. She turned around slowly and found him smirking, wearing only his boxers. Anna had never thought of herself as hot before, but the way Dan looked at her in that moment, she felt like the sexiest woman alive.

"Leaving without breakfast?" he asked.

Is he not the least bit embarrassed? Anna thought. *How can he smile like that?* "Um, yeah, I have to go to work."

"On Sunday?" He made an effort to look serious, his sparkling eyes playfully reprimanding her for lying. He didn't seem to consider the possibility that she might be making an excuse to leave because she didn't like him. No, he knew.

"Oh, it's Sunday?" She tried the playing dumb routine; he didn't buy it. He wove his fingers into hers and nearly pulled her off her feet into the house, slamming the door behind him with his bare foot. *Damn him!*

Anna's eyes traced the muscles in his forearms as he pulled out a chair at the kitchen table and motioned for her to sit. She obeyed. *What a sucker I am for a great smile, incredible eyes and damn! those forearms,* she thought.

Dan moved around the kitchen in a dance that seemed hardwired – eggs cracking, whisk twirling. It took every bit of willpower Anna could summon to stay seated. She felt heat in every inch of her body as she envisioned herself jumping on his back and twisting him to the floor.

The heavenly flavor of pancakes and scrambled eggs lingered on her tongue as she explained that she had to leave. Dan stood from his chair, took both her hands and pulled her to her feet. She felt his hands move to her hips as his soft lips brushed her forehead.

"You know," he whispered, "you're beautiful when you're sleeping."

"Dan," Anna began.

He pulled back and looked into her eyes. "Nothing happened, Anna," he said, putting her mind at ease. "Yet." He winked at her, then took her face in his hands and kissed her. Anna closed her eyes, imagining for a moment that this could last. Then she pulled away and walked out the door. Dan threw on jeans and a T shirt and followed her.

She stopped just outside, and he wrapped his arms around her from behind and whispered in her ear, "Were you planning on walking home?"

Anna rolled her eyes. *I am such an idiot,* she thought. "Will you take me home, Dan?"

He kissed her ear and trailed his lips down the side of her neck before turning her slowly to face him. "Sure," he said, suddenly all business. "I'm at your service, my lady." He took a slight bow, then strolled back into the house for his keys. He led Anna to the Land Cruiser and opened the door for her. "My lady," he said, as she climbed in.

Anna laughed. Dan winked as he closed the door.

The headache arrived the moment Dan stepped off her front porch, as if his presence had somehow made her immune to the symptoms, but once she was away from him, the hangover crushed her. She dragged herself through the front door, not bothering to take off her sweater or shoes, and made her way to the kitchen. She filled a large glass with water, downed four ibuprofen and dropped two Alka-Seltzer into the remaining water. While the tablets dissolved, she carried the glass to her bedroom, slid under her sheets, shoes and all, and pulled the covers over her head to block out the sunlight. She ignored her ringing cell phone until she heard the beep. She couldn't resist checking the message.

"Hey, it's Dan."

Just the sound of his voice made her smile.

"You're smiling, aren't you?" he said.

Damn him!

~

Sandy served Mitch his eggs and oatmeal and waited in silence while he ate. He said nothing as he stood and headed up to bed, leaving his dishes on the table. Sandy cleared the table and washed the dishes in the sink, careful not to let them clink together for fear she would wake him. He usually slept soundly after working the night shift, but Sandy wasn't taking any chances.

After inspecting the kitchen to make sure she hadn't missed anything, she sat down at the table with a glass of ice water and a stack of Saltines. No need for a test – after four pregnancies, Sandy didn't need a doctor to tell her what was happening inside her body. According to her calculations, she was about six weeks along. She had noticed the missed period, but had assumed it was stress, as usual. But this morning there was no denying it – morning sickness had arrived with a vengeance.

She rested her hand on her abdomen. "It's going to be ok, little one," she whispered. "Mommy's going to make it all ok." Tightening her ponytail, she stood and retrieved the neatly folded classifieds from their new hiding place under the trash can. She couldn't afford to risk Mitch finding them again, not after his reaction when he had found them behind the flour. She rubbed the dark shadow around her left wrist then pulled the cuff of her sleeve down over the bruise.

"*Retail Sales,*" she read again, circling the ad. Craig wandered into the kitchen. Sandy folded the classifieds, sat up straight and smiled. "What are you doing up so early, kiddo?"

"I couldn't sleep," he said. Even though he was her oldest, Craig was the most sensitive of all four of her children. At seventeen, he still slept with a night light and insisted on having the bedroom door cracked open. Todd, his younger brother, had argued over and over that he wanted the door closed, but in the end, Sandy had convinced Todd to let Craig have his way.

"What's going on, buddy?" she asked, as he moved into her arms. She cherished the scent of her children, and she drew in a slow, deep breath as he rested his chin against the top of her head. Craig was small for his age, almost as if he had stopped growing at twelve. Mitch had tried to push him into sports – first soccer, then baseball, then basketball – but Craig had no interest. He would rather spend his time alone in his bedroom creating comic books. Sandy worried that Craig didn't go out with friends; he didn't fit in. He had never once asked to go to a sleepover or have a friend stay the night. Sandy knew why, and she blamed herself.

Mitch had finally given up on his dream of having an all-star son, and had eventually stopped interacting with Craig altogether. He was a disappointment to his father, but to Sandy, Craig was a gift. All of her children were, and this new one would be no different.

"I had another nightmare," Craig said. Sandy felt him shudder in her arms.

"Do you want to talk about it?" she asked, knowing better than to press him to recall something that had frightened him.

"Not really," he said, lifting his chin from her head and taking a seat beside her at the table. "Do you think you could make pancakes?"

"Of course," Sandy said. Pancakes were Craig's favorite. He asked for them on his birthday, on Christmas morning, on Sunday mornings, and every time he was upset about something. Sandy figured she made pancakes for Craig about 360 mornings a year. She rose and began the preparations, as Libby, Todd and Cecilia thundered down the stairs into the kitchen. *Oh Lord, please don't wake your father,* Sandy thought.

"Libby woke me up again," Cecilia whined.

"Did not," Libby said.

"Did so."

"Are you making pancakes?" Todd asked.

"I am," Sandy said, and the bickering ceased, the childish resentments dissolving like the lumps in her batter. Sandy knew it was time, no matter what.

EIGHTEEN

The fading sunlight filtered through her blinds and Anna groaned, realizing she had slept away the entire day. She climbed out of bed, thanking the ibuprofen, and tried to push Dan out of her mind. She picked up her fleece blanket and walked out to the porch. The last golden sliver of sun dipped below the horizon, and the evening sky erupted into a hundred different shades of orange.

I wasted the whole damn day, Anna thought. *Damn him!* She turned to the weathered porch swing, longing to find her mother there. "Oh Mom," she whispered. "I could really use some advice right now."

"Needs paint," a cheerful voice called out.

Anna spun around to see Sunshine skipping up the brick walkway. "What are you doing here?" she asked.

Sunshine bounded up onto the porch and, not waiting for an invitation, hopped up onto the porch swing and began pumping her legs back and forth.

"Uh, have a seat," Anna said.

Sunshine smiled then patted the swing, inviting Anna to join her. "You look terrible," Sunshine said.

"Thanks," Anna said, lowering herself onto the swing. "It's nice to see you too."

"How was your date?"

Anna's eyebrows shot up. "How did you know about my date?"

"He's cute," Sunshine said, beaming.

"Yes," Anna said, remembering his smile. "That he is."

"You like him, don't you?" Sunshine said, moving closer.

Anna leaned away and gawked at the girl. "What are you talking about? Of course I don't like him!"

"Yeah, yeah." Sunshine said. "Dan and Anna sittin' in a tree..." she chanted.

"Stop!" Anna rose from the swing. "I do not!"

"Do so!" Sunshine said, and stuck her tongue out at Anna.

"You did NOT just stick your tongue out at me!"

Sunshine did it again.

"You're crazy," Anna said and stomped into the house, slamming the door and latching the deadbolt. *She's crazy,* Anna thought, her heart racing. *How dare she! That child is delusional. Of course I don't like him.* But even as the thoughts surfaced in her mind, Anna knew she was lying to herself. What Anna needed was her mother to talk to about these things, not a child. She leaned her head against the door. *Oh Mom, what do I do?*

She wandered into the living room and sat down in her father's chair. *"I remember you because you're impossible to forget."* Dan's words echoed in her mind. *I'm not who he thinks I am,* she thought. *I'm a wreck.* She decided then and there that she would not let him in. *No way,* she thought. Because in her heart, she knew if she did, he would eventually see the real Anna and run for cover. And she couldn't survive another heartbreak. *It's better this way,* she told herself. *He deserves better.*

She stood and walked to the front door and peeked out through the peephole to see if Sunshine had left. The porch swing was empty. *Good riddance,* she thought, but her heart sank.

She climbed the stairs to her parents' bedroom and stood in the doorway, feeling her chest drop as a sigh escaped. *Am I doing the right thing by pushing him away?* Girls had their mothers for these things. Anna had no one. She rested her head against the doorjamb and closed her eyes. *I need you Mom.* The silence pressed hard on her.

She opened her eyes and walked over to her parents' bed. Running her fingers over the bare mattress, Anna sat down and imagined the tiny embroidered knots that had formed swirls on her parents' bedspread. She longed to curl up beneath the soft cover and watch her mother's ivory sheers float on the breezes that drifted through the open window. The movement of the sheers had hypnotized Anna as a child as she relaxed on her parents' bed, listening to her mother hum cheerful tunes in the bathroom.

Standing and walking to the door, Anna turned and let her gaze sweep the bare room once more; she sighed. *Oh Mom, I need you.* She turned and leaned into the doorjamb, staring up at the attic hatch in the hall, as she had done so many times before. She knew they were up there – relics of their life as a family had always been so close; Anna had known where to find them, but she had never been strong enough to face them.

Her mother had spent countless hours in the attic "organizing memories," as she had called it. Memories in the attic – treasured moments tucked safely away, the painful ones shoved out of sight. Anna had tried to talk herself into climbing that ladder so many times, yet every time she approached it, she froze. It hurt to look back. It hurt to look forward. So she had remained stuck.

Tonight, though, Anna wanted nothing more than to wrap herself in her parents' bedspread and imagine herself in her mother's arms. *It's got to be up there,* she thought. "Come on," she told herself. "You can do this." She took a deep breath and marched to her bedroom to retrieve the flashlight she kept beside her bed.

Reaching up for the cord that hung from the attic hatch, Anna lowered the ladder carefully, ducking instinctively in case a dead bat or a skull tumbled down onto her head. "Let's do this," she told herself and gripped the edges of the rickety wooden ladder.

As she climbed, the ladder creaked, and Anna was certain she heard a rat scurry across the floor above her. *Breathe in, breathe out,* she thought to herself. She stopped and waited for her adrenaline to lower back to normal levels.

Poking her head up through the opening, she clicked the flashlight on and took a moment to get her bearings. She crept up onto the attic floor and sat down in the quarter inch of dust that had settled over the past twenty-five years. *It's not so bad up here,* she thought, though her ears were still on high alert for rodents.

She circled the beam of light around the attic, stopping at the back corner where she noticed a faded blue suitcase covered in cobwebs, a stack of neatly labeled boxes and a guitar. *I wonder who played the guitar,* she thought. She stood and bumped her head on the low ceiling. "Dammit!" She rubbed the top of her head as she carefully made her way to the boxes. "Camping Gear," one label read; Anna laughed. Perhaps her father had thought there was hope of convincing her mother to sleep in a tent. *Yeah right,* Anna thought, smiling. Her mother had made her opinion clear about that.

She shined her flashlight on the other two boxes – "Anna's Baby Clothes" and "Anna's Schoolwork." None of these likely held her parents' bedspread. She sat back down and tried to think. *Aunt Teresa probably just threw it out,* Anna thought. *I'm wasting my time.*

Hunched over to avoid further head trauma, she crept cautiously toward the ladder. Scanning the opposite wall, her flashlight illuminated a low shelf full of old books and photo albums. Anna felt her heart flutter. She approached the shelf and carefully removed an album marked 1967 – *the year I was born,* she thought. Taking it under her arm, she lowered herself down the ladder, raised the hatch and watched as a cloud of dust puffed out around the edges when the door reached the ceiling. She dusted herself off and walked to her bedroom, sat down on her bed and opened the album.

The caption beneath the first photo read "Welcome to the world," and Anna instantly recognized her mother. Tears burned her eyes. Her aunt had stripped the house of all evidence of Anna's happy family; it had been over two decades since Anna had seen an image of her mother, but she knew her face like it was her own. In the photo, her mother was lying in a hospital bed holding the tiny pink bundle that was Anna. *She looks so content,* Anna thought, touching her mother's eyes with her fingertips.

"Grandma's little girl," the next caption announced. *Who is this woman,* Anna wondered. The caption suggested that it was her grandmother, and the resemblance to her mother was striking. How proud she looked. Even in the photo, the glow of love was unmistakable. *How did she die,* Anna wondered. *Why didn't I ever ask them?*

On the few occasions Anna had asked about her family over the years, her aunt would simply roll her eyes and turn her back. The only time her aunt ever spoke of Anna's father was when she reprimanded Anna with slurred words – *"You're spoiled, just like your dad was."* Then she would grumble about how their mother had always liked Raymond best. "Mommy's golden child," she would say as she staggered away, retreating to her bedroom and her fantasy world where Anna didn't exist.

Anna had finally given up and tucked her questions away safely in her mind. Now it seemed they were determined to escape, by forcible means if necessary. She silenced the ringer on her phone, laid the open album on her chest and closed her eyes, resigning herself to the dream that would surely come. "Bring it on," she said, lacking the strength to fight it.

NINETEEN

Sunshine's shimmering blue eyes pierced the red haze. She released Anna's hand and turned her face toward the sky. Anna copied her, allowing the red raindrops to paint her skin. The cool drops trickled down her cheeks, caressing her neck, dripping from her hair down her back. Sunshine opened her arms wide and began to spin. Anna watched as the girl's spin evolved into a fluid dance. The drops glistened on her pale flesh, blue and orange blending with the red, creating swirling rainbows in her golden curls. She took Anna by the hand and pulled her through the rain. They slid back and forth through the colorful mud, spinning and sliding until they collapsed onto their backs, delirious, watching the colors flash through the sky like fireworks. Sunshine picked up a handful of vibrant mud and smeared it into Anna's eyes. Anna laughed as she wiped it away, and then she saw him. "Daddy!"

Anna kicked off her covers as she fought to stay in the dream, but consciousness won the battle. *Why do I have to keep losing them over and over again?* But this dream had left her with a different feeling somehow. She had danced and laughed in the rain; she had felt alive for a brief moment. *It was just a dream,* she thought.

The blinking light on her cell phone brought her back to reality. She rolled over and picked up her phone.

"Are you ever going to call me back?"

Anna rolled her eyes at the sound of his voice. *He's not going to make this easy, is he,* she thought.

"I think I'll just have to start singing into your voicemail until you return my call. Believe me," he said, "that would *not* be pretty. So call me."

Anna laughed in spite of herself. *I'm surrounded by crazy people,* she thought as she hit delete. *Damn him.* She laid her cellphone back on her nightstand and rose to prepare for work.

As she opened her front door to leave, she groaned. Rainy days were not kind to her hair. She ran back upstairs to grab her raincoat.

"Good morning James," Anna said, as he shuffled into her office.

"Damn," he said, setting his umbrella by the door.

"What's the problem, James?"

"This shit is getting out of control."

"The cursing?" Anna asked, biting her bottom lip to stifle her grin. As much as James was upset, seeing him did lift Anna's spirits.

"Hell yes, the cursing," he said.

"Why don't you have a seat and we'll see what we can do about that."

"Fine," he grumbled.

Anna studied James as he lowered himself into a chair and stared at the floor. He was wringing his hands so hard that Anna winced just watching him. She had never seen him this distraught before. She felt a tug that told her she needed to know more. "What's going on, James."

Slowly, almost painfully, he lifted his head and looked into her eyes. The usual fire had been replaced by something dark, something devastating. "You are a beautiful young woman, Anna," he said, then turned toward the window. Anna squirmed in her chair, embarrassed by the compliment and suddenly a little uneasy in James' presence. "My wife is beautiful too," he whispered. He seemed mesmerized by something outside, and Anna turned to follow his gaze. A lone mourning dove sat in the rain on a branch just outside the window.

"I don't think she loves me anymore," James said, so softly Anna could barely make out his words.

"Your wife?" Anna said, looking at him again.

"Yes."

Anna noticed that the cursing had stopped, but now James seemed consumed by a sadness, a loneliness so deep that her heart wanted to crawl out of her chest and snuggle up next to him. She knew how he felt. She knew this deep and desperate loneliness. She knew the feeling of not being loved. She wanted to hug him and comfort him. She wanted the old, cursing James back. She leaned toward him. "Why don't you think your wife loves you anymore?"

"I hurt her," he said, still gazing out the window. "It was a long time ago, but I hurt her in the worst possible way." Anna waited for James to continue, but he didn't. He was obviously confused; he had only been married a couple years, and Anna's heart broke as she witnessed confirmation of her suspicion – dementia. But to correct his thoughts would only add to his distress, so Anna played along.

"Has she forgiven you?" she asked.

"I don't know," he said, entranced by the dove.

"What does she say about it?" Anna asked.

"Nothing," he said.

"She won't talk about it?" Anna said.

"No," James replied absently.

Anna turned back to watch the dove. She was reluctant to push him any further. If he wanted to share, he would. If he needed her to just be there, she would. And truthfully, she wasn't sure what to say anymore. She listened to the dove's melancholy call and found herself searching the branches for its mate.

Lost in the lonely world of the dove, neither of them saw her enter, but Anna felt the chill and looked up to see the mischievous smile. "Sunshine! You can't be in here," Anna hissed, hoping James wouldn't hear. If he heard, he didn't show any reaction.

Patient confidentiality was the first commandment in Anna's profession, counseling 101; it had been pounded into every lecture in graduate school. It was non-negotiable, and Sunshine's even *seeing* James in her office broke all the rules. Anna wasn't sure how to get the girl out without alarming James.

Sunshine pranced over and stood directly in front of Anna, staring at her, smiling, waiting for her to get up from her chair. Anna shook her head, but Sunshine didn't budge – a standoff. Anna shook her head again, more emphatically this time, but Sunshine simply smiled. Anna rolled her eyes and stood, and Sunshine promptly pounced into the soft leather. "Would you like to join me for a walk outside," Sunshine said.

James turned, looked directly at the girl and grinned.

Anna started to apologize for the interruption, but James didn't seem to mind. She considered the rain and was about to object when she noticed that the fire had returned to James' eyes.

"Sure," he said. He rose and strolled out of the office, leaving his damp umbrella propped up beside the door.

Was he skipping, Anna mused. She grabbed her raincoat and hurried out the door behind him. Shivering in the downpour, Anna couldn't help but chuckle to herself, watching an eighty-two year old man shuffling down the sidewalk, stopping at every mud puddle to make a huge splash.

"What are you waiting for?" he called over his shoulder, smiling like a child. Anna turned her face to the sky and felt the cool rain on her cheeks. *What the hell,* she thought, and let her raincoat fall to the ground.

~

Taylor placed the tray on the wheeled table beside the bed. Ruth looked up at her. "Where's your husband?" Taylor asked.

Ruth's expression didn't change.

"Are you hungry?" she asked, but Ruth didn't respond. *How awful to be stuck in a body that doesn't work anymore,* Taylor thought. *I wonder what goes on in her mind.* She straightened the comforter across Ruth's chest, brushing away a stray down feather. "Well, I'll leave you to rest, but please try to eat something." Taylor recognized her mother's words as they fell from her own lips.

Ruth slowly lifted her hand and placed it on Taylor's. Taylor froze, captivated by the woman's eyes, seeing a longing that hadn't been there just a moment before. Taylor gently pulled her hand away and turned to make sure no one was outside Ruth's door. She quietly picked up the plastic chair, carried it over beside the bed and took a seat next to the frail woman.

Taylor offered her a spoonful of broccoli cheddar soup, but Ruth refused to open her mouth. "Please," Taylor said. "You need to eat." Ruth turned her head toward Taylor and slowly lifted her hand again. She pressed her fingers against Taylor's wrist, guiding the spoon away from her own mouth toward Taylor's.

She's telling me to eat, Taylor thought, suddenly feeling selfish. She had everything money could buy, in addition to youth and good health, and here was this sweet old woman giving up her own meal for her.

Taylor accepted the spoon and took the soup into her mouth. The warmth soothed her, and without stopping to think, she dipped the spoon back into the soup and brought it to her lips again. She closed her eyes and savored the creamy broth, then immediately dropped the spoon onto the tray. Her eyes flew open. *Oh my God,* she thought. *What am I doing? I'm eating this woman's lunch!* She quickly set the spoon next to the bowl. "I'm sorry," she said. "I'll get you another bowl of soup." She stood to retrieve the tray and Ruth abruptly raised her hand, letting it fall on the edge of the tray. "What?" Taylor asked.

A flicker of light passed over Ruth's eyes. Taylor's heart fluttered in her chest. *Wow,* Taylor thought. *She's happy.*

Taylor raced to the kitchen and fetched another bowl of soup and a spoon, then hurried back to Ruth's room. When she came through the door, she found Ruth sitting up in bed with the table rolled across her lap. *She wants to have lunch with me,* Taylor thought. Butterflies danced in her belly as she switched out the bowls of soup and took hers into her hands, lowering herself again onto the plastic chair next to the bed.

Taylor smiled in between bites as she emptied her bowl. The soup warmed her body; Ruth's concern warmed her soul.

~

Drenched and euphoric, Anna dumped her can of vegetable soup into a bowl and heated it in the microwave, praying Dr. Patterson wouldn't waltz into the break room and see her there looking like a soggy puppy. *I can only imagine what he would say,* she thought as she snuck outside to the picnic table. A large awning protected the table, and though Anna had thoroughly enjoyed the romp in the rain, she was grateful to be dry while she ate.

The large raindrops pummeling the metal awning brought back memories of summer camping trips with her parents. Her mother had refused to sleep in a tent on the ground, so they would rent a cabin – the same one every year. Anna loved listening to the rhythm of the rain falling on the metal roof, especially at night. When they woke up to rain, Anna and her father would charge outside in their pajamas and dance in the downpour, sliding across the mud, trying to drag each other down. Eventually her mother would call to them, hose them off and sit them down to eat.

The cabin had a modest kitchen with a basic stove where her mother would make eggs for breakfast and her mouth-watering fried chicken for lunch. *Not like the unlimited shelf-life chicken they put in canned soup,* Anna thought, stirring her vegetable soup.

After she finished her lunch, she crawled up onto the picnic table and lay back to listen to the rain, her mind falling effortlessly back in time.

July, 1975

"How's it going, Shirley?" Anna's father said, shaking the water from his raincoat on the covered porch. Katherine looked up at him and glared, her hair curled into tight ringlets, courtesy of the rain. "Don't worry, honey," he said. "You're much cuter than Shirley Temple." He placed a quick kiss on her nose and spun around to make a speedy getaway. She dropped her crocheting beside her lawn chair and chased him inside.

Anna lay by the fireplace reading. She startled to attention at the ruckus. Her father stopped in the kitchen, his hands raised in surrender, and her mother took advantage of his exposed mid-section, landing a fake punch to his abdomen. He collapsed to the floor and curled up in a ball. Anna gasped. She darted over to check on him and placed her hand on the side of his face. "Daddy! Are you ok?" He didn't answer. She squatted down next to him, and he reached up, growling like a monster, and grabbed her. He pulled her to the floor and tickled her until she thought she would pee her pants. She fell for it every time.

~

Ron glanced up from the file on his desk. *That woman has completely lost her mind.* Through the window he could see Anna lying flat on her back, soaking wet. He chewed the end of his pen leaving permanent tooth marks. *She seems to like being wet on her back,* he thought, then forced his eyes back to the few notes he had made in the new file.

This next patient was an interesting case. When the man called, he had explained that he needed help working through some problems with his temper. Ron had asked him a few questions including, of course, how he intended to pay for his sessions. When the man offered that he had coverage through the police department, Ron had immediately cleared a spot in his Day Timer. *A cop with anger issues,* he thought. *Finally something good.*

He looked at his clock; the jerk was already ten minutes late. *Typical,* he thought. *Give a man a badge and a gun, and suddenly he thinks he's a badass.* He leaned back in his chair and intertwined his fingers behind his head as he turned his attention back to Anna. *On her back, where she belongs.* He watched her for half an hour, lying motionless with a smile on her face, and lost himself to the memories.

June, 1953

She had left a box of cereal on the table for him, and her coffee cup sat in its usual spot on the counter. The dish rag hung over the edge of the sink, just like it always did. Everything was normal, except that the voice he heard wasn't his mother's.

A tiny drop of water clung to the faucet, slowly growing into a heavy teardrop before losing its grip. "Plip." He watched another one form where the first one had been. "Plop." Over and over he watched the teardrops grow then fall... "plip... plop..." The sound comforted him, and he resented the interruption. He didn't want to listen to the woman, he just wanted to watch the teardrops fall into the sink.

"Ronny, honey," the woman said, "I'm Shirley Jamison and this is Officer Franklin. We're going to take you to stay with a nice family in town until we can, um... until we find your mother." She placed her hands on his shoulders and tried to guide him out of the kitchen.

He didn't budge. He turned and stared at the back door, waiting for his mother to come bursting through it. She would explain to this Shirley woman that she had just run out for groceries. He was sure his mother would come running through that door any second. He stared. He waited. "plip... plop... plip... plop..."

He felt someone wrap a blanket around him and turn him by the shoulders. He never saw who it was. He didn't see anything for days.

"He sure is a scrawny little shit," the man hissed.

"Be nice," the woman said.

"Why doesn't he talk?"

"Who knows."

"He doesn't even say thank you when you make him dinner."

Ronny pushed the instant mashed potatoes around on his plate with his fork, mixing them with the mushy canned peas.

"Something's wrong with this one," the man said. "Someone needs to teach him some manners."

"Come on now. Be nice," the woman said.

Anna sat up, and the spell was broken. Ron pulled his mother's photograph out from under his keyboard and lit a cigarette. He looked at the clock again. *A no-show,* he thought. *Asshole cops think they own the world. I cleared my schedule for this jerk and he stands me up. It's no wonder they can't catch the rapist.* He blew the smoke out through his nose and crushed the cigarette butt on his mother's face.

~

James stopped by his apartment to change out of his wet clothes before visiting his wife. He raised the blinds throughout the space, allowing the daylight in for the first time. He opened the top drawer of his dresser and touched the hat box reverently, then dug through the other drawers in search of dry socks. He fished out a black Merino wool dress sock and rooted around for its mate. *Ruth used to keep the clothes so well organized,* he thought. James didn't bother matching his socks before putting them away. *At least I put them away,* he thought, chuckling. He found the matching sock in the last drawer he checked. He chose his grey Italian wool two-button suit jacket and matching pants. *It's an important day,* he thought, tweaking his tie in the mirror. "This will to have to do." Turning his back to his reflection, he retrieved the hat box and headed for the door.

The rain had stopped, and he took that as a good omen. He approached his car and paused, then dropped his keys into his pocket and strolled toward the sidewalk on foot. He felt the sun smiling down on him and removed his suit jacket, draping it over his shoulder, enjoying the sound of his oxfords on the wet concrete. *I haven't felt this alive in years,* he thought. *Not since...* He halted his thoughts. All of that was in the past. She was still Ruth, and he felt in his bones that today was the day he would reach her again. *The letters,* he thought. The letters would convince her that she was on his mind every moment while he was away. The letters would show her that he never stopped loving her. *She needs to know the truth,* he thought. *And maybe, just maybe, the letters will bring her back to me.* His pace quickened as he approached the nursing home.

Ruth was staring toward the open window when James entered her room. She turned and watched him as he pulled the chair up next to her bed and set the hat box on the nightstand. Julia entered, smiled and nodded to James, then left, closing the door behind herself.

"Good afternoon, Angel Eyes," James said. "I brought something to share with you." Ruth's eyes followed his hands as he lifted the hat box and placed it on the bed beside her. She slowly raised her hand and caressed the box. James' heart soared. "Oh Ruth," he whispered.

She lowered her hand and stared at him, waiting.

He removed the lid and lifted the first letter. After carefully unfolding it, he took a deep breath and began to read. When he had finished, he nervously raised his eyes. He had been so sure that this was the right thing to do. Now his heart felt as if it were beating out of his chest. *How will she respond?*

As his eyes met hers, she blinked once, then closed her eyes. She didn't open them when Julia brought her lunch or her dinner; she didn't open them when James stood to close the window after the sun had set; she didn't open them when he leaned over to kiss her goodnight. *What was I thinking,* he thought. *I've hurt her all over again.*

His stomach churned as he brushed the hair from her forehead then raised her hand to his lips. *I'm a fool,* he thought. But as he lowered her hand back to the bed, Ruth opened her eyes. A single tear rolled down her cheek. She slowly lifted his hand to her mouth and pressed her motionless lips against his skin.

TWENTY

Anna felt her phone vibrate in her pocket, but she let the call go to voicemail as she closed her front door and dropped her keys in her purse. Her leather pumps were trashed, but it had been worth it. She smiled, recalling James, soaked and beaming as he splashed through the rain. Sunshine had lifted him up, and in the process, she had made Anna feel lighter too. She kicked off her shoes and hung her jacket on a coat hook then hurried over to the couch, picked up the photo album and curled up on her side.

"Daddy's little girl," read the caption beneath a photo of her father holding her newborn body, a pacifier in his mouth and a tiny knit hat balanced on his head. *What a goofball,* Anna thought, chuckling. *You were always such a goofball, Daddy.*

She hugged the album to her chest and closed her eyes, picturing her father straightening his tie in front of the mirror that last night.

"What do a bird and an elephant have in common?" he asked her, as he lifted her onto the counter then gave his tie one last adjustment. Anna giggled and raised her shoulders toward her ears. He stood up tall, ran his hands over his lapel then grinned at her. "They both can fly..." he said. "Well, except for the elephant." Her father had loved telling jokes, especially the kind that left people scratching their heads, wondering if they were missing something. He had told that particular joke at least a hundred times, and Anna had laughed every time.

He helped her down off the counter. "We'd better let your mother get started with the primping, or we'll never make it in time for our reservation."

Anna sighed. She knew she needed to face the rest of the memory. As a psychologist, she understood the damage she was causing herself by blocking it out. Sunshine had given her a glimpse of happiness, but in order to embrace it, Anna was going to have to confront the pain head-on.

Let's do this. I can handle it, she thought. *I hope.* She rolled onto her back on the couch and laid the album across her chest, clutching it tightly – a life preserver. She closed her eyes and willed herself to return to that night.

May 28, 1977

"Is your birthday card ready?" Her father rubbed his hands together like an eager child. Anna held up the card proudly, and he took it in his hands, admiring the bubble letters and vibrant flowers before handing it back to her. "Baby, it's beautiful. She's going to love it."

"Thanks Daddy. I hope she does," Anna said, laying the colorful card on the couch. "So where are you guys going tonight?"

Her father groaned and winked at her. "I'm taking her to a *musical."* He said the word as if it had been soaked in vinegar.

"You hate musicals," Anna said, giggling. "You say they're cheesy."

Her father chuckled and leaned down close to her ear. "They *are* cheesy," he whispered. Then he stood back up and held his index finger to his lips. "I just can't say no to your mother," he said. "Especially on her birthday."

"Well, you look handsome," Anna said, "if that helps."

"Why thank you, young lady," he said, and took a bow. "You really think I look good in this penguin suit?"

"You look like a movie star," Anna said.

When her mother descended the stairs in her dazzling red dress, Anna stood spellbound. *Two movie stars,* she thought, and forgot all about her card.

Stephanie turned away from Kurt, wiped the tears from her cheeks and tried to smile at Anna.

Anna's eyes darted from Stephanie to Kurt; she took in the pain in Kurt's eyes, and he turned his gaze to the floor.

Fuzzy Bunny toppled down the stairs ahead of Anna's limp body. Her head slammed against the treads as she tumbled down the same stairs her mother had descended in her red dress just a few hours earlier. Kurt raced toward the stairs and caught her at the third step from the bottom. He carried her into the living room and laid her on the couch. Stephanie ran to the kitchen for ice.

"Anna," Kurt said. He held her face in his calloused palms. "Anna, talk to me."

Anna slowly opened her eyes and sat up, then turned away from the man in the disheveled uniform kneeling in front of her. She wrapped her fingers around the birthday card that lay on the couch at her side. She brought it into her lap and stared at it as Kurt spoke.

"Anna, I'm so sorry," he began. "There was an accident."

Anna stared at the card.

"Honey, your mother didn't survive."

Anna stared at the card.

"Your father is in pretty bad shape. He's at the hospital."

Anna's eyes shot from the card to Kurt. "Can I see him?" Her heart pounded in her tiny chest.

"Anna, his injuries are life-threatening." Kurt felt a sob threatening as he spoke those words, and he had to stand and walk outside. Anna followed at his heels.

"I want to see him," she said, tugging at the hem of his untucked shirt. "Take me to him," she shouted. "Now!"

Kurt nodded and led her to his police cruiser.

Kurt pulled his cruiser up to the curb at the emergency room entrance. He walked around and opened the back door for Anna; she sprang out of the car and shot into the hospital.

"Where is he?" Anna shouted at the woman behind the counter. "Where is my daddy?"

"Sweetheart, I..."

"Anna," Kurt said when he caught up with her. "He's in the emergency room."

Anna read the sign and sprinted toward the ER.

"Honey, slow down," he said. "Anna, you need to understand..." Kurt tried to catch his breath. "He looks pretty bad..." She pushed through the double doors before he could finish warning her.

"Daddy!" she shouted, throwing the curtains back one by one. On the third try, she found him.

The space reeked of the rubbing alcohol her mother used to clean her cuts and scrapes, and the bright lights burned her eyes. A clear bag of liquid hung from a hook beside the bed, and her eyes followed the tube that ran from the bag to the back of her father's hand. *It's stabbing him,* she thought. *Get that thing out of my daddy!* She ran to his bed. "Daddy!"

Her father slowly turned his head toward her and tried to smile.

"I'm sorry, Officer," the nurse said. "We have to get him into surgery immediately."

"Wait," Raymond said, his voice little more than a whisper. "I need a moment with my daughter."

Kurt looked at the nurse. "Would just a minute be ok?" he asked.

"Just one minute," she said and led Kurt away, quietly pulling the curtain closed as they left.

"Anna," her father said.

She buried her face in his chest.

"Anna, please look at me." Anna looked up at him. He wiped the tears from her cheeks with his bandaged hand. "Baby, if I don't make it through surgery–"

"Daddy stop! Don't talk like that!" Anna was sobbing now.

"Baby, please, listen to me. I love you. You are so strong, just like your mother. You two will be fine no matter what. You hear me?" He felt a tear slide down his own cheek now, but didn't bother wiping it away.

Anna continued to sob, clinging more tightly to her father when the nurse came in. "I'm sorry dear, but we have to get him to surgery now." When Anna refused to let go, Kurt peeled her off; she turned and punched him, kicked him and then collapsed into his arms. She watched through blurry eyes as they wheeled her father past the curtain, and she promised herself in that moment that she would never love another man. She would keep this one special love, just for her father.

She had managed to. Until now.

"Oh Daddy," she whispered. "I'm so sorry. Why didn't I make that nurse wait so I could tell you I loved you one last time? Why didn't I…" There were so many things she wished she had said differently, done differently. *Dammit,* she thought. There was no way to change the past; Anna knew that. But the future? She had no interest in a future without her father.

She stood, her arms limp at her side as she made her way to the foyer. She dug her phone out of the pocket of her jacket, held it up in front of her face and stared at the blinking light. *I don't want to hear his voice,* she thought, but her fingers disagreed. She dialed her voicemail and entered her pin. "Anna, it's Dan," he said. "I was hoping you might be free for lunch tomorrow. Maybe we could meet at Blakely's at noon?" He paused, as if waiting for a response, then continued. "I promise not to sing if you show up."

She hit delete.

~

Kurt guided his cruiser down Main Street, searching the shadows for anyone who looked suspicious. *This is a waste of time,* he thought. Whoever this man was, he was smart. *I've got to think like a criminal if I'm going to catch this bastard.* But Kurt Malone was incapable of thinking like a criminal – he didn't have an ounce of evil in him. He would never dream of raising a hand to a woman, let alone taking her against her will. He thought of Cathy. He had been angry with her on a few occasions over the years, very few, but he had never once been tempted to harm her.

A group of college girls staggered out of Riley's as Kurt turned right onto Martin Street. He made a quick U-turn and followed them at a distance, watching as they stumbled toward Chancellor Hall. *I can't follow them all home,* he thought, but he couldn't allow another girl to be harmed. *I've got to stop this man,* he thought. *But how?*

When the front door to Chancellor Hall swung shut, Kurt drove back toward Riley's, passing two other police cruisers as he navigated the four blocks. He had instructed all of his officers to make routine trips down Main Street during their night shifts, and he was glad they were following his orders. At the very least, Kurt hoped the constant police presence would deter the attacker and buy him time.

He parallel parked in front of Riley's and noticed Mitch's cruiser scouring the area a few blocks away. Mitch might be a monster of a husband to Sandy, but he was a dedicated police officer. Kurt hated to admit it, but Mitch seemed just as committed to catching the attacker as Kurt was, though he guessed that Mitch's dedication to the case had more to do with personal gain than with putting an end to this nightmare.

He knew his son-in-law was gunning for his position. Everyone at the police department was aware of Kurt's eagerness to retire, and it was generally assumed that once this case was solved and the attacker was behind bars, Kurt would announce his departure from the force. Mitch seemed to have the mayor and town council charmed, and personally apprehending a serial rapist would go a long way toward convincing everyone that he was the obvious choice for the new Chief of Police.

Kurt removed his cap and wiped the sweat from his forehead. *Over my dead body,* he thought. He placed his cap back on his head, vowing that he would not retire until the attacker was caught *and* Mitch's true nature was exposed. Kurt Malone would never allow a man like Mitch to lead the police department, and he wouldn't stop until he found a way to set his daughter free.

TWENTY-ONE

Like clockwork, Sunshine showed up as Anna was preparing to take her lunch break. Anna smiled in spite of her mood. She really wasn't interested in being cheered up today, but this little girl always seemed to do it effortlessly.

"Back again?" Anna asked.

"Come on," Sunshine said, grabbing Anna's hand and pulling her out of her chair.

"Where are we going today?"

"It's a surprise," Sunshine said, her face glowing as she dragged Anna out the door.

They rushed down Main Street, and Anna struggled to keep pace with the child – her gait a cross between skipping and running. "What's the hurry?" Anna asked. Sunshine said nothing as she pulled Anna along.

As they skip-ran past the Gateway restaurant, Anna shrugged off the memories of her date with Dan. They passed the spot where Sunshine had made the silly newspaper hat and hurried into a restaurant that had opened just a few weeks earlier. "Have you been here before?" Anna asked.

"Nope," Sunshine said, staring toward a table across the room.

Anna followed the child's gaze and felt her heart stop for an instant. "You tricked me," she hissed.

Dan looked up, caught Anna's eyes and stood to pull out a chair for her.

"Look Dan," Anna said, as she approached the table, but he stopped her mid-sentence.

"Did you come to hear my latest single?" he asked, standing and pulling out her chair.

"Dan," she started again, but the waitress came by and asked for their drink order. Dan motioned for Anna to sit, and waited for her to order, but she had lost her appetite. "Can you give us a minute?" she said to the waitress.

"Take all the time you need," the cheerful woman said to Dan, even though Anna was the one who had asked.

"I'm glad you decided to come," Dan said, "because I really am a horrendous singer."

"It wasn't... I mean I didn't..." Anna couldn't speak. His smile warmed her, and she turned away, searching for the little brat who had gotten her into this situation.

"You look beautiful, Anna," he said, looking self-assured. *How does he do that,* she thought, feeling her defenses crumbling. This man was impossible to fight off.

The waitress returned. "Are you ready to order?" she asked Dan. Anna bristled. *Find your own man,* she thought. But Dan's eyes never left Anna as he waited for her to choose her lunch.

Anna ordered the soup and salad and asked if they had milkshakes.

"No, but we have ice cream," the waitress responded absently.

"That will be just fine," Anna said.

The waitress finally took her eyes off Dan and turned to Anna. "You want that *with* your meal?"

"Uh no," Anna said, rolling her eyes at the woman. "I want that as my appetizer, of course."

Dan smiled. *That's my girl.*

~

With three hours to spare before she needed to pick the kids up from summer school, Sandy drove to Maple Manor. She parked in the farthest spot from the entrance and pulled out the newspaper again – "*...seeking volunteers to play piano...*" Sandy's hands shook as she closed the paper and placed it on the passenger seat. She checked her face in the rearview mirror, rubbed her fingers over the dark circles under her eyes, took a deep breath and opened her car door.

The nurse behind the reception desk glanced up at Sandy and smiled. "May I help you?"

Sandy felt out of place in the bright, cheery lobby. She had expected a sterile space full of mumbling elderly folks pacing the halls. This place was warm, welcoming. Sandy felt herself relax a little.

"May I play the piano?" she asked quietly.

The nurse's face lit up. "You read the article, didn't you?"

Sandy nodded.

"That would be lovely," the nurse said. "My name is Julia. Come with me."

Sandy followed Julia down the long corridor and into a spacious room filled with pastel floral print couches and love seats, chairs grouped in circles around small oak tables with a vase of fresh flowers on each one. A teenage girl was laying out a tray of cookies on one of the tables, and Julia called her over. "Taylor, we have a pianist today."

Taylor looked at Sandy, sizing her up. Sandy looked down at her hands. "Hey," Taylor mumbled. "Piano's over there." She gestured with her chin in the direction of a baby grand and walked away without saying more.

When Sandy spotted the piano, her heart soared, hanging suspended momentarily – the way it had when she was a child, riding with her father over hills on the country roads. Up they would go, then drop down as the car crested the hill. It always took a second longer for her heart to settle back into her chest.

"Don't mind her," Julia said. "You know how teenagers are." She reached over and touched Sandy's shoulder; Sandy flinched. Julia pulled her hand back, her eyes silently apologizing for making the timid woman nervous. "You're just in time," she said. "The residents have social hour in ten minutes. Would you like to go over and warm up?"

Sandy nodded. "Thank you," she whispered, and wandered toward the piano. Placing her fingers on the keys, she sighed; so many years had passed since she last played, and she hadn't thought to bring sheet music. Her hands trembled as she lowered herself onto the piano bench. She looked around the room at the residents eyeing her. *Oh my gosh,* she thought. *What was I thinking?* She closed her eyes and tried to focus on her breathing.

Taylor looked over at the mousey woman who had come to entertain the residents; she was in dire need of a makeover. *I could work wonders with that lady,* Taylor thought. *Pale skin, a terrible fashion sense, and a definite lack of confidence. Poor thing looks nervous, like a trapped cat about to run up a tree and hide.* Taylor took pity on Sandy and walked over. "Sheet music's inside the bench," she muttered, before disappearing back into the kitchen.

"Thank you," Sandy whispered to Taylor's back, forcing the air out through her lips. She lifted the seat and pulled out a small stack of music. Sorting through the stack, she decided on a basic piece. She sat down and began to play the notes lightly. Every head in the room turned toward her. Residents slowly emerged from their rooms and made their way to the various chairs and couches. Sandy gradually felt her heart and her fingers take control, and by the time she had finished her warm-up, she realized she no longer needed the sheet music.

As Sandy's fingers gave life to Mozart's Piano Sonata No. 16, Taylor appeared in the kitchen doorway and hesitantly made her way to Sandy's side.

Music filled the air, and Sandy's lips relaxed into a soft smile. A few of the residents hummed along, some swayed in their chairs, and by the time Sandy finished the piece, every person in the building had packed into the community room to hear her play. Applause erupted; Sandy's fingers buzzed.

Taylor leaned over Sandy's shoulder. "That was..." Taylor always struggled with compliments. "Really good," she finally said.

"Thank you," Sandy said, holding her chin up a little higher now. She rose to leave, and Taylor stayed by her side.

"Will you be back to play again?" Taylor asked, like a child begging for another scoop of ice cream. She had never heard music like that. She was amazed that such a plain woman could bring so much happiness to this boring place... to her own soul.

"I'll try," Sandy said.

"Can I walk you out?" Taylor asked.

"Ok," Sandy said.

As they wove through the crowd toward the door, one of the residents reached up and touched Sandy's jumper; a few others wiped tears from their cheeks. Sandy, herself, struggled but failed to keep her own tears from falling. These were different tears though, not the ones she cried every night in bed. These tears liberated her, and she promised herself she would return just as soon as she could sneak away again.

"I hope you'll be back soon," Taylor said. "The residents really enjoyed your music." *I did too,* she thought, surprising herself.

Sandy nodded.

As they approached Sandy's car, Taylor startled Sandy by reaching out and hugging her. Sandy pulled back out of instinct, and Taylor apologized. "I'm sorry. I don't know where that came from." Sandy lowered her gaze and got into her car. "Please come back," Taylor said, unsure why she felt so strongly about this woman, but knowing she needed to hear that music again.

"I'll try," Sandy whispered, her eyes avoiding Taylor's as she closed her car door and backed out of the parking space.

This short glimpse of what life could be like if she were allowed to be herself, this brief moment of being *Sandy* again, brought her back to time before Mitch.

She entered her house, made her way to the kitchen and pulled the classifieds from their hiding place, her pre-Mitch confidence urging her on.

~

"How long are you planning on staying?" Anna asked, as Dan placed a dozen eggs, a head of lettuce and a package of brie in her refrigerator, then laid out the ingredients for seafood chowder.

"Good question," he said. "You sit. I'm making dinner."

Damn him!

Anna rolled her eyes when he set the bowl on the table in front of her. "Go on," he said. "Try it." Anna faked a scowl as she lifted the spoon to her mouth.

Pleasure rippled through her body from the spot on her tongue where the first drop made contact. Dan grinned victoriously when he saw her lips blossom into a smile – the smile she had been fighting with every muscle in her face.

"Ha!" he shouted. "I knew you'd like it!"

Anna's eyes moved from his stunning eyes to his tilted smile. *What the hell,* she thought. *I give up.*

After dinner, he took her hands and gently pulled her from her chair, the way he had the morning after their first date. He kissed her forehead and led her to the couch. He wrapped his arms around her, and she leaned her head against his chest.

"You know Anna," he whispered. "You were beautiful even when we were kids."

Anna pulled back. "I'm sorry, Dan," she said. "I don't remember many people from those years. I guess I was just too caught up in my own problems."

"I remember," he said. "I remember your incredible smile, and the way it faded after your parents died. I remember wanting to beat the crap out of that kid in the cafeteria who made light of your loss. I was so mad at myself for not defending you that day."

Anna thought back to that day, the first day back to school after the summer her parents were killed. She had felt so alone that day, and every day after.

"I remember watching you on the playground," Dan said, "wishing there was some way I could make you smile again."

Anna folded herself into his arms. "You do now," she said, smiling up at him. He leaned down and kissed her softly. "You make my head spin," she whispered.

"Ditto," he said.

Anna studied his face. He looked so radiant, so content. His eyes were full of excitement, full of life. She couldn't help but wonder if the time he had lived in the mountains had given him his intoxicating perspective, so different from her own. "Dan," she said, "tell me something."

"Anything," he said.

Anna hesitated. "If it's too personal…"

"Ask me anything, Anna."

"I was just wondering," she said, resting her head on his chest again and taking his hand in hers. "Why would you come back to a place like Bloomfield when your life in the mountains sounds so amazing?" She felt his chest rise abruptly as he sucked in a breath.

"It's complicated," he said, then exhaled slowly.

"I'm sorry," Anna said, sitting up straight. "I shouldn't pry."

Dan looked into her blue eyes, so full of concern and compassion. He had seen that look in her eyes as a child, and had watched it cloud over after her parents were killed. He sighed and pulled her close for strength. "No, I want you to know," he said. "But I don't want you to think I'm crazy."

"Well, I *know* you're crazy," she said. "That's one of the best things about you."

Dan smiled. "I'm crazy about you," he said, then looked away. He ran his hands through his hair before continuing. "I'm divorced, Anna." He looked down at her. "Does that bother you?"

"Wow," she whispered, turning to meet his gaze. "I never would've guessed. Of course that doesn't bother me, Dan," she said. "Can I ask what happened?"

Dan looked away again. "We met in graduate school," he said, "and married right after graduation." He paused, and Anna waited. "I guess we both thought that's what people were supposed to do next in life." Anna reached for his hand. "We both found positions with the same clinic in Colorado and moved the week after the wedding. But it didn't take long to realize that we had very little in common; we rarely spoke unless it was to discuss the housework or the bills," he said. "It was miserable." Anna heard his voice crack.

"I'm sorry," she whispered.

"It got to the point where I dreaded going home," he said. "I would ride the trails for hours searching for answers, but the more I asked, the less I understood. It was as if something was missing and I was just going through the motions. There was a hole in my world, and nothing I did seemed to fill it. I felt alone, even when I was with her." He faced Anna again. "Does that make sense?"

Anna nodded.

"I tried talking with her about it, hoping we could somehow find the answers together. But every time I brought it up, she would just get up and walk away. So I finally had divorce papers drawn up, packed my truck and left."

"Do you ever hear from her?" Anna asked.

"No," he said. "I think it's better that way."

"I'm sorry," Anna said.

"Don't be, Anna. I'm exactly where I want to be." He brushed her hair from her forehead and looked into her eyes. "I came back here because I didn't know where else to go. I felt lost. I had always believed I would get married and spend the rest of my life with that one person. I felt like I had failed. So for the last two years I just poured myself into my work. And then I saw you again at the conference," he said. His eyes locked on hers. "I can't explain it, Anna. It was like all the pieces fell into place in that moment." He ran his hand through his hair. "Is that too much?"

"Not at all," she said.

His shoulders relaxed as he began to speak again. "When I approached you at the conference," he said, "I could tell you didn't remember me from when we were young. I was so nervous to ask for your number, but then you gave it to me and I felt like a kid on Christmas morning."

Anna laughed. *I'm no Christmas gift,* she thought.

"Are you laughing at me?"

"I wouldn't dare," she said. "Go on."

"Ok," he said. "But no laughing, you hear?"

"Loud and clear," she said, raising her hand to her forehead in a salute.

"You're trouble, you know that?"

"Who me?" she said. "No way! I'm just waiting to hear the rest of your story."

"Fine," he said, his face relaxing into a smile. "So when I walked away with your phone number, that feeling I had before, like there was a hole in my world? I no longer felt it. That sounds ridiculous, doesn't it?"

Anna's heart felt light. "Wow," she whispered.

"You *do* think I'm crazy!" he said.

"No, Dan. I think you're amazing."

He sat up straight and looked at her. "So that's my story," he said, shifting uncomfortably in spite of his efforts to look casual. "Now let's talk about you."

Anna studied his face again. For the first time, he looked nervous, vulnerable, like a little boy. He had let her in, and now he needed her to be vulnerable too.

She hesitated. "What do you want to know?"

"I want to know everything about you," he said. "Aside from what I already know – that you're beautiful and smart and have always been both, and your incredible spirit lights up every space you enter."

Anna eyed him, unsure how to respond. *How did I miss this man back then,* she thought. *Was I blind? Deaf? Completely clueless?!*

He smiled at her and lifted her fingertips to his lips, kissing each one softly. "I want to know everything," he said.

Dan's eyes never left hers as she shared the happy memories – the family trips to the cabin, skipping stones and catching tadpoles with her father. She filled him in on each of her patients, then told him about the painful times – her parents' death and the eight years she had been forced to share her home with her aunt. Except for the few vague facts James had tricked her into disclosing, Anna had held the memories close, private scars and treasures locked away... until now.

She felt the shackles unlock and fall away from her heart as she told Dan about her dream of a family and her sense of failure at never having accomplished that dream. He kissed away a tear that rolled down her cheek, and she continued. She talked for hours, and he never once interrupted, occasionally tucking her hair behind her ear. He never once looked away from her eyes. It occurred to her that she must have sounded like one of his babbling patients, though he never made her feel that way during her monologue.

Dan listened as Anna spoke well into the night, and once she had emptied her heart of all the hurt and loneliness, he reverently undressed her, then removed his own shirt and jeans. He took her into his arms and held her tight, and they fell asleep on the couch, Anna's bare heart secure in Dan's embrace.

TWENTY-TWO

Kurt's pulse pounded as he nodded to the receptionist at Midwestern Memorial. After so many attacks, he should have been used to this by now, but this one was different. This victim was a minor – a high school student and, Kurt realized, young enough to be his granddaughter. "Room 387," the receptionist said. He thanked her and walked toward the elevator.

He studied the numbers on the plaques outside each room as he made his way down the third floor corridor: 381, 383, 385... He rubbed his fingers along the braille beneath the number 387 and took a deep breath before entering.

"Chief Malone," Dr. Carson said, looking up from the chart in his hands. "She's still unconscious. Her brain shows no signs of swelling from the trauma to the head, which is good. Her neck was cut, but it's just a superficial wound." Kurt approached the bed and studied the bruises on the girl's face. "He didn't take anything," Dr. Carson said, then looked down at the floor. "Nothing of material value, I mean." He straightened again and continued. "The field investigator found a card in her purse for Dr. Anna Cunningham," he said. "We assume Dr. Cunningham is her therapist."

"Have you been able to contact the girl's parents?" Kurt asked.

"One of our nurses tried the number listed in the phone book, but the answering machine picked up. She left a message."

Kurt considered the ignorant bliss the girl's parents were enjoying at this moment. He knew that once they got word of what had happened to their daughter, their hearts would never completely mend. A parent's heart doesn't heal after their child suffers like this.

Is that what I've been doing, he thought. *Have I been trying to remain ignorant of what Mitch is doing to Sandy? Am I really that selfish?* Kurt didn't want to hear the answer his mind would surely give. "Will you please have someone call Dr. Cunningham?" Kurt asked. "I'd like her here when we get a statement."

"Of course," Dr. Carson said, and left Kurt alone in the room with the young woman.

Kurt placed the back of his hand on her cheek. She was so thin – too thin, in his opinion. Her neck was bandaged, and he wondered if the wound would scar. From raising a daughter, Kurt knew that girls could be extremely self-conscious about their looks, especially in high school. He pulled up a chair and sat down beside the bed. He took her hand in his, bowed his head and prayed.

~

Anna opened her eyes and took in the beautiful man lying next to her on the couch, his arms wrapped protectively around her. *No dream last night,* she thought. *This man must scare them off.* She gently moved his arm off of her waist, sneaking out of his cocoon.

"Trying to get away again?" he whispered, opening his sleepy eyes.

"I wouldn't dare," she said, smiling. *Damn it feels good to smile,* she thought, realizing she had smiled more lately than in the last twenty-five years combined.

"Good," he said and pulled her back down into his arms before kissing her forehead then releasing her. "I'm in the mood for an omelet."

Anna laughed. *Lordy this man loves to cook.* She lifted his button-down oxford from the floor, slid her arms into the sleeves and rolled up the cuffs. Dan pushed each button through its hole, one by one, pausing to kiss her after each one.

"That shirt looks much better on you than it does on me," he said as he pushed the last button through. Anna pulled the collar up and inhaled his divine scent.

She was tempted to pinch herself as she followed him to the kitchen. She watched his sensual movements as he prepared yet another gourmet feast in nothing but his boxers, and he smiled knowingly as he placed the plate in front of her. "Try it," he said, and she obliged.

Holy shit! "You should really open a restaurant," she mumbled through a full mouth as she chewed slowly, savoring the bite. Her cell phone rang, and she quickly swallowed and wiped her mouth with her napkin then reached over to check the caller ID. Not recognizing the number, she set the phone back down on the table.

"You should get that," Dan said. "It might be important."

Anna rolled her eyes and reluctantly hit "Send." She brought the phone to her ear.

"Dr. Cunningham?"

"Yes," Anna said, lifting a forkful of her omelet and smiling at Dan.

"This is Clara from Midwestern Memorial. I'm sorry to call so early."

Anna's fork dropped to the table, eggs and brie splattering across the oak tabletop. She clung to the phone as if it were a lifeline keeping her head above water. Drowning. She knew this feeling.

"We have Taylor Wellington here."

"Taylor?" Anna whispered.

"Yes ma'am, she was attacked last night. She is stable but still unconscious. Chief Malone asked if you could be with her when she gives her statement."

Anna hung up without waiting for more information. She threw on her jeans and raced out the door. Dan bolted after her.

"What is it?" he asked, grabbing her by the shoulders and turning her to face him.

"I've got to get to the hospital. One of my patients. Wait here for me," she said as she jumped into the driver's seat.

No matter how hard she pushed the gas pedal, her car moved forward as if she were driving through quicksand, and the self-recrimination returned. *Why didn't I take more time with Taylor? How could she go out at night with that lunatic out there? Why didn't I know she was going out at night? She's seventeen! She should be at home after dark. I knew her parents were out of town. I should have checked on her!*

She jammed her car into park at the red curb in front of the Emergency Room entrance. A security guard shouted at her as she darted into the hospital. "Ma'am, you can't park there!" Anna ignored him. She spotted the front desk and raced to it.

"Where is she?" Anna demanded, her eyes wild.

"Who?" the receptionist said.

Anna pounded her fists on the desk. "Taylor Wellington!"

"Ma'am, I understand you're upset, but I have to check my intake records."

Anna took a breath and stepped back.

The receptionist eyed Anna nervously as she typed Taylor's name into the computer. "Here she is, room 387," she said. "Are you family?"

"No," Anna shouted. "I'm her goddamn therapist!"

"Right this way, ma'am."

Anna pushed past the woman and sprinted toward the elevator. She pounded the button with her palm. "Dammit!" She ran to the stairs. The receptionist chased after her.

"Ma'am, please, you're going to upset the patients!"

Anna didn't hear her. She could smell him. She knew he was close. *Where is he?* She looked frantically through each doorway as she continued down the hall. "Where is he?" she shouted. "Where is my father?"

"Ma'am?" The receptionist said, breathless as she caught up with Anna.

Anna looked through the doorway into the room where Taylor was sleeping, then turned and kept running. "Where is he?" she shouted again, sobbing as she raced toward the next room.

"Ma'am, *she's* in here," the receptionist said, stopping outside room 387. She waved her hands above her head to get Anna's attention.

Anna stopped. She turned and looked at the woman as if she was speaking a foreign language, then the years melted away, and Anna was back. Wiping the tears from her cheeks, she calmly walked toward the receptionist, holding her chin up and avoiding eye-contact.

"What happened?" Anna asked as she entered the room.

Dr. Carson lowered Taylor's chart and looked up at Anna, taking in her disheveled hair and oversized shirt. "Dr. Cunningham?"

Anna nodded impatiently.

"Thank you for coming. It seems Miss Wellington was attacked last night. It appears that he tried to slit her throat, but the wound isn't deep."

"Dammit!"

"Excuse me?" the doctor said.

"Dammit! Dammit! Dammit! This is all my fault!"

The doctor studied Anna as if wondering when her *own* therapist would arrive. Shaking his head, he continued. "She's bloody and bruised, but she will heal. I'm more worried about the psychological trauma than the physical. She has yet to regain consciousness, but Chief Malone thought it would be best if you were present when she does. Thank you for coming so quickly." Anna had her doubts whether the doctor was actually glad she was there, but she wasn't concerned with his opinion of her. "Right now though, she needs her rest," he said. "There's nothing you can do for her until she wakes up." He motioned toward the door then hesitated. "Dr. Cunningham, do you know how to get in touch with her parents?"

Of course I don't, Anna thought. *If I did, I would be a good therapist. I'm a shitty therapist. I don't even know where they're vacationing this time!*

When Anna didn't answer, the doctor spoke. "Dr. Cunningham, I have to ask you to wait in the lobby."

Anna rode the elevator to the main floor then stepped out into the lobby. She found an empty loveseat and collapsed into it. When Sunshine skipped through the double doors and over to the loveseat, Anna wasn't the least bit surprised. "I did this," Anna mumbled.

Sunshine's mouth dropped open and she stared directly at Anna, her eyes wide. "Where'd you get the knife?"

Anna groaned and grabbed a magazine from the coffee table and opened it. She curled up on the loveseat and laid the magazine over her head. She was in no mood for this girl.

"Dr. Cunningham?"

Anna sat up, startled when she felt Dr. Carson pull the magazine off her head.

"Dr. Cunningham?" he repeated, his cheeks flushed with embarrassment. "I was beginning to think something was wrong," he said. "I've been trying to wake you, but you weren't responding."

Anna hadn't meant to fall asleep, and now she was the one who felt embarrassed. She smoothed the collar of Dan's shirt and stood.

"Miss Wellington is awake," he said. "Would you like to see her now?"

"Absolutely," Anna said, attempting to fluff her hair. She had no idea what she would say when she saw the poor girl, or how she would find the words to apologize for letting her down.

Taylor was alert when Anna entered the room, despite what her body had been through during the last eight hours. *While I was whining to Dan about all my problems,* Anna thought. *How did I become so self-absorbed?*

"Dr. Cunningham!" Taylor said. "Why are you here?"

"How are you feeling?" Anna asked.

"Foggy. What happened?" Taylor asked.

"You're in the hospital."

"I figured that much out," Talyor said, glancing around the room. "How did I get here?"

Anna's gaze followed the IV line from the back of Taylor's hand to the hanging bag of clear liquid; she shuddered as she recalled her father's IV that last night. She shook her head to bring her mind back to Taylor. The young woman seemed quite relaxed and free from physical pain, so Anna guessed it was fentanyl or morphine in the bag. "I don't know the details. Do you remember anything?" she said.

Taylor stared at Anna for a moment, then covered her face with her hands, and Anna regretted pressing. After a few minutes, Taylor dropped her hands and spoke. "Why are you here?"

"They found an old appointment card in your purse and called me."

"Oh," Taylor said, and turned to stare at the ceiling.

"And," Anna took a deep breath, "Because I care."

Taylor looked at Anna. "I didn't know anyone did," she whispered.

"Well I do," Anna said. "So get used to it." Taylor smiled for the first time since she had woken up, and Anna stayed by her side until Kurt entered the room.

"Anna," he said, "thank you for coming."

"Of course," Anna replied. "But Kurt, do we have to do this right now? She needs time."

"I'm fine," Taylor said, adjusting herself in the bed to make herself appear taller. "But thank you."

Anna tucked Taylor's hair behind her ear, remembering Dan doing the same for her last night. She took Taylor's hand as Kurt spoke.

"Are you sure you don't want to wait for your parents?" Kurt asked.

"We'd be waiting a while," Taylor said. "They're in Italy." Taylor looked at Anna, "I have family here." She squeezed Anna's fingers.

"In that case, Social Services will need to be notified," Kurt said. "An alternate caretaker will need to be assigned before you can be released."

Anna spoke up. "I'll take care of that, Kurt."

Kurt nodded. "Ok then," he began. "Taylor, I know this is hard to think about, but anything you can remember will help us catch the man who attacked you."

Anna watched Taylor's face as the beautiful young woman recounted what she could remember about the night before. There was no anger or fear in Taylor's expression. *So innocent,* Anna thought. *So brave.*

When Kurt finished making notes, he eyed Taylor. "Miss Wellington," he said, "can I ask how you got into Riley's when you are only seventeen?" Kurt realized he sounded more like a grandfather than the Chief of Police now. Taylor glanced down at her hand in Anna's, and Kurt smiled. "Hey," he said. "I was young once, too." Taylor looked up at him, and he winked. "We will catch him," Kurt said. "That's what matters."

Kurt left, and Anna stayed with Taylor until the young woman succumbed to the pain medication and drifted back off to sleep.

Kurt thanked the nurse behind the counter and turned when Anna walked out of Taylor's room. "Anna, do you have a minute?"

"For Taylor, I have all the time in the world," she said. *I will not let her down again.*

Kurt spoke quietly. "It's good to see you after all these years," he said. "I just wish it was under different circumstances."

"It's good to see you too," Anna said. "It's been a long time." Anna thought back to all the work Kurt and Cathy had put into planning her parents' funeral, in spite of their own grief. And for weeks afterward, Cathy had stopped by with casseroles and cookies, and Anna had watched from the top of the stairs as her aunt shut the door in Cathy's face every time, rejecting her gestures. Eventually Cathy had stopped trying, and Anna had been relieved. She resented the constant reminder of all she had lost. But now, looking into Kurt's tired eyes, the deep creases across his forehead, the lines edging his mouth, Anna realized how much time she had wasted. "How's Cathy?" she asked.

"She's fine," he said. "I'm sure she would love to see you." Anna saw his expression relax, the lines softening when he spoke of his wife.

"And Sandy?" she asked.

Kurt rubbed the spot between his eyebrows, and Anna noticed the creases across his forehead stiffen again. "She's doing ok," he said. "She has four children –"

"Four children?" Anna said. "That's great to hear. Is she still with Mitch?"

Kurt nodded and turned away. He closed his eyes and took a deep breath before looking back at Anna. "Anna," he said, glancing toward Taylor's room. "I'm hoping I can pick your brain about this monster. I keep running into road blocks. He seems to be one step ahead of me no matter what I do. Just when I think I know what he's going to do next, he does something different. And," he looked toward Taylor's room again, "he's becoming more violent with each attack." Kurt leaned his weight into the counter, and Anna saw exhaustion and desperation in his eyes.

This poor man has the weight of the world on his shoulders, she thought. "How can I help?"

He massaged the crease between his eyebrows. "Do you have any idea what would make someone do this?" he said. "I know there's something I'm missing. I need to understand the way this man thinks."

"I don't have any profiling experience," Anna said, "but let me do a little research."

Kurt hesitated. Anna noticed his torn expression.

"Is there something else?" she asked.

He rubbed the crease between his eyebrows again. "Anna?" he began. He wanted her advice on Sandy, but now was not the time. He shook his head. "No," he said. "That's all."

"Ok Kurt. I'll come by as soon as I can," she said. "I hope I can provide some insight."

"Thank you, Anna," he said, and escorted her to her car.

~

Anna picked up the handwritten note on the kitchen table:

Anna,

I hope everything went ok at the hospital. I'm worried about you. I tried your cell phone a few times but got your voicemail. I'll call you later to see if you're up for company.
Dan

She checked the call log on her cell phone. *Four missed calls.* She set the note back down on the table and wandered out to the front porch. She lowered herself onto the porch swing and rested her head against the chain, letting the wooden slats carry her weight. How had she allowed Taylor to get herself into that terrible situation? The poor girl lived most of her days alone in that enormous house while her parents traveled the world. *She must have been so lonely,* Anna thought. *I should have realized what was going on. I should have paid more attention.*

She thought of James and his lonely nights at home while his wife slept at Maple Manor. *I haven't been much of a friend to him either,* she thought. She had been so wrapped up in her own pain, her own loneliness that she had shut out everyone else's needs. She pulled up James' number on her cellphone. *He's probably sleeping by now,* she thought, and set the phone down beside her.

Then she thought of Dan. He was so full of enthusiasm, so content. He didn't need her problems. He was clearly on track. He appreciated good food and exciting adventures. He knew the value of his life. Anna, on the other hand, wondered anew if her life had value to anyone. She scanned the yard; it was far too late for a ten year old girl to be out, but she needed Sunshine right now. She waited, listening for the girl's soft footsteps, squinting in the dim light to see down the brick walkway. She heard nothing but the chirping crickets and cicadas looking for love.

She silenced her cell phone and went inside to bed.

~

Kurt pinned Taylor's photograph next to the others. "Why a child?" he whispered.

Taylor had been so brave as she recounted the details of her attack – the few details she was able to remember. She had blamed herself for being irresponsible walking home alone at night, but Kurt was comforted to know that she had seen a police car on patrol before she left. At least his officers were following his orders. *Why hadn't she just asked him for a ride home,* he thought. He would be sure to suggest this to his officers. *We need to protect these young girls,* he thought. *So young, so naive.*

Kurt took Taylor's photo back down and held it delicately in his hands. He shuddered as he recalled the single tear Taylor had shed when giving her statement. It wasn't when she told him about her intoxicated friend deserting her for a college kid, leaving her alone at the bar; it wasn't when she described being grabbed as she turned the corner of Martin and Main; it wasn't when she recalled the pain of the knife across her neck or the blow to her face just before she lost consciousness. No, Taylor had recounted these details with the grace and composure of a woman twice her age. The tear had come the one time she had averted her gaze from Kurt's and whispered that she had been a virgin.

"Bastard!" Kurt shouted and put his fist through the drywall.

A moment later, the door to his office flew open. "Are you ok?" Jane asked. She looked at Kurt, then at the wall, then at his bloody knuckles. "I'll get bandages and ice," she said.

"I'm fine," Kurt said, waving her away with his throbbing hand.

"Please Kurt, there must be something I can do," she said.

"Can you get the crime lab to rush those damn DNA results?" he snapped, and instantly regretted taking his anger out on Jane. He apologized and looked back at Taylor's photo. "I just need to be alone. Will you hold my calls please?"

"Ok," Jane said. She turned to leave then hesitated. "Kurt," she said. "I know you'll get this guy."

Which one, Kurt thought. It was his responsibility as a public servant to catch the rapist, and it was his responsibility as a father to get to the bottom of the situation with Sandy and Mitch.

TWENTY-THREE

The dream returned that night.

"Why aren't you dancing?" Sunshine asked.

Anna didn't answer.

Sunshine took her by the hand and led her away from the creek toward home, but Anna pulled the girl in the opposite direction. Sunshine shook her head but followed, holding Anna's hand tightly as they entered the dorm room.

The scent of beer and pot filled the air, and Anna searched the room for a familiar face. She clung to Sunshine's hand. In an instant, Sunshine and all the others vanished, and she saw him.

He pushed her onto her back on the bed, crawled on top of her and began kissing her. Not the soft kisses of a gentleman trying to seduce a lady, but the mechanical kisses of a college kid trying to get what he wants. He yanked her jeans down with one quick motion, and held her wrists firmly above her head with the other hand. When she felt her panties ripped away, she began kicking and screaming, "Stop!"

He pinned her legs down with his knees.

"Stop!" She repeated, over and over, tears streaming down her cheeks past her ears and onto the bare mattress beneath her, as he crushed her - body and soul.

"Stop!" Anna shouted, jolting herself awake. She rolled onto her side and curled her arms around her knees, pulling them tight to her chest. *Damn him!*

Thoughts of Taylor came rushing back to her. "Oh Taylor, I'm so sorry," she whispered.

Anna stayed in that position, clutching her knees, shaking, vowing over and over that she would never be hurt like that again. The light on her cell phone blinked incessantly, and Anna reached over and deleted the message without listening to it. *He doesn't need my shit.*

She dialed each of her patients and cancelled their appointments for the day. She walked to the bathroom and glared at herself in the mirror. "You are a complete failure," she said, staring deeply into her own eyes.

"Easy now," a little voice called out. Anna spun around.

"How the hell did you get in here?" Anna hissed.

"It's not polite to curse."

"Well I'm not in the mood for company. Just go."

"Sorry. I can't."

"Why the hell not?"

"Because I care."

I didn't know anyone did, Anna thought, and her heart broke for Taylor all over again.

"And because I don't like hearing you talk to yourself that way," Sunshine said.

"Well, Sunshine, it's high time I admit it. I *am* a failure. In my life *and* in my work. It's time for me to look for a new profession."

Sunshine stepped closer. "Why?" she asked.

"Because I'm worthless as a therapist," Anna said.

"Why?" the girl repeated.

"I just don't see how a person like me could help anyone."

"Why not?"

"Sunshine, look at me! I'm a failure! I failed Taylor. I've failed all my patients. I am thirty-five years old, no husband, no family, no friends, nothing of my own," Anna shouted, waving her arms around wildly, wondering at the same time why she was explaining all of this to a child.

"Nothing?"

"Yes, nothing!" Anna stomped her foot like a two-year-old, her fists balled up tight.

"You've got me," Sunshine said.

Gee, that makes it all better, Anna thought. *I have some little pest who shows up at the worst possible times, who doesn't know the first thing about loss. Yippee! Now I feel better.*

"That's not true," the girl said.

"What?"

"The part about me not knowing about loss."

Dammit! Had she said that out loud? The blood rose to her cheeks. "I didn't mean that," she said.

"I know," Sunshine said, and focused in on Anna's eyes.

"But seriously, Sunshine," Anna said. "How can you be my friend when you won't even tell me your real name?"

"Who said Sunshine wasn't my real name?"

Anna took a step back. "I guess I…" she stammered.

"So things are pretty bad for you right now, huh?" Sunshine said, rescuing Anna from the uncomfortable moment.

"Yes, but you wouldn't understand." Anna turned back to the mirror to escape the child's gaze.

"Why not?" Sunshine said, peering at Anna's eyes in the mirror.

"Ok then, let me tell you," Anna said. She whirled around to face the girl again. "My parents died when I was ten, and I had to live with my alcoholic aunt and her lovers, I have no friends, I suck at my job, I will never have the children I've always wanted. I am completely alone. There." Anna took a deep breath realizing she hadn't stopped to inhale during her tirade.

"Well that stinks," Sunshine said.

Anna recoiled. "That's it? That's all you have to say after everything I just told you?"

Sunshine didn't respond right away, she just stared into Anna's eyes for what felt, to Anna, like an eternity. Finally she said, "You have a house."

Anna rolled her eyes. "Yeah, and I love my house, but it's only mine because my parents died. I had to lose the only two people I ever loved. That's why I have a house." *Children can be so simple-minded,* Anna thought, careful to not speak her thoughts out loud this time.

"You have patients who depend on you," the girl said, tilting her head to the side.

"They depend on me to let them down!"

"You have soup to eat whenever you want it," Sunshine said, and the smile returned to her face.

"Canned. Condensed," Anna said, refusing to be cheered up.

"You have a beautiful tree right outside your office that blooms every summer, and you have a man who is trying so hard to love you, if you would just let him."

Damn her!

"Come on. Let's get out of here," Sunshine said, grabbing Anna's hand.

~

Sandy stared at the clothes strewn across her bed. *There's nothing here that will work,* she thought. Mitch had limited her wardrobe to the point where everything she owned made her look matronly. *Maybe retail sales isn't for me.*

Sighing, she sat down on the edge of her bed and closed her eyes. "Eenie, meenie, miney, mo." She opened her eyes and assessed the plaid jumper her index finger rested on. "It is what it is," she said, picking up her white turtleneck and carrying both pieces to the bathroom to dress. *Maybe I could borrow Mom's mascara,* she thought, but then decided against it. She knew she couldn't tell her mother what she was up to without inviting questions. *I don't want to have to lie to her again,* she thought.

She pulled into a parking space in front of Washburn's department store and closed her eyes to bring back the courage she had experienced after her visit to Maple Manor. She had felt so strong, so free, so optimistic – confident that she could finally get her children away from Mitch and start a new life, but now she was having doubts. She looked at herself in the rearview mirror. "You have to be strong for them," she said, and opened the car door.

"May I help you?"

Sandy raised her eyes, and a fashionable middle-aged woman smiled.

"Um, yes. I saw the ad in the newspaper," Sandy said, trying her best to appear confident in spite of the obvious disparity between the two women's styles. "May I please have an application?"

Her hands trembled as she accepted the sheet from the friendly woman who directed her to the break room so she could sit as she completed it.

"Name... Address... Education... Work History." *I have no idea what to write*, Sandy thought. *I have no work history! Can I list cooking, cleaning, helping with homework and trying to raise kids with strong values in spite of their father being a demon?* Sandy sighed and crumpled the application into a ball. *Who am I kidding?*

The fashionable woman entered the break room as Sandy stood to leave. "I'm Susan," she said, taking her lunchbox from a cubby then pulling out the chair next to the one Sandy had vacated.

Sandy didn't want to be rude, but she needed air. She needed to get out of this place. *Mitch was right,* she thought.

"Washburn's is a great place to work," Susan said, gesturing for Sandy to sit back down. She pulled an apple from her lunchbox and offered it to Sandy.

"No thank you," Sandy said and returned to her chair as instructed.

"They have health insurance and paid time off if your kids get sick," Susan said. She looked at Sandy with loving eyes, not judging, just commenting, "and a 40% discount on clothing."

Sandy took no offense. She knew she needed to update her wardrobe, but honestly, that was so far down on her list of priorities that she couldn't imagine spending even one cent on clothes for herself. The health insurance was attractive, though. She hadn't thought that far ahead.

Susan continued, "Alexa is the store manager, and she's wonderful. Very supportive, not like some of the other managers I've worked for." She took a bite of her apple, taking the time to chew and swallow before speaking again.

Sandy remained silent.

"You really don't need any experience. Alexa is a great trainer." Susan took another bite of her apple, and Sandy slowly opened the ball of paper in her hand.

I guess it's worth a try, she thought. She pressed the application flat against the table, running her palm over it to smooth out the creases.

Susan erupted into a burst of laughter, small chunks of apple flying from her mouth. "I'll go get you another one," she said, her mouth still half full.

How embarrassing, Sandy thought.

Susan returned with a new application and handed it to Sandy. "It's ok," she said. "I felt the same way when I applied for my first job after staying home with the kids."

"I think I'll take it home to complete it," Sandy said, standing and pushing the chair under the table.

Susan took another bite of her apple and nodded. "I'll tell Alexa to be expecting it."

TWENTY-FOUR

Anna rested on her back in the soft grass between her parents' graves and closed her eyes. The sun warmed her face, and she felt her muscles slowly relax. The grass tickled the back of her arms, bringing back memories of summer days as a child, two giddy girls rolling over and over on their sides down the hill in front of Sandy's house, coming to a stop on their backs. They would lay there on Sandy's lawn talking about anything and everything that came to mind. Eight year old Anna had confessed her undying love for a boy in their class named Nick, and Sandy had said he had cooties. They had giggled until their bellies hurt.

Sunshine stretched out beside Anna and gazed up at the clouds. "Look!" she said.

Anna's eyelids sprang open. "What?" she snapped, startled out of her happy memories.

"There!" Sunshine said. "Right there!" She pointed to a puff of a cloud that floated alone above the rest. "It's a bird."

"It's a cloud," Anna corrected.

"Watch," Sunshine said.

The cloud slowly widened and grew thin. Anna continued to watch as it thinned out more and more until it finally faded completely. "What is it now?" she asked.

"Gone," Sunshine whispered.

Anna considered this. It had been a cloud, maybe even a cloud shaped like a bird as Sunshine had suggested. And it had evolved, changed, and then was gone.

"Everything changes," Sunshine said. "We can't hold onto a cloud, even a beautiful cloud shaped like a bird. It was beautiful, and we were lucky to see it, but it's no longer there, so now we let it go."

Anna closed her eyes and contemplated all the things *she* needed to let go. She needed to let go of the pain, the guilt, the self-pity, but the feelings gripped her so tightly that she sometimes found it hard to breathe. *Why can't those awful feelings go away like the cloud did?*

"When you're wanting something to go away," Sunshine said, "you're still holding onto it. The trick is to let it go. When I think about the balloon that floated away when I was four, it's real for me again. I feel sad. The sad feeling is real, but the balloon is gone. So I release the memory. I let it go. It doesn't exist anymore. It's not real, and I'm not sad."

Anna knew she was continuing to make her pain and loneliness real by dwelling on them. "How do you know all this?" she asked.

"We all do," Sunshine said. "I just listen. You grown-ups don't."

"Who do you listen to?" Anna asked, thinking she might finally get a little background on the wise child.

"My heart."

Anna sighed. She realized in that moment that Sunshine might never tell her about her family or her life, and for the first time, Anna was ok with that. She didn't need to know any more than she knew about this child. All she needed to know was that Sunshine was with her in this moment, and that felt right.

"When we only think about what we don't have," Sunshine said, "we can't see what we do have… right now."

Once again, Anna was stunned. This little girl who had barged into her life was quite the little sage; the things she was saying made perfect sense. Maybe Sunshine was right. *Maybe we all do know this stuff, we just don't listen to our hearts,* Anna thought.

Sunshine spoke again. "Remember the happy times, Anna, but let go of the pain. You can't live in the past if you hope to be happy right now. You can't be in two places at once. Your happiness is here, now. You can't feel it because you keep remembering the sad stuff. You can't change the past by making yourself feel the pain over and over. You can't hold onto your parents by holding onto the pain. Your parents are gone, but they will always be with you. The happy memories are yours to hold onto, but the sadness doesn't help you right now. Every time you think of the hurt, you make it real again. Like my balloon. If you keep thinking only of the sadness, that's all you'll ever feel. Let it go Anna," Sunshine said. "It's been long enough."

Sunshine fell quiet and Anna relaxed again, feeling at peace with the silence when she was with this girl. She knew that this was a sign of a healthy relationship – when the silence is comfortable. It felt good to feel that way with someone again. Anna took a slow deep breath. Her body seemed to float as the sun warmed her eyelids. She felt the sun's energy thawing her soul.

Sunshine spoke again. "You have so much love to give, but you can't give it to other people until you remember how to love *yourself*. And you can't do that until you let go of the pain. You blame yourself for your parents' deaths. You punish yourself for not being in the car with them that night. You beat yourself up because you didn't tell your dad you loved him that one last time. You're mad at yourself because you haven't kept the promise you made to your mom," Sunshine said. "Your parents loved you, Anna, just the way you are."

Anna felt a tear roll down her cheek and drop off into the grass. It was time to set her parents free. She needed to, but who was she without them? If she let them go, she would be truly alone.

"They are a big part of who you are," Sunshine said, "but you are still Anna without them. And you were born with a gift," she said. "We all are. But you can't feel love and share your gift until you let go of the past, forgive yourself and live now, today."

Like the cloud, everything changes. Anna sighed. She knew it was time to say goodbye. She had never done this, not truly, not with her heart. She pictured the cloud as it had dissipated and become nothing more than a whisper on the breeze, and she thought again of Sunshine's words. *"You can't change the past by making yourself feel the pain over and over. You can't hold onto your parents by holding onto the pain."* Sunshine was right. It was time to let go.

"Goodbye Mom and Dad," Anna whispered, and her heart broke. It hurt to say goodbye. She wanted to hold on to them forever so she wouldn't have to feel *this* pain – the pain she was feeling *right now*. She didn't know who she was without them, and so when they died, she had allowed herself to die along with them.

"But you're alive now," Sunshine said.

Anna let go then, and the tears came freely. These were cleansing tears – a baptism, a rebirth. Anna said goodbye to the past, and made a commitment to the present. "Love yourself first," Sunshine said, and Anna heard her mother's voice too. "The rest will come naturally."

Sunshine fell silent again.

Anna opened her arms wide so that all the pain could be washed away into the vastness of the present moment. She imagined her pain as the cloud, and watched in her mind as it grew thinner and faded, little by little, until it was completely gone. She turned her face to the sky and opened her eyes. "Goodbye Mom and Dad."

When she finally dried her eyes and sat up, Sunshine was gone. Anna smiled. She knew the little girl was too full of life to sit still for long; Sunshine wanted devour every moment. *Just like you did Mom,* Anna thought. What a blessing to get out of bed every morning excited about what the day might bring. Stepping into not knowing, not *needing* a particular thing to happen, trusting that everything will work out. That, Anna realized, was faith. That was freedom.

She drove home from the cemetery along the same streets she took every day on her way to work, but today everything looked different. The edges of the leaves seemed impossibly sharp as they fluttered in the breeze, and the grass edging the sidewalks glowed. Every stoplight turned green as she approached, and the other cars flowed right along with her. She turned off her air conditioning and rolled down the window, leaning her head out, enjoying the wind in her hair. She felt light, free. She pulled into her driveway and stepped out of her car. The warm, damp air caressed her skin. The sunlight rained down in pieces, breaking through the voids between the branches of the tall oak she had parked under a thousand times – tiny spotlights illuminating her mother's neglected flower bed in front of the porch.

She walked over and dropped to her knees. "Goodbye, Mom," she whispered as she ran her fingers through the thick mat of crabgrass that strangled every sign of life. She clutched a clump and pulled. She dug into the cool dirt, over and over, clutching and pulling, clutching and pulling. She wiped sweat from her forehead, smearing dirt across her brow. The tears fell, and she made no attempt to stop them. *Goodbye Mom.*

She pushed her fingers into the earth at the base of the last clump and pulled it out. A tiny crocus bud stared up at her. *Oh Mom. I love you too.*

Dan answered on the first ring. "Hey stranger."

"I'm sorry I haven't called you back before now," Anna said.

"Can I come over?"

"Please."

"I'll be there in an hour."

TWENTY-FIVE

Ron peered through the kitchen window. *Where is she,* he thought. The overgrown holly pricked his thighs as he inched his way over to the family room window. *Not there either.* He knew she hadn't left. He had been parked around the corner since she pulled into her driveway. At one point, as he followed her home from the cemetery, he had driven a little too close, and he thought she had seen him in her rearview mirror. But she had continued to drive, and he had risen from his ducking position in the driver's seat. He hadn't lost sight of her until she entered her house.

Now he was risking the neighbors seeing him and calling the cops, so he returned to his car to wait, to watch. He sank down into his seat, keeping his head just high enough above the steering wheel to see her front door. It was becoming more difficult to find places to park that still had a good view of her house. He couldn't take a chance by parking in the same spot each time; what if someone noticed him? Ron knew it was risky, but he had no choice. She had *given* him no choice, especially with this new guy. Ron hated to admit it, but when that jerk was around, Anna looked… happy. The thought disgusted him. Ron decided he needed a plan. *How can I get rid of that idiot?* If he didn't find a way, he knew what would happen next… *if* he allowed it. But he wouldn't allow it. She would not leave him again.

He sat up straight when he saw the dork's truck pull into her driveway. His eyes burned; his pulse pounded in his temples. He took a long drag of his cigarette, pulling until he could taste the filter melting. Then he blew the smoke out in a burst. He jammed the burning butt into the back of his left hand and tightened his grip on the steering wheel. He started the engine and slammed the gas pedal to the floor. *I will put an end to this,* he thought, chucking the butt out the window. *There is no way that bitch is leaving me again.* His tires squealed as he tore past Anna's house toward town.

As the flashing neon word "Riley's" came into view, Ron's mood began to lift. He had never been much of a drinker, but lately he had discovered an affinity for whiskey. *Look what that little tramp is driving me to,* he thought.

He parked out front and scanned the bar through the windows. *Maybe the redneck will be here,* he thought. He had seen the man sitting at the bar a number of times since the night he had taken Anna to bed, every time sporting the same plaid flannel shirt, but Ron had never had the desire to interact with scum like that. Tonight though, he just might pull up a barstool next to the pathetic loser and commiserate while Anna was off with the new guy. Ron didn't want to think about her with that dork, and he certainly didn't want to watch. Anything that made Anna happy was sickening.

No, tonight he would befriend the flannel wearing redneck, buy him a few shots and get the play-by-play of his one-night stand with Anna. Ron hadn't been able to see much of the action that night through the thick bushes in front of the redneck's windows. Yes, tonight Ron would get the loser wobbling drunk and convince him to retell each and every detail of that night. Then he would take him outside and beat the shit out of him.

~

Dan appeared at Anna's door exactly one hour later, excitement dancing in his eyes. "Grab a sweater," he said, raising his hand and gently wiping the dirt from her forehead.

"Where are we going?" Anna asked.

"It's a surprise," he said, and led her to his truck.

He closed the passenger side door behind her, and she rested her arm on the bottom of the open window. A cool breeze caressed her face, and she sighed. "What a perfect evening," she whispered.

"Sure is," a chipper voice called out. Anna's gaze shot toward the overgrown hedge that ran up her property line. Sunshine was peeking over the top, giggling, her small hand cupped over her mouth.

Anna glared at the girl. "Stop being so nosey," she mouthed. Sunshine kept giggling. Anna rolled her eyes at the girl, but couldn't force her face to look stern. "You're crazy," she mouthed. Sunshine nodded, still giggling, then ducked down behind the bushes.

Dan got in on the driver's side and looked at Anna. "What's so funny?"

Anna shook her head and smiled. "It's nothing," she said. "Just a silly neighborhood kid."

Dan leaned over and took her face gently between the palms of his hands. "You're beautiful when you smile," he said, then released her and turned the key in the ignition without giving her a chance to respond.

Neither of them spoke as Dan drove, and Anna reveled in the lingering feeling of his warm hands on her cheeks... and the word "beautiful." She didn't feel the need to ask where he was taking her. She was letting go.

Fifteen minutes later, they pulled up next to a boat rental shop at the reservoir just outside of town. Dan walked around to open Anna's door and led her to a small dock where a glossy green canoe awaited them.

"Hop in, my lady," he said in a pitiful attempt at a British accent.

Anna tried her best to look graceful as the canoe teetered under her weight. Once she was safely seated, Dan stepped into the hull with ease. Anna noticed a cooler behind his seat, and he opened it and pulled out two pale ales. "My lady," he said, as he pried the cap off the first bottle and handed it to her. He turned his back to her then, placing his own bottle between his thighs, and began paddling.

The ripples sloshed against the side of the canoe, and Anna reached her hand down into the water. It felt warmer than she had expected for this time in the evening.

"Careful, my lady," Dan said in the silly accent he was faking. "Don't want to tip the boat."

Anna ignored his warning, enjoying the feeling of her fingers trailing through the water as he paddled. She watched his movements, graceful and strong, and knew in that moment that she was one incredibly lucky woman.

"In a couple months all this green will be gold and orange," he said over his shoulder, his paddle creating tiny whirlpools in its wake.

Autumn was spectacular in Bloomfield. People drove from miles around to see the changing leaves every year. The crowds had always irritated Anna, but somehow this year she had a feeling she wouldn't mind them so much.

"Fall is the best time of year," Dan said.

"My dad used to say the same thing," Anna said, falling into memories of bonfires and hayrides, pumpkin patches and crisp night air. "Goodbye, Daddy," she whispered.

As the last of the daylight evaporated, Dan pulled the paddle into the canoe and turned to look at Anna. His eyes shimmered in the moonlight and he smiled. Anna's heart skipped. She felt as if she had known him all her life. In a way, she supposed she had, though no matter how hard she tried, she still couldn't remember him from school. But his eyes were so familiar, and his arms felt like home to her. She found herself wishing they weren't in a canoe so she could feel those arms around her. Dan recognized the look in her eyes and stood and began teetering her way.

"Stop!" Anna shouted, covering her eyes with both hands as she laughed.

"No! Must be with woman!" he said, in a new caveman voice.

"Don't say I didn't warn you," she said, and grabbed the edge of the canoe, jolting it to the side.

"You wouldn't dare," Dan said, his eyes wide.

"Wanna bet?" Anna said, and pushed down with all her strength. Dan tried to steady himself. He failed.

A cloud of sleepy birds poured from the treetops, circling the canoe, bellowing in protest at having been awakened by the loud splash and Anna's subsequent fit of laughter. When Dan's head popped up above the shimmering water, he scowled at her. Her laughter ceased immediately. She watched him swim to the side of the canoe.

Dammit! What have I done? She searched his eyes for forgiveness as he placed his hands on the side of the canoe and glared up at her. Drops of water trailed from the ends of his hair, down his temples, over his cheekbones and curled around his set jaw. *Oh my God,* she thought. *He's even hotter when he's mad!*

Dan's fingertips curled around the edge of the canoe, and a sneaky smile spread across his face. With one swift motion, he tipped the canoe to the side so forcefully that Anna went in head first. Once she surfaced, she grabbed his head and dunked him in revenge. He grabbed her feet from under the water and pulled her down. She felt his arms around her, and his lips pressed hard into hers.

When they came up for air, she gasped, but he pulled her mouth to his again, holding her tight as he expertly treaded water, supporting them both.

"Are you cold?" he whispered. Anna nodded, just now noticing her shivering limbs. "Let's get you warmed up," he said.

They abandoned ship and swam to shore, and Dan ran off to the canoe shed. He returned with an armful of towels and draped each one around her until she resembled a snowman. "There," he said. He wrapped his arms around her girth and looked into her eyes – a lost boy finally home. "I love you Anna," he whispered. "I always have."

Anna swallowed hard.

~

"Didn't I make myself clear?" Mitch growled, shoving the classifieds into Sandy's face. "You think anyone would hire a tramp like you?" Sandy stood frozen, grateful that she had already tucked the kids safely into bed. Her eyes dared not meet his; instead she studied the gash in the linoleum – lingering evidence of the morning shortly after Craig was born, when Mitch had searched the refrigerator for milk. Finding none, he had flown into a rage.

"I see who you care about," he had shouted, snatching a jar of breast milk out of the refrigerator. He dangled it in the air. "I do all the work in the family. You do nothing. And you can't even keep the fridge stocked." Sandy had worried that his shouting would wake the baby. "What does that little brat do? He keeps me up. I need my sleep, and that baby whines and cries all night. And *he* gets milk!" Mitch shouted. "If I can't have milk, neither can he!" He hurled the jar across the kitchen at her.

Sandy jumped out of the way, and the jar crashed into the cabinet and shattered, spraying the breast milk all over her, glass fragments crashing to the floor. Sandy's hair dripped, and Mitch glared at her. "Look at you! You're disgusting." He approached her, took a long sniff and said, "You smell like trash." He grabbed Sandy by her ponytail and yanked her head back, slamming it into the cabinet; she fell to the floor ducking out of his wrath. "Trash," Mitch said. "That's what you are." Sandy had stayed on the floor on top of the broken glass. She didn't dare move. She remained on her bloody knees, praying.

When Mitch had gone back upstairs to shower, Sandy crawled to the phone and dialed her parents' number, then hung up after the first ring.

"Answer me!" Mitch shouted. "Who the hell would hire someone like you?" He grabbed Sandy's chin, forcing her to look up at him. "This is NOT going to happen," he growled. "You can barely keep this house running now, there is no way in hell you're getting a job." He released her face, snatched his cap off the table and left, choking the classifieds in his fist.

Thank God he has the night shift tonight, she thought, refusing to give in to the tears.

She quietly made her way to the boys' room. She knew Craig needed the door open to ease his endless fears, but she always worried that the boys would hear their father's shouting. Padding silently to Craig's bed, she pulled up the covers he had kicked off and kissed his damp hair. She touched his sweaty cheek. "I love you," she whispered. He stirred slightly, but didn't wake.

Craig was her angel. Being the oldest, he had taken it upon himself to protect the other children when the yelling started. He would lead the girls to his room with Todd following close behind. He would read to his three younger siblings to drown out their father's harsh voice, and he would tuck them in at night when he knew his mother was too bruised to. Craig had seen far too much in his seventeen years. Sandy knew why he had the nightmares and why he was still afraid of the dark – she *would* make it better for her children, if it was the last thing she did.

After checking on Todd and kissing her girls goodnight, she retreated to her bedroom. Not bothering to brush her teeth, she climbed into bed and pulled the covers up tight. Her hand settled on her abdomen. "Good night, little one," she whispered. She closed her eyes, knowing her pillow would be tear-soaked in the morning.

~

Anna tossed from her left side to her right side and back again, then finally flipped onto her back. She stared at the ceiling as she wrestled with the thoughts in her head and the feelings in her heart. *He loves me?* Her heart fluttered, and she rubbed her eyes, fighting the fog. She would not give in to sleep for fear of what she might dream after hearing those words. *"I love you Anna. I always have."* She repeated his words in her mind, over and over until her eyelids grew so heavy she could no longer resist; they fell shut.

Bright lights and brilliant colors whirled behind her eyelids. She felt herself spinning, dancing as one with the kaleidoscope of blues and pinks, and she knew in her soul as she surrendered, that this would be a different kind of dream altogether.

TWENTY-SIX

Anna swayed back and forth on her porch swing as vibrant hues encircled her – pinks, blues, yellows, purples – no red. She inhaled the colors and felt her body absorb them. She glanced down and noticed a radiant glow emanating from her hands. She looked over at the lilac bush in full bloom.

A bright fluttering caught her eye and she turned – Enormous orange wings flapped on either side of a tiny body, thin legs running, jumping. A fast run, a jump, a landing, more running, more flapping, another jump...

Anna rose from the swing and stood watching, as Sunshine turned and ran back up the slight hill and did it all over again. Over and over, wings flapping, legs fluttering and jumping.

Finally, when she ran out of steam, she shed her wings and plopped down at the bottom of the hill. Anna approached cautiously so she wouldn't startle the child. "Want to give it a try?" Sunshine said.

"Where did you get these lovely wings?" Anna asked, lowering herself beside the girl and inspecting the wings. She admired the balsa wood frame beneath the cardboard meticulously painted with the bright orange and black pattern of the monarch butterfly.

"My daddy built them for me," Sunshine said.

"They're beautiful," Anna said. "Why did he build them for you?"

Sunshine looked up at Anna. "Because I told him that if only I had wings, I could fly. My daddy believes in me," she said. "He told me to just keep trying to fly no matter what. And so I am. I'm trying. I'm sure it will happen. I just need to build up strength. He said I just have to believe." And with that, she got up, donned the wings, ran to the top of the hill and shot off once again, flapping and fluttering.

Over and over she tried, until she finally collapsed to the ground next to Anna, pulled the wings off and handed them over.

Studying the bright wings, Anna pondered the father who would go to so much trouble, knowing full well that there was no way his daughter could fly... Or was there?

Anna slipped the elastic around each of her arms, then stood and gave the wings a little swoop. She walked to the top of the modest hill and held her breath, closed her eyes and took off running and flapping like a wild woman. She flapped and ran, ran and flapped, and for one brief moment she felt her feet leave the ground, her body suspended in mid-air. The wind caught beneath the wings and lifted her. She opened her eyes and looked around. *"I'm flying!"* she shouted.

She reached for a lone white cloud and it vanished. She glanced down and saw Sunshine staring at her in awe. A blue jay circled her, and the wind flowed down her body like ripples in a stream. Everything looked so small and insignificant below her as she flew higher and higher. Every worry evaporated, the loneliness disappeared and it was just Anna floating through the sky. Completely free.

Sunshine's voice was the first thing Anna heard as the pain seared her forehead. *"Are you ok?"*

"What are you talking about?" Anna said, struggling to catch her breath. She realized then that she was face down at the bottom of the hill, her head rough against the curb. She sat up and wiped her forehead; blood dripped from her palm as she pulled it away. She was bleeding. She was hurt. She was happy! *"Did you see me?"* Anna said. *"Did you see me flying?"*

"I sure did!" Sunshine's eyes were as alive as Anna's. *"You were up there for some time!"*

"But then how did I end up like this?" She wiped her forehead again.

"Does that matter?" the girl asked. "You flew!"

Yes I did.

Anna opened her eyes and rubbed her forehead with her fingertips, then pulled them back to examine them. No blood. *It was just a dream,* she thought. It had felt so real, but she didn't really fly. She sighed, closing her eyes to bring back the feeling of weightlessness. She had felt herself floating, soaring, free from all that had bound her to her misery. And she had shared in the magic of a father who loves his child so much that he would spend his day building wings for her, just because she insisted she could fly. And despite the laws of physics, he believed in his daughter.

She wrapped her arms around herself and thought of Dan's confession. In his arms she felt loved, and that, she realized, wasn't just a dream.

~

"Get up, you lazy bitch!"

Sandy jumped out of bed and looked at the clock. 6:12. *Darn it!* She scanned the room to make sure the children weren't around. *Thank God,* she thought. Mitch's bloodshot eyes burned into Sandy's.

"What the hell are you still doing in bed?"

Lowering her eyes to the floor, Sandy grabbed her robe and moved toward the door, hoping if she got started on his eggs right away, he might calm down. She knew better. He slammed the bedroom door shut just as she reached it.

"You need to get your priorities straight," he shouted. Sandy's gaze stayed glued to the floor. "Get this crazy idea of a job out of your head and get my breakfast made!" She reached for the doorknob, but he grabbed her shoulders and shoved her against the wall. Her head snapped back. "You need to learn where you belong." He pushed her toward the door, and she stumbled. When she hit the floor, he kicked her firmly in the ribs.

The baby! Panic gripped her. She felt her throat constrict; she folded her arms around her abdomen to protect her unborn child. Mitch kicked harder. When the assault ceased for a moment, Sandy froze. Mitch knelt down on the floor, grabbed her hair and pulled her head up. "Look at me when I'm talking to you!" She instinctively lowered her eyes, and he slapped her.

Sandy had never seen Mitch this angry, and she suddenly feared that this time the beating might not stop. He wrapped his fingers around her neck and forced her face into the carpet. Then he stood and landed one more blunt kick to her abdomen; Sandy didn't move. Mitch left the room, mumbling about Marcy's Diner.

Sandy waited until she heard the back door slam before she tried to stand.

~

Cathy sprang out of bed and raced to the bathroom. She threw the toilet lid up just in time. Over and over she retched until her body collapsed from exhaustion. Her arms shook; beads of sweat lined her upper lip. She pressed her cheek to the cool tile. Her pulse pounded in her throat and she felt another wave coming on. She struggled to an upright position and threw up one last time before dropping back down to the bathroom floor.

Something's wrong, she thought, as a dark feeling consumed her. *Something's terribly wrong.* She curled up into a ball at the base of the toilet and closed her eyes. She felt another surge of nausea and suddenly recognized the sensation. *Sandy!*

She pulled herself up onto her hands and knees and crawled back into the bedroom. She fumbled for the phone on Kurt's nightstand and knocked the handset to the floor. She dialed her daughter's number. After six rings, she threw the phone down, shook off another wave of nausea and rose to dress. Cathy knew her daughter was in trouble; she needed to get to her. "Hang on honey," she whispered as she raced down the stairs and out the door.

The children were huddled together in the corner of the living room when Cathy burst through the door. "What's wrong?" Cathy shouted, running to her grandchildren. She dropped to her knees. "What is it?" She searched their faces– Libby was folded in Cecilia's arms, and Craig held all three of his siblings close. "Craig?" Cathy said. "Where is your mother?"

"In her bedroom," Craig said softly, his eyes downcast.

Cathy felt the blood drain from her face. "Is she ok?" She didn't wait for an answer. She raced up the stairs, threw open her daughter's bedroom door and spotted her in the bathroom, frantically cleaning blood from her bottom lip. "Sandy! What happened?"

"Oh Mom," Sandy said and ran into her mother's arms. Cathy stroked her hair as she cried, and her mind raced back in time to the night her teenage daughter had confided her pregnancy. *Twice,* Cathy thought. *I've let her down twice.* Sandy's thin body heaved against her mother's.

Cathy took her by the shoulders and stared into her eyes. "Did Mitch do this?"

Sandy didn't respond.

"Sandy, talk to me."

Sandy wiped her nose with a flat hand. "Mom, can you take the kids to school?"

"Of course, honey, but please tell me what happened. You need to get to the hospital. I can drive you."

Sandy stiffened. "No Mom," she said. "I don't want the kids to see me like this." She pulled away from her mother and returned to the mirror. She picked up the washcloth and wiped fresh blood from her lip. "Please," she said as she hurried toward the bedroom door. "Please just take them to school."

"Ok honey," was all Cathy could say as she followed her daughter down the stairs and watched her sneak out the back door to her car.

Taking a deep breath, Cathy walked into the living room; her grandchildren rose and ran to her. She gathered them into her arms and held them close as they cried, just as she had held her daughter, standing strong to support their quivering bodies.

"Your mom's going to be fine," she finally said, forcing a smile. "She just needs to see a doctor. Let's get you guys ready for school." *Normalcy,* Cathy thought. *They need normalcy right now.* But she couldn't help wondering if this *was* normal to them. *How long has this been going on?*

"Grandma," Craig said, interrupting her thoughts. "Can you make us pancakes?"

~

Sandy was waiting by the door when Anna pulled into her parking space at the office. Even after all these years, Anna recognized her instantly.

"Sandy," she said as she stepped out of her car. "What are you doing here?"

Sandy didn't speak or look up to greet her. As Anna approached, the fresh blood beneath her bottom lip and the red marks around her neck spoke the words Sandy couldn't. She was holding herself around her middle, sobbing.

"Was it Mitch?" Anna asked.

Sandy nodded.

Anna fished around in her purse for a pen and scribbled a note to her morning patients on the back of an old receipt. She wedged it behind the lockset and wrapped her arm around Sandy's waist. She helped her into the passenger seat and drove toward the hospital.

Sandy stared blindly out the window as Anna drove.

"He didn't..." Anna paused and turned toward Sandy. "Did he hurt the children?"

Sandy shook her head.

Anna felt her heart slow some. "Where are they?"

"Summer school."

Thank God, Anna thought. "Sandy, there's a shelter in town –"

Sandy interrupted her. "Anna," she said, "I'm sorry I wasn't there for you after your parents –"

"Sandy," Anna said, "That's not important right now."

Anna checked Sandy in at the front desk then took a seat beside her.

Sandy studied her hands, and Anna struggled to find words to comfort the woman she had once considered a sister. She turned to look at Sandy, and felt her eyes burn at the sight of fresh blood forming under Sandy's lip.

There was nothing Anna could say to make things better now. In spite of all of her training and ten years in private practice, Anna was at a complete loss for words. She thought of her conversation at the cemetery with Sunshine. Now was not the time to share that wisdom with Sandy, not while she was in the midst of the crisis. *What am I supposed to say?*

Out of the corner of her eye, she saw Sunshine peeking around the edge of the front desk, scowling at her, urging her to comfort Sandy. "I don't know how, " Anna whispered.

"Yes you do," Sunshine whispered back, her eyes wide in emphasis.

When Anna didn't budge, Sunshine shook her head and marched over. She crouched down in front of Sandy and placed her small hand under Sandy's chin, lifting it gently, forcing her to make eye-contact. With the tenderness of a mother and the confidence of a child, she said four simple words: "You can do this." Then she stood and skipped out the door.

A quiet sigh escaped Sandy's lips and her shoulders relaxed. "Thank you," she said, placing her hand on Anna's.

When the nurse called her name, Sandy looked directly into Anna's eyes, squeezed her hand and said "I *can* do this." She stood, then turned back to Anna. "You don't need to wait here, Anna. I'll call you when I'm done." And walking taller than she had in years, Sandy disappeared with the nurse through the double doors.

Anna returned to her office, took down the note and shut herself in her office. She needed to breathe. She needed to be alone. *I wish Sandy had come to me for help,* she thought. *How long has he been abusing her?*

Anna thought back to her one and only encounter with Mitch Watson.

She had ditched her eighth period calculus class and was sitting alone on the football bleachers carving a giant "X" into the metal bench with the broken tip of her ball-point pen. Mitch had walked past her and glanced up, hesitated, then casually climbed the steps and sat down two rows below her. He didn't look at her when he spoke.

"You skipping too?" he said.

Anna didn't respond. She hated Mitch for what his father had done.

"Yeah," he said. "School sucks."

Anna continued carving.

Mitch pulled out a cigarette and turned to offer it to Anna.

She continued carving.

He lit the cigarette and took a drag. After a long, slow exhale, he turned to face the football field again. "He was a drunk bastard, Anna."

She continued carving.

"I wish I could take it back," he said. "What he did, I mean. To your parents."

Anna continued carving.

Mitch took another drag then stood. "I'm sorry," he whispered before clunking down the bleachers in his steel-toe boots.

Mitch had never spoken to her again. She had seen his vulnerable side and she knew he was embarrassed, but she would never accept his apology for what his father had stolen from her.

Dr. Patterson waltzed in, interrupting Anna's reflection.

"I notice your hours are becoming somewhat..." he scratched his chin, "sporadic." A mist of spit sprayed from his mouth as he said the word. "You know I have a long list of highly qualified *professionals,* who are waiting for an opening at my practice." And with that, he turned and walked out the door, stopping to close it firmly behind himself.

Anna rolled her eyes. After what she had been through with Sandy this morning, his threats had no effect.

She glanced at her clock and sighed, then picked up her cell phone and crossed the fine line between professionalism and friendship.

"Chief Malone."

"Kurt," she said. "It's Anna. I need to talk to you about Sandy."

~

Dr. Carson inserted the ultrasound probe, and a tear rolled down Sandy's cheek.

"Mrs. Watson," Dr. Carson said, "I'm afraid there is no heartbeat."

Sandy already knew. She had felt the baby's soul as it lifted itself from her body on the floor in her bedroom. She had felt a breeze blow by her, the windows closed – a warm breeze that grazed her cheek as if kissing her goodbye, and in that moment, she had also said goodbye, but not before she had whispered "I'm so sorry."

"You will experience some cramping and bleeding as the tissue passes," Dr. Carson said. He paused and scanned the room. "Mrs. Watson –"

"It's Miss Malone," Sandy interrupted.

"Miss Malone," he said, "would you like to speak with a police officer?"

"Yes she would," Kurt said, shoving the door open wide.

"Daddy!" Sandy attempted to straighten her hair, as if doing so would somehow hide the cuts and bruises.

"It's over, baby," Kurt said, as he approached her. Dr. Carson quietly left the room.

"Daddy... I ..." Sandy couldn't speak. Her father leaned over and swallowed her in his arms.

"Let it out," he whispered. "Just let it out."

Sandy released it all – tears of exhaustion, tears of loneliness, tears for her children and the child she had lost, but not tears of pain. She didn't feel the pain.

Her heart had shut that out a long time ago.

"It's ok," he whispered, smoothing her hair. "I will fix this."

"I'm so sorry Daddy," she said between sobs.

"No," Kurt said, taking control. "I'm the one who should be apologizing. I should have intervened a long time ago. I knew in my gut what he was doing to you, and I understood why you didn't want to tell me, but there is no excuse for my letting it go this far." He released her and looked into her eyes. "I will make this right." He kissed her cheek and turned to leave. Pausing for a moment, he faced her again. "Sandy," he said, "would you and the children like to come stay with us?"

"Thank you Daddy," she said, "but that's the first place Mitch will come looking for us." She felt brave as she said his name. "Anna offered to take us to the shelter. We'll be safe there."

"Ok honey," he said. He studied the bruises again. *This is all my fault,* he thought. "I'll stop by the shelter to see you after you get settled."

"Thank you Daddy."

Kurt shrugged off his daughter's gratitude. *I don't deserve it.*

~

"I will make this right." Kurt replayed the words in his head as he walked to his cruiser. *"We will catch him."* The promises he had made to his daughter and to Taylor. Two promises, two monsters. Kurt had his work cut out for him, but if nothing else, Kurt Malone was a man of his word. His cell phone vibrated and he pulled it out of his pocket and hit send.

"Kurt," Cathy said. Kurt could hear the panic in his wife's voice. "Kurt, something's wrong with Sandy. She wouldn't tell me what it was, but it has something to do with Mitch. Kurt, I think he beat her up!"

Oh God, Kurt thought. *She knows. How can I tell her that I know, that I have suspected for months. She will never forgive me for not telling her.* "I know honey," he said, his voice breaking. He closed his eyes and continued. "She's at

Midwestern Memorial. I just left her." Time stood still as he waited for his wife to respond. He could hear her rapid breathing, and then a soft question –

"You know?"

"Cathy,"

"You know?" she said, louder now.

"Honey," Kurt said.

Cathy interrupted him. "What do you know?"

Kurt searched for words, and his silence fueled Cathy's anger.

"How long have you known?"

Kurt couldn't respond.

"You bastard!" Cathy shouted, and the phone went dead.

TWENTY-SEVEN

Anna snatched up her cellphone the instant it rang.

"Sandy?"

"Yes Anna, it's me."

"Are you ok?"

"Not really." There was a long pause. "Can you come get me?"

"Of course. I'm on my way." She grabbed her keys and raced out of her office.

Sandy was waiting outside the Emergency Room entrance when Anna pulled up.

"Are you going to press charges?" Anna asked, as she helped Sandy lower herself into the car. Sandy remained silent for a long time as Anna drove toward the school. She looked at the clock – 2:44. They still had time to make it to pick the kids up by 3:00.

"Yes," Sandy finally said.

Anna exhaled in relief. "In the meantime," she said, "we need to get you and the children to the shelter."

"I know," Sandy said, studying her hands in her lap.

"For now, you can leave your car at my office." Anna said. "We don't want it parked anywhere near the shelter. I'll make arrangements with your dad to move it someplace safe."

"Thank you, Anna," Sandy said. "You're a good friend."

Bloomfield's one public school served every child from kindergarten through twelfth grade. The building was thirty years old; the narrow rectangular windows were trimmed in bright orange aluminum; the matching metal roof sloped halfway down the side like a red-head's bangs.

Anna and Sandy walked in silence as they approached the entrance. A stream of chattering students poured out, and Anna saw Sandy's eyes light up when she spotted her four beautiful children coming toward her.

"Hi Mom," the oldest boy said, and gave her a gentle hug, averting his eyes from the stitches under her lip.

"Hi guys," Sandy said as she released her son. "I want you to meet my friend Anna."

The children looked at Anna with surprise, and Anna realized that they had probably never met a friend of their mother's before.

"We're going on a little vacation," Sandy said. The children seemed to know what this meant, and Anna wondered how much these poor kids had witnessed.

Sandy's daughters clung to her hands, Todd shuffled nervously, and Craig wrapped a protective arm around his mother's shoulder as Anna pressed the doorbell. Nancy Meyers, the shelter director, looked out through the peephole. When she saw Sandy and her children, she opened the door immediately. She studied the marks on Sandy's face then led them all inside and introduced herself.

"Is there someplace I can speak with Anna in private?" Sandy asked. Nancy looked around, then gestured toward the sitting room. Sandy instructed her children to wait with Nancy. Craig knelt and held his sisters close while they waited for their mother to return.

"Anna," Sandy said, studying the floor. The Berber carpet showed wear in circles around the edges of the room, evidence of endless hours of pacing feet. "You've done so much for me. I'm so sorry I wasn't there for you after your parents died."

"Sandy," Anna said, "that was a long time ago. We were just kids."

"But all those years, I should have been there for you."

"It's ok," Anna said. "None of that matters now. It's in the past."

"I know," Sandy said, "but…"

Anna took Sandy's chin and lifted her face so that their eyes met, just as Sunshine had done at the hospital. "I forgive you," Anna said. "It's time for you to focus on yourself and your children." She took Sandy's hand and led her back to the foyer.

Craig stood, and Cecilia and Libby ran to their mother, wrapping their arms around her waist. "Thank you Anna," Sandy said, her eyes brimming with tears.

Anna gave her a gentle hug. "Are you going to be ok?"

Sandy smiled. "We're going to be just fine."

Anna released her friend, hoping she was right.

~

Kurt's face went ghost white when he pulled into the driveway and saw the vacant spot where Cathy always parked. *She wouldn't,* he thought. *Would she?*

He raced through the front door and took the stairs two at a time to the bedroom he shared with his wife. An overflowing closet brought him relief and he placed his hand over his chest, feeling his panicked heartbeat slow back down. *She hasn't left me,* he thought, though he wouldn't blame her if she had. Kurt had never heard anger like that in his wife's voice. *She deserves better,* he thought. *She deserves a real husband.*

He wandered into his study and sat down at his desk. *I failed my wife,* he thought. *I failed my daughter. What kind of a man am I?* He picked up the crystal paperweight he had been awarded the night he was inducted as Bloomfield's Chief of Police. He studied the engraving; *"Kurt Malone, Chief of Police,"* he read. *Failure,* he thought. He glanced around the room at all the

195

awards and plaques he had earned over the years – *"Twenty-Five Years of Outstanding Service," "Protecting and Serving."*

"Bullshit," he growled and hurled the paperweight into the plaque on the wall, gouging the word *"Protecting."*

He had known. He had known all along. He had tried to protect Cathy from the truth, but he had done nothing to protect his daughter. *What kind of father am I?* Dropping his face into his hands, he thought back to the day he first knew – the day he should have taken a stand.

Mitch had come in to the station late. Kurt had given him the benefit of the doubt; he was his son-in-law, after all. But something about the way Mitch looked at him that day had haunted Kurt, and it wasn't until later in the afternoon that he realized what it was.

Kurt had stopped by Sandy's house to surprise her with lunch, and she was slow to answer the door. When she finally greeted him, Kurt noticed that she was holding her side; she dropped her hands when she saw him eyeing them. She claimed to have cramps, and Kurt hadn't pressed, not comfortable with discussing women's issues. But during the visit, she had fidgeted and avoided eye-contact. Sandy had always been closer with her mother but she had never been this uneasy around him. He knew something was wrong but he couldn't quite figure it out. When he returned to the police station, he had asked Mitch if Sandy was feeling ok.

"She's fine," Mitch had said. "You know how women are." Mitch had turned to walk away, then stopped and glanced over his shoulder looking Kurt up and down, a raised eyebrow, a smirk and a smug expression on his face, an expression that said "You may be the boss here, but I am the boss with your daughter."

From that day on, Kurt had watched his son-in-law's every move, hoping to catch him in an indiscrete act, something, *anything* he could use against him. But the man was good at his job, and short of confronting Sandy, Kurt hadn't known what else he could do.

So I stood by and did nothing, Kurt thought. He folded his fingers around the pewter-framed picture on his desk. His wife looked so proud – her daughter was a bride. Cathy had barely slept during the two short weeks she had to plan the wedding. Sandy had pleaded with her mother for a simple wedding, perhaps embarrassed by her burgeoning baby bump, but Cathy had insisted on family, friends, flowers, music and an outrageously expensive wedding dress.

Kurt picked up the photograph and looked closely. Mitch had his arm wrapped tightly around Sandy's shoulders... a little *too* tightly, Kurt now realized. As he focused in on his daughter's eyes, his head began to spin. The evidence he had been searching for had been there all along, right there in her eyes – terror.

He slammed the frame down, the glass and his heart shattering as one.

~

"You did great," Sunshine said. "Your parents would be so proud."

"Thank you," Anna said, pulling her legs into her body on the porch swing. The cool evening breeze caressed her cheeks. She imagined her mother's soft fingers wiping the tears away as she let her emotions go.

Sunshine turned and stared at her. "Why are you crying?"

"I don't know," Anna said.

"Yes you do," Sunshine said, reaching up to touch Anna's tears. She pulled her fingers away and studied the glistening drops on her fingertips.

Anna thought of Sandy and her children. In spite of everything they had been through, they were happy; they were together.

The evening was full of hope – male cicadas searching for their mates, oblivious to the fact that once they succeeded in finding their perfect partner, they would die. Anna feared that was just how life was – endless searching that always ends the same way. But things were changing for Sandy, and that gave Anna hope. She knew that her friend had a long road ahead of her, but she had seen the love in the children's eyes when they looked at their mother, and Anna realized how lucky Sandy was in spite of the abuse. And how strong.

"I'll never be as brave as Sandy." Anna said. Perhaps it was being a mother that made her friend so strong. Anna sighed as she remembered her own mother, and how safe she had always felt in her presence. *I'll never be that strong,* she thought. "I'll never be the woman my mother was," she whispered.

"You're right." Sunshine said. "You can't be."

Anna stiffened. "Gee thanks," she said, turning and glaring at the girl.

Sunshine continued. "Anna, you can't be who your mother was, because you're not her. You're Anna. Perfect just the way you are. Your mother saw that in you, and now it's time for you to see what she saw."

Anna sighed. "I don't feel perfect," she said, letting her back fall against the swing, shifting her gaze toward the stars once more.

"Maybe that's the problem," Sunshine said. "We're all perfect, Anna. We're all capable of great love, but you're too busy thinking about what you lost, what you aren't, that you can't see what you have, what you are."

Anna searched the night sky for Orion once again, knowing she wouldn't find him there… just like her father.

"He's there," Sunshine said. "Even though you can't see him."

Anna felt a flutter in her chest and she sat up straight, staring at the wise child's silhouette. "Who?"

"Orion."

Anna sighed and slumped against the back of the swing again. Sunshine's legs dangled from the edge. The cicadas' quiet song rose around them, growing deafening, then receding.

"I miss them," Anna finally said. "Saying goodbye sucks."

"I know."

Anna pulled her fleece blanket tight around her shoulders. "And I'm terrified."

"I know," Sunshine said. "You're afraid you'll be alone forever."

Anna nodded and thought of Dan's confession. He believed he loved her, but how was that possible? He barely knew her. *"Love yourself first, and the rest will come naturally."* Anna replayed the words in her head. *It sounds so simple,* she thought, *but it's not.*

"You're right," Sunshine said. "It's not simple, but you have to start somewhere, and it starts with forgiving yourself and letting go. That's the only way you can begin to truly love yourself and trust your heart; your heart will guide you in the right direction, and everything will work out from there."

Anna relaxed her gaze and allowed the stars to blur. "I'm trying," she said, wondering if she would ever truly forgive herself. She was letting go, but in letting go, she felt more alone than ever.

"You're not alone, Anna," Sunshine whispered. "You never have been."

TWENTY-EIGHT

Kurt marched straight through the double doors of the police station without looking up to greet Jane. He closed his office door and walked over to study the pictures on the wall. A soft knock startled him from his thoughts.

"What?" he snapped.

Jane ducked inside apprehensively. "Kurt," she said, "Officer Blake was unable to serve the warrant." She hesitated, then continued. "Officer Watson seems to be missing."

Kurt turned to face her. "I want every available officer out looking for him."

"Ok," she said. "But Kurt,"

"Jane," he interrupted, "Go home. It's late. You should have left hours ago. Thank you for everything."

"I just wish I had known about Sandy," she said. "Maybe I could have helped. I'm so sorry." Kurt looked down at the floor, and Jane closed his door quietly.

Alone now, Kurt returned his attention to the pictures of the victims – young women on the cusp of life. With the exception of Taylor, all were college students. Why did this man go after college students? Was it possible that the attacker was also a student? Was he meeting them in the bar and convincing them to leave with him? But that didn't make sense, because each of the victims reported leaving the bar alone, then being grabbed from behind and forced into a car before being knocked unconscious. *Not one girl has been able to get a good look at the man,* Kurt thought. He flipped the top page on his desk calendar and counted back. Four weeks had passed since he sent the first DNA sample to the state crime lab. He picked up his phone and dialed.

"Tom Williams."

"Tom, this is Chief Malone from the Bloomfield PD. Any idea on when we will have results on the DNA samples I sent you?"

"Chief Malone," Tom said, "I'm sorry. You know we're overwhelmed with a backlog of biological evidence. We're working night and day."

"Meanwhile this bastard continues to attack innocent women," Kurt said.

"I'm sorry, Chief. I'll call you the minute we have the samples processed."

Kurt knew these things took time, but he didn't have time. He had to solve this case with or without a DNA match. He would take personal responsibility for every woman this man attacked while he floundered. His job as Chief of Police was to protect; his job as a father was to protect. He had to get one of the two right.

"Do you have a suspect?" Tom asked, breaking into Kurt's thoughts.

"Unfortunately we don't, but I'm hoping CODIS will reveal a match," Kurt said. "So anything you can do to expedite the results would be appreciated."

"We'll do our best."

Kurt hung up the phone and walked over to the photos on the wall. He traced his finger around the edge of the first victim's picture. She, too, had a father who loved her and who was probably blaming himself at this very moment for not protecting his daughter. That's what fathers are supposed to do... "at least the good ones," he whispered. Then he thought of Mitch. In addition to domestic assault, murder charges were an option, since Mitch's blows to Sandy's abdomen likely caused the baby's death. *Did he know she was pregnant? Is that why he kicked her so hard,* Kurt thought. *What kind of father murders his own child?* Kurt walked over and looked out the window into the dimly lit parking lot, searching the shadows for signs of his son-in-law. He rubbed the crease between his eyebrows. *Where is that little bastard hiding?* Kurt snatched up his keys. *I'll find him myself.*

~

Sandy rested on the bottom bunk with her four beautiful children encircling her. "… and they all lived happily ever after." She closed the book and pulled them close. *Thank you, God,* she thought. They were safe. They were starting over.

Her mother's visit this evening had comforted the children, but they still had so many questions. Cathy had brought the tattered Mr. Wiggles and three bags of clothes she had purchased on her way to the shelter. She had shared stories of Sandy's childhood, and they had all laughed together, taking turns hugging the threadbare stuffed animal. Mr. Wiggles had lost most of his stuffing over the years, now a limp bag of worn fur. The children had held him reverently as Cathy told them how much he had meant to their mother as a child.

Sandy tucked her two girls and Mr. Wiggles into the bottom bunk, and Todd climbed onto the top bunk. Craig curled up on an air mattress on the floor beside Sandy's twin bed. Sandy turned out the light and focused on the comforting sound of her children breathing. *How can I keep them safe,* she thought. She doubted Mitch would serve much time in jail, if any. She also doubted he would just allow her to walk out of his life. In his mind, he owned her, and Sandy was well aware of how Mitch's mind worked.

Don't think about that now, she told herself, and turned her attention back to the sweet sound of her children sleeping peacefully, as her mind drifted back to the conversation with her mother earlier that evening.

"How did you know I was in trouble?" Sandy had asked, as her mother embraced her in the foyer.

"Mothers sense these things," her mother had said, releasing her. "I came to check on you and bring you a few things." Then she had hesitated, a flicker of hope in her eyes. "And to let you know that I've decided to take the house off the market in case you and the children would like to stay with us for a while." Her mother had smiled expectantly, but when Sandy didn't respond right away, her expression turned to concern. "Honey, how long has this been going on?"

index finger down the keys, hearing the music in her mind.

Her heart felt lighter as she finally stood and made her way back to the bedroom to check on her children. The door was cracked open just a little. She sighed. *Will they ever feel safe again?* She pushed the door open and found her four children huddled together on the twin bed, staring at the door. *Waiting for me,* she thought, her heart feeling heavy again as she realized that they still had a long way to go.

"Let's see if they have pancake mix in this place," she said. Her children jumped to their feet and followed her to the kitchen.

~

Kurt needed time to think, but he still needed to do his job. He shook his head to clear his mind of all his worries about Sandy and Cathy. He took a thumbtack out of his desk drawer and placed it on the map where yet another college student had been attacked last night. *While I was asleep on the couch,* Kurt thought.

Two drunk kids had discovered the unconscious young woman on the sidewalk around the corner from Riley's. *He just dumped her there,* Kurt thought. *Just like all the others.* He pushed the tack in harder. It was the sixth thumbtack close to Riley's. There were two tacks a few blocks away, but the pattern had been obvious for the past couple weeks. *How,* Kurt thought. *How does he manage to get his hands on these girls when every officer on duty is casing that bar?* And then a sick feeling seized his gut as the realization hit him – he had ordered all his officers to search for Mitch last night. Without question, they had obeyed, pulling off the surveillance around Riley's.

"I keep screwing up," he whispered, and dropped his face into his hands.

~

"Hey," Taylor said as she knocked and walked in all at once. "You ready for me?"

"Always," Anna said, smiling. Taylor was coping so well with her trauma, and Anna found strength in the young woman's resilience.

Her parents had not yet returned from Italy, even after receiving the news of Taylor's attack, and Anna found this unfathomable. *Such a strong young woman,* she thought.

Taylor came in and sat down, looking healthier than Anna had ever seen her. The color had returned to her cheeks, and the dark circles under her eyes had faded.

"You look great," Anna said. "What did you have to eat this morning?"

"I had a glass of orange juice," she said. "And..." she paused to build suspense, "I put peanut butter on my toast!" She smiled at the woman who had become such a good friend since the attack.

Anna had stocked Taylor's kitchen with *real* food, not meatloaf. She brought her peanut butter and fish sticks, chicken nuggets and applesauce. Anna knew what teenagers liked – macaroni and cheese was Taylor's new favorite.

"That's a start," Anna said, grinning at the girl. She hated to rob Taylor of her good mood, but Taylor needed to talk about the attack. Anna hadn't brought it up during her house calls, and Taylor hadn't mentioned it. But Anna feared if Taylor didn't work through her experience, she would repress the devastating emotions and relapse back into her eating disorder. "How are you feeling about what happened?" she asked gently.

Taylor's smile faded and she mindlessly brushed her fingers across the bandage on her neck. She wasn't ready to talk about it, and Anna respected that. She would give her time. Taylor looked away.

Anna sat quietly for a moment, her eyes studying her office, truly seeing it for the first time. "Let's get out of here," she said.

The shocked expression on Taylor's face quickly gave way to a look of animation, her eyes bright. "Where are we going?"

"You'll see," Anna said.

"What are we doing here?" Taylor asked, as they approached the nondescript home that served as the women's shelter.

"I want you to meet someone," Anna said, pressing the button beside the front door. Seconds later Nancy peeked through the peephole. She immediately opened the door, embraced Anna and invited them in. Taylor hesitated, and Anna took her hand, guiding her to a plaid love seat in the sitting room.

"What is this place?" Taylor whispered. She took in the children's artwork on the walls, the mismatched furniture, the women scattered about, reading or knitting. She heard children giggling in the next room and turned toward the cheerful sound.

Taking this as her cue, Anna asked Nancy if she could introduce Taylor to the children. Nancy nodded and escorted them into the room where the kids were playing.

"Libby, come meet our guests," Nancy said.

A young child turned shyly and stood. Taylor figured she was only six or seven. Blonde curls trailed down her back, and her eyes studied the ground as she slowly approached the women.

"Libby came here with her mother and three siblings," Nancy explained to Taylor.

In the far corner of the room, Sandy's two boys and Cecilia had stopped their card game and were watching Taylor closely. Taylor's eyes met Craig's and he looked away. Her cheeks burned. She took a deep breath and redirected her attention to the little girl in front of her.

"Hi Libby," Taylor said, squatting down to the child's level.

"Hi," Libby said, her eyes turning toward her siblings in the corner. She nibbled at the skin beside her fingernail and shifted from foot to foot.

"You can go back and play if you'd like," Nancy said, and Libby shot off to the corner of the room where her brothers checked her over to make sure she had escaped unscathed. Craig looked up at Taylor again. He was wringing his hands, and Taylor saw something in his eyes that resembled shame.

"What are they doing here?" Taylor whispered, turning away from Craig.

"Their father was abusive and your friend, Anna, convinced their mother to come stay with us," Nancy said, tipping her head toward Anna and smiling.

"Really?" Taylor said. Her stomach knotted into a tight ball and she glanced back over at Craig. He was staring at the floor. *I never knew,* Taylor thought. The other kids at school had been so cruel to Craig, and though Taylor had never been mean to his face, she had never done a thing to defend him. She suddenly felt like crying.

Anna nodded. "How are they today?"

"The boys won't talk to me," Nancy said.

"They look very chatty with each other," Anna said.

"They're doing much better than when they arrived," Nancy said. "They're eating and playing. Our hope is that each day they will come out of their shells a little more. Libby is the most outgoing, but she still only answers in one word responses."

"Where is their mother?" Taylor asked, scanning the room.

"Right here," Sandy said, her eyes bright as she walked through the doorway.

"It's you!" Taylor said, instantly recognizing the woman who had touched her heart with her beautiful music that day at Maple Manor. "You're Craig's mother?" Taylor said.

"I am," Sandy said. "Do the two of you have classes together at school?"

"Yes," Taylor said, looking down. *But I never reached out to him,* she thought. She remembered the many times she and Jodi had whispered jokes about the kid who never spoke to anyone, who wore secondhand clothes and never had a girlfriend. Again, she felt the urge to cry. *What a jerk I've been,* she thought.

"Taylor?" Sandy said.

Taylor looked up at the beaming woman in front of her and forced her mood to match Sandy's. "Do they have a piano here?" Taylor asked.

"They sure do," Sandy said, nodding in the direction of the upright in the next room.

The three women followed Sandy to the piano, and Sandy sat down and began to play Mozart from memory. Her eyes were closed, a peaceful expression on her face.

Another strong woman, Anna mused. *I seem to be surrounded by them.*

When Sandy finished playing, Taylor noticed the same reaction she had seen at Maple Manor – the women wiped away tears and the children stared at Sandy as if she were a celebrity. Sandy rejoined the group and wrapped her arm around Taylor's waist, whispering in her ear.

Anna thanked Nancy for her time. "Taylor and I need to get back to the office," she said.

"If it's ok," Taylor said, "I'd like to stay for a while." She glanced at Craig once more. He was shuffling the cards, ignoring her.

Nancy saw Sandy's hopeful expression and smiled. "Sure," she said.

Taylor hugged Anna, and Sandy took the young woman by the hand. They walked over to Libby and her siblings. Taylor kneeled on the floor just outside the circle the kids had formed and watched as they resumed their card game. After a few minutes, Craig looked at Taylor and handed her the deck of cards without speaking. She moved into the circle, shuffled and dealt. Sandy sat back watching as, one by one, her other three children lifted their eyes and looked at Taylor. *They're beginning to trust again,* Sandy thought.

Anna turned to leave, knowing that Taylor was healing, and so were Sandy and her children. So was she.

THIRTY

Anna's heart skipped when she saw Dan's car as she pulled into her driveway. She hadn't seen him in days, not since his confession, and she missed him. *Does he regret those words,* she thought.

He watched her from the porch swing and stood when she opened her car door.

"What are you doing here?" Anna asked, trying to tame her childish grin.

"Good to see you too," Dan said, giving her a quick hug. "I have a surprise for you."

"Another one?" she said. "Should I wear my swimsuit this time?"

"No, but you might want to pack it," he said, offering her his hand.

"Pack it?" Anna said, looking at his extended hand with suspicion. "Where are we going?"

"I told you, it's a surprise." He took the keys from her and unlocked her front door. Once inside, he pulled her close and kissed her hungrily. Anna surrendered herself to him... Then he stepped back abruptly, leaving her breathless, wanting more. "Plenty of time for that," he said, kissing her forehead before directing her upstairs to pack. "Let's get going." Anna rolled her eyes and stomped up the stairs to her bedroom, smiling.

She tossed her swimsuit, her robe, her favorite jeans, a couple T shirts, a sweater, a blouse and a sundress onto her bed. *How am I supposed to pack when he won't tell me where we're going,* she thought. Then, realizing that she really didn't care where they were going, she dropped it all in her suitcase and zipped it closed. She wasn't worried about wrinkles or whether she had packed the right things, she just wanted to be with this man.

Dan met her at the top of the stairs and took the suitcase from her. "I've got it," he said, his eyes burning into hers. She melted in his stare.

Anna watched the trees whiz by. When Dan finally slowed and took a right onto a gravel road, she turned to him. "Where are we going?" she asked.

"Shhh..." Dan said. He glanced over at her, smiling mischievously. "Close your eyes."

Anna's heart fluttered.

After a few more minutes, he spoke. "We're here. You can look now."

She saw the porch swing first. "Oh Dan," she whispered. The forest still surrounded the cabin on all sides; Anna was happy to see that the owner hadn't let the loggers in as so many others in the area had. Smoke rose from the chimney, and Anna attempted to form a question. "What... How..." She was speechless.

They walked hand in hand up the steps onto the small covered porch, and Anna noticed a mason jar filled with lilac clippings on a log table next to the swing.

"You thought of everything, didn't you?" Anna said, leaning into his arms. "Where did you find lilacs this late in the season?"

"I have my connections," he said, obviously proud of himself. "It was either those or carnations." He winked. "I know how much you love carnations."

"You're terrible," Anna said.

Dan smiled and gave her a quick kiss. "Let's go inside and see if it looks the way you remember." He lifted her into his arms.

"What are you doing?" Anna said, giggling like a child.

"Carrying my woman over the threshold."

"Dan! You're going to hurt yourself!" she said.

"Baby, you're dealing with a *real* man here."

July 4, 1974

"Rise and shine little rosebud," Anna's mother sang as she opened the blinds, allowing the bright morning sun to pour into Anna's bedroom. "We've got a big day ahead." The aroma of bacon hung in the air, and Anna rubbed her eyes. Her mother laid a red, white and blue striped sundress on the foot of her bed, then kissed the top of her head and left her alone to dress.

When Anna entered the kitchen, her father pulled out her chair and gestured for her to sit. Anna covered her mouth to hide her grin as she took in the sight of him in her mother's apron, trimmed in soft pink lace with a fuchsia heart on the chest. "What?" he said. "You don't like my apron?"

Anna shook her head.

"I think it looks quite manly on me," he said, placing a plate in front of her. Anna's mother wrapped her arms around his waist and kissed him on the cheek before taking her own seat at the table.

As they ate, Anna's parents discussed the plan for the day. They were packed and ready to head to the cabin right after breakfast. Anna found it hard to sit still and finish her scrambled eggs. "Easy now," her father teased. "We've got all the time in the world."

Anna's mother rested her hand on Anna's shoulder as they walked through the door. Anna inhaled the familiar musty air. Her father followed with the suitcases, then made trips back and forth to the car, carrying in the food and supplies. Anna helped her mother put everything in its place, stocking the small refrigerator and filling the cabinets with all the ingredients she would need to create her culinary masterpieces for the week. Anna heard the sound of the axe striking wood and wandered outside to watch.

"Don't lose a finger," Katherine called from inside the cabin. Anna's father looked toward the door.

"She doesn't think much of my survival skills, does she?" he said.

Anna giggled and took a seat on the edge of the porch. She felt the warm sun on her face as she watched her father expertly split the logs for the fireplace. When he had chopped more than enough for the week, he propped his axe against the stump and joined her on the porch.

"See?" he said, tilting his head toward the fruits of his labor. "Your mother just doesn't realize how skilled I am."

"Who wants fried chicken?" Katherine called from inside.

"Your mother, however, has some amazing chicken frying skills." He lifted Anna to her feet. "First one in gets the drumsticks!"

They barreled through the front door and slid into their chairs at the kitchen table.

"You two!" Katherine said, chuckling as she took her seat. "There are two drumsticks and two of you. Surely you can figure out a way to make this work."

"No!" Anna's father said. "I want them *both*!" He grabbed the drumsticks off the platter and pretended to take a bite.

Anna jumped out of her chair and grabbed them from him.

"No fair," he whined, "she always gets the drumsticks."

Katherine slapped his thigh under the table. "It's almost time for the fireworks," she said. "Do you think you two can get along long enough to watch, or do I need to separate you?"

Anna and her father looked each other in the eye and nodded. "We've called a truce," he said.

Anna's father unfolded the small pink lawn chair and placed it on the porch as the first "boom" rang out. He hurried back to the car to unload his wife's chair and she brought out a tray of snickerdoodles. They stuffed themselves with cookies as the sky lit up red and blue and gold.

When the night fell silent and the gray trails of smoke had drifted away, Anna crawled into her mother's lap. Her mother stroked her hair, and Anna fell asleep to the sweet sound of her parents' quiet conversation.

THIRTY-ONE

Carrying Anna through the cozy living room, Dan headed straight for the bedroom. She felt weightless in his arms. He gently lowered her onto the bed and sat down next to her, gazing into her eyes. She was still giggling, but when he reached down with his fingers to brush the hair away from her eyes, her breath caught in her throat. His stare was so intense. He was a man deeply in love. Anna knew that look. She had seen it in her father's eyes every time he looked at her mother – Anna was home.

Slowly, lovingly, Dan leaned over and kissed her. Then he pulled back and stared into her eyes again. "You're the one, Anna," he said. He lowered his body next hers and propped himself up on his elbow. "You've always been the one."

He moved his fingertips across her cheek and down her neck. He took his time unfastening each button on her blouse. She sat up, and he eased her shirt down her back then gently lowered her head to the pillow. His kisses trailed around her jawline, and Anna closed her eyes. Every touch of his lips sent electricity through her body. His mouth moved slowly across her chest and down her stomach as his fingers carefully unbuttoned her jeans, sliding them off like silk.

Anna looked down at the man who had turned her world on its head. She tried to rationalize what was happening, but when his lips brushed the inside of her thigh, she let go. She let go of all the worry, all the pain, all the overthinking… and she gave herself to him completely.

When Anna woke, Dan was lying next to her, entranced. She followed his eyes as he studied her chin, her lips, and then found her eyes. She pulled him down to her. In Dan's arms, all was right. Every lonely moment she had lived vanished like Sunshine's cloud, and Anna remembered the wise girl's words – *"Love yourself first, and the rest will come naturally."* Anna was beginning to love herself again. She was allowing herself to exist as "Anna." Dan loved her, the way he looked at her confirmed it. He saw what Sunshine saw, what her parents had seen, what she was beginning to see – Anna.

"I made dinner," he whispered.

"When did you have time to do that?" she asked.

"While you were sleeping," he said.

Anna glanced around the room. He had also brought in her suitcase and unpacked it, and her sundress and blouse were hanging neatly in the small closet. "Aren't you just full of surprises," she said, reaching up to touch his cheek. She tried to pull his face down to hers again, but he gently peeled her hands off the back of his neck, kissing the palm of each one before releasing them.

"Dinner's getting cold," he said. Anna groaned. He smiled as he pulled her off the bed and guided her out of the room.

The kitchen was just as she remembered, though the stove seemed even smaller than it had when she was a child. *How can anyone cook on that thing,* she thought. Dan slid out her chair and motioned for her to sit. Anna admired his forearms once again. He walked over to the stove and gave the simmering Alfredo sauce one last stir.

Anna's body ached as her eyes took in every inch of the man working so efficiently, hair mussed, wearing nothing but his boxers. *Good God this man is hot,* she thought and smiled again at her own good fortune.

She thought back to May 28th – sulking on her porch swing, running through all that was wrong in her life. She recalled seeing Sunshine for the first time, and considered how much that little girl had changed her life.

Dan's cellphone rang, pulling Anna from her thoughts. He picked it up off the counter and checked the number, and for a moment, Anna thought she saw his face go pale. He silenced the ringer and turned back to her.

"Everything ok?" she asked.

"Everything's just right," he said. "How about a glass of wine?" Anna hesitated, and the tilted smile spread slowly across Dan's face. "Just kidding," he said, reaching into the refrigerator and pulling out two pale ales.

Anna shook her head. "You're amazing."

"I know," he said as he drizzled the Alfredo sauce over the noodles.

"Modest too," she teased.

After dinner, Dan led her to the couch in front of the fireplace. He put another log on the fire then sat down beside her.

"You know, Dan," Anna said, smiling. "It's not really cold enough for a fire."

"And that matters why?" he said, pulling her close. "You love fires, so we will have fires." And that was that. "So," he said. "What should we name our kids?"

Anna laughed, knowing he was just being silly... *or was he?* The thought gave her goose bumps.

They made love that night, and again in the morning. Anna had never felt so exhausted or exuberant in her life. She joined Dan in the shower, then he left to make her tea while she dressed.

She wiped the steam from a small spot on the mirror and checked herself over. She didn't bother with make-up – she knew she didn't need to with Dan. In his eyes, she was beautiful just as she was. She smiled at her reflection.

Stepping out of the bedroom, she heard his voice, rough and angry; she hadn't heard him use that tone before.

"Don't call me again," he said.

He whipped around and clicked off his phone when Anna entered the kitchen, and this time she was sure his face was pale. He ran his hand through his hair then smiled at her and handed her a cup of tea. She followed him out to the covered porch, thinking about what she had overheard. She hadn't meant to eavesdrop, but she was having trouble pushing it out of her mind.

Let it go, she thought. He obviously didn't want to talk about it, so she wouldn't press. *If he needs my help, he'll ask.* She lowered herself onto the swing beside him and forced her mind away from the calls, focusing instead on the amazing man beside her.

"Thank you for the tea," she said. Dan knew her. He paid attention. He didn't bother with coffee or wine. Looking down at her steaming cup, she thought again of Sunshine. As much fun as she was having with Dan, she missed the girl. She had grown accustomed to seeing her every day, and she suddenly found herself wishing Sunshine was there with them. Anna could hear the child's sweet giggles in her mind; she could picture her face aglow. *She would be so happy for us,* Anna thought. "I'll be right back," she said, and stood and walked into the cabin. She picked up her purse and sat down at the kitchen table. *Where are they,* she thought, digging through her purse for the stones.

Dan walked up behind her and placed his hands on her shoulders. "You ok?"

"Just perfect," she said, pushing her purse aside and turning to him.

"Yes you are," he said. "Perfect for me."

Anna blushed. "I'm not perfect, Dan," she said as she stood. "Let's go back outside."

Dan took her hand in his. "I don't want you to be perfect, Anna," he said as they sat back down on the porch swing. "I want all of you – the good, the bad, every little wonderful part of who you are."

He tightened his grip on her hand, and they sat listening to the birds serenading them. Anna thought back to the day in the cemetery with Sunshine, watching the clouds. Silence with Dan felt just as comfortable as it had with Sunshine. She considered the phone calls again. *Let it go,* she thought.

When Dan finally spoke, his voice was full of boyish excitement. "You like the porch swing?" he asked.

"I love it," she said. "It wasn't here when I was a child." She squeezed his hand and smiled at him. "Other than that, the cabin is exactly as I remember. It feels like home to me." Anna pictured her father splitting logs for the fireplace, her mother taking refuge inside while he wielded the axe.

"I was hoping you'd say that," Dan said, breaking into Anna's memories. "You've told me so much about your time with your family here."

"My mother would have loved this porch swing," she said.

Dan's eyebrows shot up, and he sat up straight and rubbed his hands together like a little boy. "It wasn't here until yesterday," he said.

"Yesterday?" Anna said. She thought about what he was saying, and then it dawned on her. "Did you put it up?"

"Sure did, my lady," he said, pumping his bicep. "I told you, you're dealing with a *real* man." His face was serious and manly, and Anna had to laugh. "What? You didn't know I was so talented?"

"Oh, I know all about your many talents," she said, and lifted his hand to her lips. She kissed each of his calloused fingertips, and he gave her a warning glance. "What?" she said. "I'm just admiring the tools of the trade."

"You're bad," he teased, taking her tea from her and setting it on the log table beside the swing. "Wouldn't want you to spill this and burn yourself." He stood and lifted her from the swing and carried her toward the door.

"You are insatiable," she whispered in his ear. She laughed as he tried to turn the doorknob with his knee.

"You, my lady, are irresistible," he said, finally kicking the door open, breaking the jamb.

"Dan!" Anna shouted, laughing harder now. "We'll have to pay for that!"

"It's ok," he said. "This is an emergency." He lowered her to the couch and pulled her sweater over her head. He was frantic, passionate, full of longing, and yet his kisses were still reverent, his touch gentle.

"What are we going to do about that door?" Anna asked.

"You're thinking about the door after *that?*" he said. He kissed her forehead. "This mind of yours never stops, does it?" he said, kissing her forehead again. "I love that about you."

Anna pushed him off of her playfully, and he rolled to the floor. "You're cruel," he teased.

"I know," she said. "It's one of my best qualities." She sat up and patted the couch next to her. "Sit," she said. He obliged. "Seriously, did you bring your tool box?" She squeezed his bicep.

"A *real* man doesn't leave home without it," he said, flexing again. "But it can wait. My woman needs breakfast." He stood and walked toward the kitchen, and Anna studied his body.

"I'm going to get your robe," she said. "Otherwise we won't make it through breakfast."

Anna wandered into the second bedroom and spread Dan's robe across the foot of the twin bed. She sat down on the edge and ran her hand over the comforter, thinking back to the evenings here with her father, listening to the cicadas through the open window as he read her favorite stories to her over and over. She lay back and closed her eyes.

"I can picture you here as a child," Dan said as he snuggled up next to her. Anna hadn't heard him enter the room, and she didn't bother to open her eyes. He propped himself up on his elbow and traced her nose with his fingertip. "You were adorable when we were kids," he said. "You still are." Then he leaned over and whispered in her ear. "I hope our children look just like you."

Anna opened her eyes and studied his face – his jawline, his gorgeous blue eyes. "I hope they look like you," she said.

"Well," Dan said, "I love you too much to argue with you. Besides," he said, "I'm freezing." Anna looked at his body, bare except for his boxers. Then she looked at the robe she had laid at the foot of the bed and laughed.

"Sorry," she said. "I got sidetracked by the memories."

"Plenty more to be made in this cabin," he said. "But we might have to add a bunk bed or two. One twin bed won't be enough for our brood." He stood and put on his robe. "Let's eat."

~

Kurt had checked on Sandy at the shelter, and her spirits were higher than he had expected. She had asked him for the name of an attorney and seemed confident in her decision to move forward with the divorce. He hadn't wanted to worry her about Mitch's disappearance, and she didn't ask about him, but Kurt did pull Nancy aside to let her know, just in case Mitch showed up at the shelter. Mitch knew where it was, after all. Kurt figured it was only a matter of time before he figured out where Sandy and the children were staying, if he hadn't already.

His granddaughters had squealed when he walked in, practically knocking him off his feet when they both tried to jump on him at once. The women in the shelter had seemed uneasy in his presence, and he wondered what kind of encounters they had experienced with his officers in the past. A few of the children ran from the room when he entered; others hid, peeking around corners. Kurt guessed many of them had been escorted from their homes by officers in uniform, and he cursed himself for not thinking to change into plain clothes before his visit.

Nothing had come back from the crime lab, but thankfully there had been no attacks the last few nights. Unfortunately this left Kurt with more time to ruminate about his son-in-law. He had issued an APB, and if Mitch was still driving his cruiser, he should have been easy to find. But Mitch was too smart to be so obvious; he was likely hiding out, or traveling on foot. Kurt had personally notified the local news – the public needed to know that the man was armed... with Kurt's gun as well. He groaned. The thought made him sick. His officers would have a heyday with that one, once word got out.

Cathy still hadn't spoken to him. She stayed in her bedroom when he was home, and he still occupied the couch at night. He tried to give her space, spending every waking hour at the police station. *She's right*, he thought. He should have told her from the beginning. *Maybe she could have gotten through to Sandy. Maybe she could have spared our daughter this pain.* Kurt prayed that his wife would forgive him in time. One thing he was certain of, however, was that he would never forgive himself.

~

Anna hadn't felt this complete since she was a young child. As she wiped down the kitchen counter, she replayed the weekend over in her mind. Her memories of this cabin as a child were some of the happiest of her life, and now she and Dan had created more memories here.

"What are you thinking about?" Dan asked, wrapping his arms around her waist, kissing the back of her neck.

"I love this place," she said.

"I know." Dan turned her to face him and took the sponge from her hand. He laid it on the counter. "I was serious about adding the bunk beds," he said.

"You might want to check with the owner," Anna said. "After what you did to the door, he might not let us come back."

"I fixed the door!" he said, feigning indignity. "Besides," he continued, "he won't mind." He winked at Anna and stared into her eyes, waiting, watching her expressions change as her mind pieced it all together...

"You didn't!" she finally said.

"I had to," he said. "I couldn't very easily install a porch swing if it wasn't ours."

Ours. Anna liked the way that word sounded coming from Dan's lips. *Ours...* She shook her head. "I can't believe you bought it!"

"I bought it for us, Anna. For our family." He pulled her into his arms. "For our future."

"Getting a little ahead of yourself, aren't you?" she teased.

223

"I've waited this long, Anna," he said, pulling her into his arms. "I'm a patient man."

THIRTY-TWO

Anna didn't want to return to reality. She wanted to stay in the cabin with Dan and pretend nothing else existed. They had arrived home late, and Dan had insisted they go straight to sleep, since they both had to work the next day. Anna was disappointed, and she had tried to seduce him in every way she knew how, but he had remained disciplined.

Damn him, she thought, smiling.

"So how was your weekend," Dr. Patterson asked as he shoved her office door open. His voice startled her, and she quickly opened the file on her desk.

"Fine," she said. *Why the hell does he care?*

"Do anything interesting?" he asked.

"Not really," she said, studying the file.

Lying bitch. Ron was well aware of every detail of Anna's little rendezvous with the dork. He had researched the man, discouraged when he found nothing juicy – Dan Everett was a respected therapist, successful and well-liked. *Apparently he's good in bed too,* Ron thought. All weekend long he had observed their endless fornication through the windows of that pitiful excuse for a cabin. *The slut couldn't seem to get enough,* he thought. "I'm going to need you to cover for me this weekend," he said. He wouldn't allow her to go away with that jackass again. How careless he had been in allowing it to happen this time.

"Fine," Anna said, failing to mask the resentment in her voice.

Dr. Patterson's eyebrows shot up. "Excuse me?" he said.

"I mean *of course*, Doctor Patterson," she said, mocking him now. His eyes bored into the top of her head; she pretended to read the file in front of her. "Is that all?" she asked, without looking up. Ron didn't respond. He walked out, leaving the door wide open.

Anna exhaled. "Baby steps," she told herself. She hadn't been able to say no to covering his shift, but she had let Dr. Patterson know she wasn't intimidated by him. So much had changed inside her. She was proud of the strong Anna. She smiled as Sunshine's words came back to her. *"Love yourself first, and the rest will come naturally." I love the strong Anna,* she thought.

She glanced at her clock – she had a few minutes before her first appointment. She picked up her cell phone and dialed Kurt's direct line.

"Malone," he said.

"Hi Kurt. It's Anna," she said. "How's Sandy?" She hoped her friend hadn't felt hurt when she didn't come by over the weekend.

"She's doing better than I expected," Kurt said.

"I guess she's had a long time to prepare," Anna said.

"Yes," Kurt said. "And she's remarkably strong. She has always been strong," he said. "And now that she's taking a stand, for her children and for herself, I think she'll be just fine."

"It'll take time," Anna said, "but I saw that strength in her too, the last time I visited." Anna thought about a parent's love for a child – her dream about Sunshine's wings, her own mother loving her even in her worst moments as a child, and the way Sandy's eyes had come alive when she saw her children walking out of the school building. "The worst is over," she said.

"Let's hope so," Kurt said, but Anna could hear worry in his voice.

"Mitch is still on the run?" she asked.

"I'm afraid so. We have everyone on the force out looking for him, and I've issued an APB. It shouldn't be long now," Kurt said, trying to convince himself.

"Any news on the attacker?" Anna asked.

"It's been quiet over the weekend," Kurt said. "The leads are still coming in, but none of them have panned out. And with nothing back from the crime lab…" His words trailed off.

Anna remembered her promise to investigate the psychological profile of serial rapists. "I'll do some research this evening and see what I can find."

"Thank you, Anna," Kurt said.

"It's the least I can do." She suddenly felt guilty for relaxing and enjoying herself with Dan all weekend, while Kurt was back here buried in two unfathomable situations.

Anna looked toward the door as James stepped tentatively into her office. "I've gotta run, Kurt. I'll get back with you tomorrow with anything I find." She silenced her cell phone and set it on her desk. "James, what a lovely surprise."

"Anna," he said, "I didn't mean to interrupt your call."

"It's no problem," she said. "Why are you here? Your appointment isn't until tomorrow. Did we change it?" *Maybe I forgot to record it,* she thought, though she couldn't imagine that she had – that wasn't like her. Then again, she had been so distracted lately; it was possible.

"No, I don't have an appointment. But we need to talk," he said.

"About what?"

"This attacker," he said, lowering himself into a chair.

"What about him?" Anna asked, curious to know if James had insight that might help Kurt catch the man.

"What kind of precautions are you taking?" James asked. He leaned forward in the chair, and the sober look in his eyes caught Anna off guard.

"I carry pepper spray, if that's what you mean," she said. "What's this about, James?"

"It's about you," he said. "It's about my not wanting to read in the newspaper that you were his next victim."

"James, I'll be fine," she said, though she wasn't completely sure she could promise him that. Up until the last few days, the maniac had been on a rampage, and according to Kurt, he eluded every attempt the police made to catch him. Kurt Malone was the best of the best though, and Anna was sure he would solve this case in time. Anna hoped it would be soon, before another woman was hurt.

"It's just," James paused, and Anna wondered where all this worry was coming from.

"It's just what?" she asked.

"Just please be safe," he said.

"I will, James," she said. "Now, tell me how things are going with you." Anna noticed again that the cursing had stopped, and James seemed more lucid today than he had since she met him. "How is your wife?"

"She's doing pretty well," he said, but added nothing more.

Why won't he open up about her, Anna thought. "Is she talking to you again?" she asked.

"It's complicated," he said and glanced toward the waiting room. "I think you have a patient waiting."

Anna looked at the clock. "You're right," she said. "I hate to rush you."

"I'm the one who stopped in without an appointment," he said. He stood slowly and walked to the door, then turned back to face her. "Anna please be safe," he said.

She watched him walk away. She didn't want to let him leave. It felt good to have someone care, to warn her, to worry about her. *I have two men who care,* she thought, smiling as she rose to usher in her first patient.

The day flew by, and as she had promised, after her last appointment, Anna spent a few hours online reviewing academic journals and case studies of serial rapists.

She rubbed her eyes and looked at her clock – 11:20. *How did it get so late?* She checked her cell phone; Dan had called three times. *I'm sure he's worried,* she thought, smiling. She straightened up her office quickly, and dug through her purse for her pepper spray. After locating it, she thought again of Sunshine's stones. She dumped the contents of her purse on her desk. *What the hell did I do with them,* she thought. She glanced at her clock again. She needed to get home to Dan. She sighed and shoved everything back into her purse then hurried out of her office, stopping to lock the front door behind herself.

"Stay."

Anna whirled around to greet the child she had been missing so much. "Sunshine!" she called out.

Nothing.

"Sunshine, honey, it's a little late for you to be out, don't you think?" she said. "Now is not a good time for hide and seek." Anna chuckled as she peeked around the corner of her office building. "Where are you?"

"Stay," she heard again. A chill ran down her spine and her smile faded. *Come on, Anna, you're imagining things,* she thought. Nevertheless, she gripped her pepper spray tightly as she hurried to her car. She clicked her keyfob and felt the hair on the back of her neck stand on end. The chill rocketed down her arms, then down her legs and back up her spine. She knew he was there before his hand bruised her wrist; she spun around and sprayed. She kept spraying as he covered his burning eyes, the only part of his face not disguised by the ski mask. She kept spraying as she ducked into her car and pulled the door shut. She turned the key with shaking hands and pressed the gas pedal to the floor, refusing to look back.

She sped into her driveway and saw Dan's car ahead of hers. She slammed on her brakes, jumped out and ran to him. He was asleep in the driver's seat. She pounded on the window to rouse him. He startled to attention when he saw her expression and was out of his car in an instant. "What happened?" he shouted, pulling her into his arms. "What the hell happened?"

Anna couldn't speak. She had been holding her breath the whole drive home, and her legs went weak as she began to sob. Dan silently held her up, supporting her body and her heart, until she found the strength to speak.

"Get in," he ordered, opening the passenger side door of her car. She handed him the keys, and he walked calmly to the driver's side. His jaw was set as he turned the key in the ignition, and he didn't say a word during the five minute drive to the police station. Anna was grateful that he hadn't pressed for details when she had told him what had happened. All she had been able to get out was, "the attacker. I'm fine." But the way Dan gripped the steering wheel and stared out the windshield told her he was pissed.

Dan threw open the door at the police station, nearly ripping it off the hinges. Every eye turned their way. "Where's Malone?" he shouted.

"He's off duty, sir," the woman behind the counter said softly, attempting to calm him with her voice.

"Well get him on the phone and tell him to get his ass down here. Now!"

"Sir, it's almost midnight," she said.

"Do I look like I give a shit what time it is? Get him in here now!"

Anna hadn't seen this side of Dan before, and at this moment, it comforted her.

Ten minutes later, Kurt dashed through the double doors. His eyes moved frantically from Dan to Anna. "Anna," he gasped as he ran to her and swallowed her in his arms. And the world fell away at her feet.

She was ten again, and he was holding her as she cried...

When he finally released her from his arms, Anna saw tears in his eyes. Dan was still holding her hand. He hadn't released it since they walked through the double doors. He didn't release it while she gave her statement to Kurt, he didn't release it as she offered what little description she could of the attacker, and he didn't release it as he opened the passenger side door to take her home. After buckling her seatbelt with his free hand, he looked her in the eyes, squeezed her hand then released his tight grip.

Back at Anna's house, he made a fire in the fireplace while Anna stood watching, numb. He sat down in her father's chair and motioned for her to sit on his lap. He wrapped his arms around her and they fell asleep just like that – Anna safe in Dan's arms in her father's chair.

THIRTY-THREE

"How are you feeling?" Dan whispered, as Anna's puffy eyelids blinked open. He had watched her sleep all night, terrified to let her out of his sight even for a second. Every time her breath had become shallow, he leaned his head over, holding his ear close to her lips to make sure he heard her breathing. Every time she had twitched in her sleep, he had tightened his hold on her.

"Hmm?" The events of the previous night had yet to register in Anna's mind. She rubbed her back, stiff from sleeping upright. "Did we sleep here all night?"

"Yes," he said. "You looked so peaceful, I didn't want to wake you." The fire had gone out hours before, but the daylight streaming through the windows warmed the room. "How are you feeling?" he asked again.

"My back is sore," she said.

"I mean after last night," Dan said.

Anna groaned. She didn't want to let the memories in; she didn't want to spoil the moment. But they came. There was no stopping them. The warning, the chills, the ski mask. Anna buried her face in Dan's chest.

"You're safe now, Anna."

"Thank you," she said, sitting up straight and turning her head to study his face. The dark circles under his eyes told her that he hadn't slept. She felt terrible for worrying him, but she was glad to be in his arms. "Thank you for being there for me."

"But I wasn't," he said. "And that's what has been haunting me all night."

"You were there when it mattered," she said. "You can't be there all the time."

"I would like to be," he said, and kissed her softly on her forehead. "Anna, I've been finding my way back to you my whole life. I know that now. If I had lost you..." his voice faltered and he couldn't continue. He kissed her forehead again and gazed into her eyes. "Will you marry me?"

Anna inhaled sharply.

Dan's weary eyes begged, overflowing with excitement and expectation and worry all at once as he waited for her response.

"Dan," she finally said, pausing to form the right words. "We've only been dating a short time." She was making excuses and she knew it. He had told her at the cabin that she was the one, and she felt the same way. She had known it from the moment he appeared on her front porch wearing that hideous Cosby sweater, though it had taken her a while to be honest with herself.

Dan's face dropped – the excitement and expectation vanished, and now all Anna saw was the worry. He looked away.

"Dan," she said, "look at me." He slowly turned his head, but couldn't look her in the eyes. "Dan, it's about that sweater," she said.

"What sweater?" he asked, raising his eyes to meet hers again.

"The one you wore on our first date," she said. *I'm cruel,* she thought, struggling to keep a straight face.

"Anna, what are you talking about?" He pulled back in the chair and spun her around in his lap so her body was facing his. He held her at arms-length.

"The one that looks like you've owned it since high school."

"I know which sweater you're talking about," he said, "but what does that have to do with my proposal?" Anna could sense his growing frustration.

"I can't marry you, Dan," she said, looking him square in the eyes. Dan ran his hand through his hair and turned away. *Don't do that,* she thought, watching him muss up his hair. *That's my job!* She fought the urge to drag him to her bedroom. "I can't marry you," she continued, and took his face into her hands this time, forcing him to look at her, "unless you get rid of that God awful sweater."

The smile spread slowly across his face, and he wrapped her in his arms. "Deal," he said. "I'll burn it right here in the fireplace." He lifted her and carried her to the bathroom. "Let's get you showered for work."

~

Kurt had stared at the ceiling for hours after leaving the station last night. He had finally given up trying to sleep and abandoned the couch for his study. He had passed the hours at his desk, staring at the wall, blind to the plaques and awards.

He needed to get dressed for work; he was already three hours late, but his legs wouldn't follow his orders, so he just sat and stared. How could this have happened? *Why Anna?* He rubbed the crease between his eyebrows and thought of Cathy. He missed sharing a bed with his wife; he missed her eyes, her arms, her lips. Sighing, he reread Anna's statement.

Anna hadn't been able to offer anything useful, but the fact that her attack didn't fit the pattern alarmed Kurt. Not only was this man becoming more violent, he was now attacking women off campus. *Who are you, you bastard?*

"Bastard," he said out loud, repeating Cathy's last word to him. Kurt had let everyone down – his wife, his daughter and now the woman who had been like a daughter to him as a child. He stood and walked over to the window.

"Why Anna?" he whispered. He ran through her statement again in his mind. *At least she got away*, he thought to himself. The thought comforted him... and then panic fell heavy on his chest – *She got away!* "Shit!" Kurt grabbed his keys and sprinted to his cruiser, his legs finally obeying, his feet barely touching the ground.

~

The morning dragged on as Anna daydreamed about waking up in Dan's arms, watching that beautifully curved smile form on his face as she accepted his proposal.

After their shower, they had made love, but this morning he was different. Anna had never known love like that. He touched her body as if it were a gift from heaven he was afraid to defile. He was gentle, but passionate. And afterwards, while she lay in his arms, he had traced every inch of her body with his eyes as if he were studying a fine work of art. "I'm finally home," he had said. Anna sighed. Would every morning with this man feel this way? Somehow she knew that with Dan, it would.

"Anna?" James said.

"Huh? Oh, sorry James."

"Do you see them?" he asked again, pointing out the window. "There, on the branch. The doves!" Anna turned to see what James was so excited about.

"Oh wow," She said. "He found his mate."

James eyed her and grinned. "I don't think he's the only one," he said.

"What do you mean?" Anna said, blushing.

"Honey, if you think I have lived eighty-two years and can't recognize that look," he said, "then you are a fool!" He winked at her. "Congratulations."

"Oh James," she said. "This is your session. Let's talk about you."

"I'd rather talk about you," he said, leaning forward in his chair. "So have you set a date?"

It felt good to be able to tell someone, and James had grown to be the closest thing she had to family, until she met Sunshine that is… and now Dan. It felt appropriate to celebrate the news with James. "Let's not get ahead of ourselves, James," Anna teased. "He just asked me this morning."

"I can tell," he said. He took her hands in his, startling her. "You deserve this, Anna. You deserve to be happy." With that, he stood and pulled her out of her chair, embracing her like she was his own child. He released her, still holding her hands, and stared into her eyes. "Your parents would be so happy for you, Anna."

The tears came. She tried to brush them away, but his comment hurt and healed and tore open the scar she was trying so hard to mend. All the joy and the pain and the loneliness came pouring out, and James held her tight.

"I'm sorry," she said, reaching for a tissue. She turned to blow her nose discreetly.

"You're going to make a beautiful bride."

"James, thank you," she said. "Sometimes I think maybe you're the therapist here. I don't know what I would do without you."

After James left, Anna relaxed in her chair, gazing out the window, admiring the two doves perched side by side. One of the doves flew up to a higher branch, and the other – the female, Anna suspected – stayed put, pretending not to notice his absence. After a few minutes he gave up and flew back to her side. Anna chuckled to herself. *Good girl,* she thought. She pulled her hair up off her shoulders then let it fall down her back. Her heart overflowed with love and joy and she couldn't have wiped the smile from her face if she had wanted to. She didn't want to. But still, she had a feeling that something was missing. When she heard a knock at the door, she knew exactly what she had been waiting for. *Sunshine,* she thought. "Come in!"

"Anna," Kurt said as he pushed her door open.

"Kurt," Anna said, her disappointment evident in her voice. She adored Kurt, but she was hoping to see Sunshine. She wanted to share her news with the girl. She could only imagine how Sunshine would react, and she was eager to see the look on the child's face when she told her about the engagement.

"How are you feeling after last night?" he asked.

"You're the second person to ask me that this morning," Anna said, unable to hide her elation as she remembered Dan's sweet inquiry.

"You seem to be doing just fine," Kurt said, eyeing her curiously.

"Yes," she said, "I'm fine." She tilted her head slightly. "Why are you here?"

"Anna," he said. "I did a lot of thinking after you left the station last night."

"You didn't stay there all night, did you?" she said. "You were off duty when we came in. I'm sorry we had to pull you away from Cathy in the middle of the night."

"No, I went home," Kurt said. *I pushed Cathy away all by myself,* he thought, and then continued. "I couldn't sleep. I'm so sorry I wasn't able to apprehend that man before he came after you." Kurt shifted his weight from one foot to the other.

Anna couldn't read his expression. "What is it Kurt?"

"Anna," he said, moving closer now, "I don't want to alarm you, but –"

"But what?" she asked, suddenly conscious of the sound of her own heartbeat.

"Anna," he said. "Of all the women this man has attacked, you're the only one that got away."

"Yes, I was very lucky," she said. "So why do you look so upset?"

He hesitated again. He didn't want to scare her, but she needed to know. "Anna," he said, "I think he will try again." Anna's mouth went dry; she struggled to catch her breath. Kurt watched the glow fade, and her face suddenly looked pallid. "I want to trap him," Kurt continued – there was no turning back now.

"How?" Anna asked, in a voice so soft Kurt barely heard her. She didn't want to think about that monster right now. She wanted to continue to bask in the happiness of the morning. Everything was falling into place in her life, and now Kurt was here warning her that she might be attacked again? She buried her face in her hands.

"I want to follow you," he said. "I can protect you, but we need to let him get close enough that I can apprehend him."

Anna dropped her hands away from her face and looked up at him. "What are you saying?" Her head was spinning. Just twenty minutes ago she was celebrating her engagement with one of her favorite people, and now Kurt Malone was in her office telling her this? "When? Where?" She asked, barely able to get the words out.

"That's what I was thinking about last night," Kurt said. "With the exception of your attack, he seems to strike most often late at night near campus. The majority of the attacks have happened as the women leave Riley's alone. I still haven't figured out why he came after you. It doesn't fit his M.O." Kurt paused to make sure this wasn't too much for Anna. She nodded, and he continued. "He seems to stalk Riley's, but I haven't been able to figure out where he's watching from. I've checked all the cars parked outside every night since I noticed the pattern, but they're always empty."

"So what do you want me to do?" she asked, terrified of what she knew he was going to say.

Kurt took off his cap before answering. "I want you to go to Riley's," he said, "and leave alone on foot after dark." He felt sick as he watched Anna's expression change from shock to horror to resignation. "I will be there, Anna."

The numbness returned, and she said the only thing that came to mind, "Can I talk it over with Dan?"

"Of course," Kurt said. "Anna, I know I'm asking a lot."

You sure as hell are, she thought.

"You've been through so much," he said. "I hate to ask this of you, but I think this is our best chance at catching this bastard."

Anna stared at him blankly.

"I'll be at the station," he said. "Let me know what you decide." He placed his cap back on his head and turned to leave, then stopped and turned back. "Anna," he said. "Are you going to be ok?"

She couldn't respond. He closed her door and left.

THIRTY-FOUR

Dan was standing by her car when she walked out of the office building. He pretended to be there for fun, but Anna knew he was making sure she got to her car safely. She forced a smile as he approached her. *How am I going to bring this up?* She knew what his answer would be. There was no way he would agree to let Kurt use her as bait to catch a serial rapist. When she thought of it in those terms, she couldn't believe he had asked her either. She needed time to think.

"You ready to celebrate?" Dan said. His joy was contagious. Anna pushed Kurt's proposal out of her mind and focused back on Dan's.

"Whatever do you have in mind?" she asked, batting her eyelashes at him innocently.

"You have a one-track mind, my love," he said.

"*My love.*" Anna rolled the words over in her mind. Those two little words warmed her heart, and she repeated them to herself again and again. She finally decided they sounded better coming from Dan.

"Say it again," she said, reaching for him.

"What?" he asked.

"My love," she said, pulling him close.

"My love," he said, and ran his fingertips down her cheek. Anna melted into his arms. *Oh yes, I'm going to be just fine,* she thought, answering Kurt's last question.

Dan's eyes sparkled as he tried, but failed, to study the menu. "Anna," he said, looking up at her. "My love."

"Ok mister," Anna teased. "Stop that right now, or we're going home hungry."

"We wouldn't be hungry for long," he said, taking her hand across the table.

"Daniel," she said, and a thought occurred to her. "What's your middle name?"

"Why?" he said, tensing at the thought of having to share the name that had caused him so much teasing as a child.

"Why, huh? That's a strange name," she said, "but if it's yours, I like it."

"Very funny," he said, and released her hand. He picked up the menu again. His cellphone rang, and he slid it out of his pocket and silenced it. "I think I'll have the trout," he said.

The waitress appeared, and Dan waited for Anna to order.

"I'm in the mood for chicken noodle soup," she said.

Dan's mouth dropped open. "We are at the most elegant restaurant in Bloomfield," he whispered across the table, "and you order soup?"

"And a chocolate milkshake," she said to the waitress.

"What?"

"And fries."

"My God, are you pregnant?" Dan asked.

"Not yet," she said, smiling at him.

"Umm," the waitress interrupted nervously. "For you, sir?"

Anna and Dan laughed when they noticed the woman again.

"I'll have the same," he said, and the flustered waitress scurried away. "You, my love, are a bad influence," he said, leaning over the table toward her.

"You can't reach me," she teased, pulling back to avoid his grasp.

"Wanna bet?" Dan stood, moved to Anna's side of the table and slid into the booth next to her. He grabbed her around the waist and they made out like teenagers. Anna blushed when she remembered where they were and she pushed him away.

"Daniel Why," she said. "Mind your manners."

He apologized insincerely, and moved back to the other side of the booth.

How am I going to bring this up, Anna thought. They were having such a good time, and she knew Kurt's request would ruin the mood. But Kurt wanted an answer, and she wouldn't give him one until she talked it over with Dan.

Dan's smile slowly faded as he watched Anna's expression change. He knew something was on her mind. "What is it, Anna?"

Dear God, help me find a way to bring this up gently, she prayed.

When she didn't answer, Dan felt his heart drop in his chest. "Anna," he said, "you're scaring me."

Anna looked down at her hands, tracing the spot on her left hand where the wedding ring would be. "You aren't going to like this, Dan," she said, stalling until the words came to her.

"Not going to like what?" Dan could feel the heat creep up his neck. "Just tell me, Anna."

Anna took a deep breath. "Kurt wants me to help him catch the attacker." She exhaled and waited. She could feel Dan's eyes on her, but she refused to look up.

"He what?"

"Dan, please keep your voice down," she said, finally making eye contact. She pressed on. "He thinks the attacker will come back for me because I'm the only victim that got away. He wants me to help him set a trap." Hearing the words from her own mouth now, the request seemed even more preposterous.

"Is he insane?" Dan said, making no attempt to lower his voice. "After what you went through last night? No way!" He slammed his open hand down on the table.

"Dan, please," she said. "He said he'll be there. He said he'll protect me."

"How the hell can he protect you when the psycho carries a knife?" Dan's voice continued to escalate. "What's he going to do when that maniac grabs you and forces the knife to your throat?"

The thought made Anna queasy. She hadn't allowed her mind to run through the possible scenarios. She couldn't. She knew if she did, she would chicken out.

Brushing the image from her mind, she pressed on. "Dan, please think about it. Someone has to stop this monster, and Kurt thinks I'm the best option."

Dan's jaw snapped shut; his eyes flashed. "You are not an option," he hissed. "You are *not* an option!" He was shouting now, and everyone in the restaurant turned to witness the exchange. "You are not an 'option,' Anna. You are the love of my life!" He lowered his voice, attempting to calm himself down. "Don't you get that?" He turned his head and looked out the window, pouting like a three year old child. Anna waited. She would let him calm down. She would let him think this over. She would let him take all the time he needed.

The waitress approached timidly with their chocolate milkshakes, and Anna watched as she set one in front of each of them. How silly they seemed now. *What a stupid thing to order,* Anna thought. She wanted to cry.

When the soup arrived, Anna sat frozen, watching the steam rise from the bowls. Dan continued to stare out the window as their milkshakes turned from thick and frothy to soupy and room-temperature. Anna waited. The waitress didn't come back to check on them.

Finally, Dan turned slowly toward her. "I can't let you do this, Anna." His voice cracked as he spoke.

"Dan…" she started, but he raised his hand to stop her.

"Please let me finish," he said.

Anna nodded.

"I've been finding my way back to you my whole life," he said. He ran his hand through his hair, and Anna felt the usual sensual response in her body. "I can't lose you, Anna. Not at the hands of that monster." He reached across the table for her hands.

"I need to think about it," she said.

"What is there to think about?" Dan said. "It's not going to happen!" His voice was rising again, and Anna pulled her hands away.

"I was hoping you would understand," she said.

"Understand what?" he snapped.

"Dan," she said, "This man hurt Taylor. He has hurt too many women. I feel like I need to do what I can to stop him. I can't explain it. I don't understand it myself. I just feel like I'm the only one who can put an end to this."

Dan watched her as she spoke, more emphatic with each word. He knew she was strong-willed. That was one of the things he loved most about her. But in this moment, it terrified him. He could *not* lose her. "Anna," he said, resorting to a mild form of begging, "please."

"I need to think about it," she said again, staring out the window now, lacking the strength to look at him.

Dan studied her profile. She had always been so beautiful. "Anna," he said, wondering if he would regret his next words, "If you do this..." Could he get the words out? Would he really mean them if he did?

Anna knew what he was about to say.

"If you do this, Anna," he sighed and ran his hand through his hair again. "If you do this, we're over." There it was – an ultimatum. It was all he could say. It was the only thing he could think of that might make her say no to this ridiculous idea of Kurt's.

Anna detested ultimatums. She couldn't look at him. Dan pulled out his wallet, left her car keys and a fifty dollar bill on the table and walked out.

THIRTY-FIVE

Anna was numb – her body, her mind, her heart. She felt nothing – a familiar sensation. As she drove home, she saw nothing. She made the correct turns out of habit. She pulled into her driveway, got out of her car and walked toward her house, an empty shell of a person. She didn't bother to pull out her pepper spray. She couldn't feel fear. She didn't bother to look around the yard to make sure she was safe. She didn't care. She sat down on the porch swing, unwilling to go inside and look at the chair she had woken up in with Dan just that morning. She didn't want to smell the remaining scent of the breakfast he had cooked. She didn't want to feel, so she just stayed numb. Old habits die hard.

When Sunshine climbed up next to her on the porch swing, Anna didn't turn to look at her. When the girl placed her small hand over Anna's, she didn't feel it. Sunshine didn't speak.

What am I going to do, Anna thought. Dan was the one – she knew that now. He was her one chance at a love like her parents had shared. He was her soulmate. How could she risk losing him?

She pushed it all out of her mind and turned to the little girl sitting quietly by her side. "I lost your stones," she said.

"No you didn't," Sunshine said, patting Anna's hand.

"I did," Anna said. "I put them in my purse right after you gave them to me, but now they're gone."

Sunshine smiled and patted Anna's hand again. Anna was relieved that the girl didn't seem hurt by her carelessness.

"So where were you today?" Anna said.

"When?" Sunshine asked.

"All day," Anna said. "You always seem to show up when I need someone to talk to, and yet when I had big news to share this morning, you weren't there."

"I was around," Sunshine said. "Congratulations, by the way." She smiled at Anna tentatively.

"Who told you?" Anna said.

"Word travels fast."

Anna sighed. "I'm not sure congratulations are in order at this point," she said, studying her feet for comfort. She waited for Sunshine to inquire, but the girl was silent. "I have to choose," Anna said.

"You'll make the right choice," Sunshine said. "My daddy always says that there are no wrong choices. Whichever one we choose is the right one, as long as we follow our heart."

Anna remembered that her father used to say the very same thing, and she smiled. She had forgotten so many of her father's wise words.

"Listen to your heart," Sunshine said. "It will always tell you the right choice… if you listen."

Anna's pledge to her mother came back to her then. She had promised she would always love herself first, but she loved Taylor, and she knew her mother would have felt for the women this man had hurt.

"You have a gift, Anna." She heard her mother's voice as Sunshine spoke, and Anna realized that it was true. She had always known she had a gift for understanding people, for listening, for helping them through tough times. That was the real reason she had chosen her profession. She also knew she was the only person who could stop this man. She wasn't sure how or why, but she knew she had to do this.

"Trust yourself," Sunshine said. "Trust the voice in your heart that's telling you what to do. Sometimes it speaks in thoughts, sometimes in feelings like chills to alert you, but your heart is always guiding you. You know more than you think you do, Anna. Just listen."

Anna closed her eyes and listened to the cicadas' song, waiting for her heart to confirm her choice, but her mind interrupted. *How can I risk losing him,* she thought. *He completes me.*

"No," Sunshine said. "*You* complete you."

Anna sighed. *Why can't I be strong and wise like this little girl,* she thought.

"You are," the girl whispered, and when Anna opened her eyes to respond, Sunshine was gone.

~

"Sir, you can't go in there," Jane said.

"You selfish son of a bitch!"

Kurt jumped to his feet at the sound of his office door slamming back against the wall. "Dan –"

"How could you ask her to do this?" Dan shouted. "You're going to get her killed!"

Officer Lambert rushed into Kurt's office with Jane right behind him, peering over his shoulder. "I'm fine," Kurt told them, gesturing for them to leave. Kurt walked over and closed the door. "Dan, please have a seat."

"Fuck you!" Dan shouted, remaining on his feet. "How could you? She's barely had time to deal with what happened to her, and you're going to send her right back into the line of fire?"

"Dan, I know how it sounds, but –"

"You have no idea what you've done," Dan growled.

"Dan, I can protect her."

"Like you protected the other women he's attacked?"

Dan's words cut, and Kurt lowered himself into his chair, crossing his arms on his desk. "We've been working nonstop to catch this maniac. You know that.

Surely you read the newspaper."

"I read the newspaper alright," Dan said. "All the articles about how you have failed, over and over."

Kurt knew what Dan was saying was true, but he didn't see any other option. "Anna is strong, Dan —"

"Don't you think I know that?" he snapped. "She's strong and she's stubborn and she'll go through with this idiotic plan of yours, even if it gets her killed. Why would you put her in that position?"

Kurt sighed. "Dan, I wish there was another way. As a psychologist, you know as well as I do that this man is going to continue on his rampage until we catch him. He's not going to just go away."

"Well now you've made your problem Anna's," Dan said. "Because of the incompetence of this police force, the woman I love may be hurt, she may be..." He couldn't finish the sentence. "I hope you're happy," he said, and threw the door open, the doorknob smashing a hole in the wall as he left.

~

Dust danced in the beam of light as Anna's flashlight illuminated the remaining photo albums on the shelf.

"*1977*"

This was the one she was looking for – the year time stopped.

She sat down, dusted off the album and opened it in her lap. She read the caption beneath the first picture: "January 1st – Happy New Year!" A sparkling pink party hat balanced on her father's head, a bright orange noisemaker with silver tassels in his mouth. Anna sighed.

She turned the page and admired a photo of her mother in a turquoise sequined gown. *She was so beautiful*, Anna thought. Her mother's smile was infectious, and Anna felt her spirits lift. Her mother had always been able to cheer her up; apparently she still could.

Anna turned to the next page and her gaze fell upon a photo of her father holding a little blonde girl up in the air to reach a balloon that had floated to the ceiling. *Is that me,* Anna thought. She turned the page, hoping for a close-up of the girl...

She found one.

Her vision blurred as her eyes filled with tears. She closed the album and hugged it tightly. *"You're not alone, Anna. You never have been."* She laughed out loud as she wiped away the tears.

Standing slowly, she carried the album to the ladder, stopping to shine the flashlight around the attic one more time. When the beam of light reached the back corner, she froze. Behind the stack of well-organized, neatly labeled boxes, she saw the tip of a bright orange cardboard wing. She walked over, moved the boxes and kneeled in front of it. She traced the black spots with her fingers, cherishing each and every brush stroke. She lifted the wing and slipped her arm through the elastic. *"My daddy believes in me. He told me to just keep trying to fly, no matter what. And so I am. I'm trying. I'm sure it will happen, I just need to build up strength. He said I just have to believe."*

"Thank you Daddy," Anna whispered.

She carefully leaned the wing back up in the corner, picked up the photo album and carried it down the ladder to her bedroom. She opened it to the picture of her father holding her in the air, *Flying,* she thought. She laid the album on the pillow beside her, turned off the light and slept a beautiful, dreamless sleep.

THIRTY-SIX

"Are you here to see Sandy?" Nancy asked, greeting Anna with a smile.

"I am," Anna said. "Is she available?"

"I'm sure she would love to see you," Nancy said, motioning for Anna to follow her.

"Anna!" Sandy called out. She hurried over to embrace her friend.

Taylor looked up from the corner and waved, not willing to interrupt the intense Monopoly game she was playing with Craig and the other three children. She was so close to winning – Taylor showed no mercy.

"Anna, you look amazing," Sandy said.

Anna remembered her father saying those same words to her mother the night they died. "Thank you," she said. She knew now that it wasn't her hair or her eyes or her outfit, but the glow of happiness that created that look. She understood her mother's grace and beauty now, and she was ready to continue the work her mother had started. *When you bring in the light, the darkness doesn't stand a chance.* Anna was beginning to understand.

"I'm sorry I didn't stop in over the weekend," she said. "How are you doing?"

"We're good, Anna," Sandy said. "Thanks to you."

Anna examined Sandy's face. The bruises were fading and her lip was healing. The dark circles had disappeared, and the sparkle in her eyes had returned. She was the same girl Anna had played hopscotch and freeze tag with as a child. "Sandy," Anna said, "you are the one who did this, not me."

Sandy was so grateful for Anna's support at the hospital – her words of encouragement and her help in getting the kids from school and bringing them here. That day had changed her life. "I couldn't have done it without you, though," Sandy said. "Thank you."

Anna would not deprive Sandy of her need to offer gratitude, but she hoped that in time, Sandy would learn all that Anna had. However, Anna understood that it was not something she could teach her. Sandy had to rediscover her own voice, her own heart.

"Can you stay for a cup of coffee?" Sandy asked. "It's not Starbucks, but it's good enough," she said with a chuckle.

"I'd love to stay and chat," Anna said, "but I'm not a big fan of coffee."

"Goodness," Sandy said. "How do you survive?"

Anna laughed. It was wonderful to hear humor in Sandy's voice again.

"How about a cup of tea?" Sandy said.

"Sounds perfect," Anna said, and followed her to the kitchen.

Sandy fished around in the cabinets and found the teabags, then put water on to boil. She poured herself a cup of coffee and joined Anna at the table.

"It's reassuring to know I'm not alone," Sandy said, "though it breaks my heart to hear the stories the other women tell." Sandy blew on her coffee to cool it, then took a sip. "I was lucky," she said. "He never hurt my children." She paused and looked down at her cup. "When I see some of these kids come in with bruises…" She looked up at Anna and a tear rolled down her cheek. She brushed it away and smiled.

Anna was amazed that Sandy could see her own good fortune in this situation. Sandy was a fighter, and Anna knew her friend would be fine, in time. "What will you do now?" Anna asked.

"I haven't figured that out yet," Sandy said. "I've been thinking of going back to school though. My mom offered to let us stay at their house, and Taylor said she would love to nanny for my girls. She said I can pay her when I graduate and get my teaching job." Sandy glowed as she spoke, then her smile faded. "I can't leave Craig with the responsibility of taking care of his siblings.

He's been through too much already." She looked down at her coffee again.

Anna wondered how this would all play out. Would Mitch come after Sandy once he got out of jail, if the police could even find him? Would he track her down and try to get her back? Would he hurt her again? She could tell by Sandy's silence that she was having the same thoughts. "You're worried about what Mitch will do, aren't you?" Anna said.

Sandy nodded and absently brushed her fingertips over the scab below her bottom lip. The image of Taylor running her fingers over the bandage on her neck flashed into Anna's mind. *What kind of a monster would...*

Anna felt the chill and her thought cut off. *Oh God,* she thought. She heard the voice inside her – *"Trust yourself."*

The tea kettle whistled, and Sandy rose to make Anna's tea.

Anna heard Sunshine's words in her mind. *"You know more than you think you do. Just listen."* Anna's mind raced – Kurt's desperate words expressing his confusion about how the attacker seemed to know where the police were staked out; how he seemed to anticipate every attempt the police made to catch him by surprise; Taylor's statement about feeling safe as she left Riley's because she had seen a police cruiser driving back and forth down the street all night; Sandy's descriptions of Mitch's escalating rage and Kurt's concern that the attacks were becoming more violent.

Anna needed to walk. She needed to sort this out in her mind. She did know. *Dammit!*

Sandy set the cup of tea in front of her.

"I'm sorry, Sandy," Anna said. "I need to go."

"What?" Sandy said.

"I'll come back tomorrow," Anna said, breathless now.

Sandy saw the intensity in Anna's eyes. "Are you ok?" she asked.

"I'm fine," Anna said. "I'm sorry." She gave her friend a quick hug and rushed toward the front door. The chill returned, more intense now, and Anna felt her lungs constrict. *I need air,* she thought.

"You know," the voice inside her said. If Anna had learned anything from

the wise child, it was to follow the signs, to trust her heart. She pushed the door open and stepped outside.

The day was on fire; everything Anna laid eyes on glowed – every leaf, every blade of grass. Her vision was sharp, her hearing precise. Anna felt weightless as her feet seemed to float down the sidewalk.

She heard the voice again – a familiar companion now. *"You are the one who can do this."* She lowered herself into the driver's seat and closed her eyes. *"You know."* Anna took a deep breath, held it for a few seconds then released it slowly.

"Yes," she whispered. "I do." She saw nothing around her now. She felt pulled, guided. She glanced at her left ring finger on the steering wheel and sighed. "I'm sorry, Dan. I have to do this."

~

"Kurt," Jane said, poking her head inside his office, "Anna Cunningham is here to see you."

Kurt's pulse quickened. "Send her in." He straightened his desk and tried to steady his hands. *Does this mean she's willing to help me?* Kurt wondered what Raymond would think of his asking Ray's only daughter to risk her safety, and possibly her life, to catch a violent rapist. "I'm sorry Ray," he whispered. "I wish there was another way."

Anna knocked. "Come on in, Anna," Kurt said, and stood to greet her. Her expression was hard to read. She looked completely calm, a little dazed, perhaps even happy, yet Kurt could see pain in her eyes.

"I'm in," she said, and Kurt stepped forward to embrace her.

"Your father would be so proud," he said. "Your mother too."

Anna wondered if this were true. In her mind, her father would have had a similar reaction to Dan's. Her mother would most likely be upset with her for letting Dan slip away. Anna had made her mother a promise, and she was breaking it. She also felt confident that her mother would do the exact same thing.

"Have a seat," Kurt said, "and I'll go over everything with you."

Anna sat down in one of the chairs facing Kurt's desk and listened as he detailed what he knew and what he suspected. Kurt had shared most of this information with her before, but from Anna's current perspective, it sounded completely foreign. As he spoke, Kurt pointed to the photo of the first victim, and Anna's mind drifted. She wondered where Dan was at this moment. Had he moved on already? She had hoped he would call, though he said he wouldn't. Since their first date, Dan had never gone more than twelve hours without calling her.

"And you'll notice," Kurt said, pointing to Riley's on the map, "that the majority of the attacks have occurred just outside Riley's, as I mentioned yesterday." Kurt's words brought Anna back to reality. Kurt paused and looked her in the eye. "Anna, are you sure about this?"

"Yes, Kurt. I'm sure. I just have a lot on my mind," she said. "You do too."

"You're right," he said and sighed. "Anna, have you seen Sandy?"

"I stopped by to see her before I came down here," Anna said. "She's doing great, Kurt."

"Does she know Mitch is on the run?" he asked.

At the mention of Mitch's name, Anna felt the familiar chill, and for a brief moment she thought she might throw up. She gripped the arm of the chair before continuing. "I didn't tell her," Anna said. "I didn't want to scare her."

"Good," Kurt said and rubbed the crease between his eyebrows. "Now, as far as tonight," he began, but Anna turned to look out the window as her mind wandered again.

Is it possible, she thought. *Yes.* She knew, and she wouldn't doubt the feeling in her heart. Her intuition was spot on. It made sense now – the way the attacker evaded the stakeouts. He knew the plan. He was *part* of the plan. Anna released her grip on the chair. She would end this. *You have a gift, Anna.* "We all do," she whispered. "I'm finally listening."

"What?" Kurt said, and Anna turned back to face him.

"Nothing, Kurt. I'm sorry," she said, struggling with whether to let him in on her conclusion. *He needs to know,* she thought. *But will he believe me?* She studied the man across the desk from her, the man who had been like a second father to her as a child. *Yes,* she thought. *He'll believe me.* She took a deep breath and looked directly into Kurt's eyes. "It's Mitch," she said.

"I know," Kurt said. "I can't stop worrying about Sandy either. But right now we have to focus on this case."

"No," Anna said, standing now. "The attacker, Kurt. It's Mitch."

"What?" Kurt stared at Anna, trying to make sense of what she had said. He sat up straight in his chair. "How do you know?"

"I just know," she said. "You're going to have to trust me on this."

Kurt leaned onto his desk and rested his forehead on his fingertips. *Mitch?* Yes, his son-in-law was an angry, violent man, but Kurt had never considered that he could be capable of something like this. "If you're right, Anna," he began.

"I am," she said.

Kurt couldn't express what he was feeling. He wanted to kill the man. He never knew his heart could be capable of feeling that way. That made him just as bad as Mitch.

"We still have to catch him in the act," Anna said. "There is no other way. He's on the run, but if your instincts are right, that he'll come back for me, then this is our chance. Maybe our only chance," she said.

Kurt still didn't speak. He couldn't wrap his mind around Anna's conclusion.

"So nine o'clock, then?" Anna finally said.

Kurt rubbed his temples then whispered, "nine-thirty." He took a deep breath then looked up at her. "And Anna," he said. He hadn't protected his own child, but he would not fail to protect his best friend's daughter. "I *will* protect you."

"I know you will," Anna said, and turned and walked out of his office.

She wandered around town for over an hour. She wanted to get on with it; the waiting was weakening her resolve. She walked to the cemetery and knelt in the grass between her parents' gravesites.

"Hi Mom and Dad," she whispered. "Please don't be mad at me." *I wish you were here to talk with me about this,* she thought. And then she allowed herself to admit it – "I'm scared."

She felt so alone. She longed to discuss the plan and her revelation with Dan, but he had made his feelings clear. She considered stopping by Maple Manor to talk it over with James. *No,* she thought. *He'll just worry.*

She lowered herself onto her back and watched the clouds as they moved across the sky, thinking of the little girl who had reminded her how to live, how to love and how to trust herself. A lone cloud floated above the others, and Anna smiled. *I'm not alone.*

As the sun began to set, Anna sat up and straightened her hair. She checked her watch. "Two more hours," she said. Again, she thought of Dan. He had been so angry. Or was he? Anna pictured his face as he had issued his ultimatum, scouring her mind to bring his eyes back into focus. In his wild eyes, Anna had seen passion and fury, and behind that fury, she realized now, she had seen fear.

THIRTY-SEVEN

Anna glanced from the bar to the door and back to the bar again. *Please don't let Tommy be here,* she thought. She hadn't returned to Riley's since that humiliating night. She never wanted to run into that man again. Would he ask her out? Try to get her drunk? That all seemed so trivial now.

"Can I get you something to drink?" the waitress asked. Anna's cheeks flushed when she saw that it was the same waitress from that night. *Oh God, I hope she doesn't remember me.*

"I'll just have a Root Beer," Anna said. "No, make that a chocolate milkshake," she called, as the waitress walked away. "And fries." The waitress nodded and continued on to the kitchen. Anna looked around the bar and then out into the street. She saw Kurt's cruiser in the public lot a block away and wondered if this was all too obvious.

It was imperative that they catch him in the act. With Mitch on the run, and without a DNA sample, there was no other way to nail him. Once they convicted him of going after Anna tonight, they could force him to give a sample and then link him to the other attacks... and prevent another one. *Stay focused*, she told herself.

"No pale ale tonight?"

Anna's stomach knotted into a tight ball as she turned toward Tommy's voice.

"No," she said, wondering if she should give an explanation. She felt the nausea bubble up as she studied him. *Did I really...* Anna couldn't finish the

255

thought. Once again, she considered how far she had come, how much had changed in her life. She knew she was doing the right thing, but she missed Dan already. *"Sometimes the right thing is not the easy thing,"* she heard a ten year old voice say. "My daddy used to say the same thing," Anna whispered, smiling to herself.

"What?" Tommy said.

"Nothing," Anna replied. *Just go away,* she thought. She turned back to make sure Kurt was still there, and Tommy took the hint.

Kurt was watching. He had no backup; they had agreed that their plan remain confidential. *Only one other person knows,* Anna thought with a sigh, then forced her mind away from the man she loved, the man she had let slip away.

The waitress brought the milkshake, and Anna took a sip. Again, she turned to look outside. There were a number of cars parked along the street, and Anna examined each of them. The chill returned, and adrenaline rushed through her body. *He's here,* she thought. *I don't think I can do this!* She felt sweat bead on her forehead and her hands began to tremble. Panic consumed her and she sucked in air through her tightening throat. *"You can do this,"* she heard a sweet voice say. Anna released her breath, rolled her eyes and smiled. "Whatever you say, boss," she whispered. Who was she to argue with a ten-year-old?

~

"Back for more action, I see," Ron grumbled, taking a long drag of his cigarette. *And with that same redneck, no less.* Ron had enjoyed the details that idiot had freely shared about his night with Anna, though after sizing the man up, Ron had thought better of trying to take him outside. At the sight of Anna interacting with him now though, Ron felt a little relief, since this surely meant she was done with that Dan Everett guy.

Ron shuddered as he recalled the look on Anna's face after her weekend rendezvous. She had been practically glowing. And then he had heard one of her patients congratulating her. *On what?* Had that jackass proposed? No, that just would not do. Either way, it was over now. Ron had watched what looked like an argument between them at Blakely's yesterday, and then the dork had gotten up and stormed out. *Perfect.*

Now, how to get her away from that redneck and get her alone. This nonsense had gone on long enough. Ron had come much too close to losing her to that Dan character. He just needed to get her alone, then he would convince her not to leave him again. Marching into the bar and dragging her out by her hair would cause a scene, so he would just have to wait for the right moment.

Anna glanced out toward the street, and Ron's pulse pounded in his temples. Her eyes seemed to lock on his for a brief moment and everything went hazy. That face, so familiar even after all these years. *Mother...*

~

"Chief, we just received a 911 call," the dispatcher said. "It was brief and got disconnected, but –"

"Son of a bitch!" Kurt shouted, pounding his fist against the steering wheel. Mitch must have caught wind of their plan. He must have known they would be at Riley's.

"Chief," the dispatcher said, "the call came from your house."

All feeling drained from his body. Kurt turned the key in the ignition. He needed to tell Anna he was leaving. He had promised he would watch over her tonight. He pulled up in front of Riley's and ran inside. The waitress looked up at him.

"Anna," he shouted.

Anna turned toward the door.

"He's not here."

"What?" Anna was confused. She knew he was here. She had *felt* him, and now Kurt was blowing their cover.

"He's at my house," he shouted. "He's got Cathy!" He spun around and raced back to his cruiser.

"I'll be back to pay," Anna yelled as she flew out the door. She chased the blazing red lights of Kurt's cruiser, tearing around corners at speeds that would normally get her thrown in jail. They barreled down Madison Street and turned left onto Kurt and Cathy's quiet road.

Squad cars already had his home boxed in when Kurt pulled up at the curb. He surveyed the flashing lights, the officers ducking behind their cars with their guns poised above the hoods. He flew out of his car, not stopping to ask for status, and raced toward the front door. A shot ripped through the night air, and Chief Kurt Malone fell to the ground.

Anna slammed on her brakes as she saw her father's best friend collapse. She was out of her car and running toward the house before any of the officers could get to her.

"Stop, Miss! You can't go in there!"

Anna didn't hear them. She ran to Kurt, dropped to her knees and put her hand to his face. *Dammit!*

"Anna, you have no business being here." He was using all his strength to speak.

She held her finger to his lips. "Kurt, breathe." Anna felt Sunshine lifting her up now, and she knew what she had to do. She took a deep breath, stood and faced the house. "Mitch!" She called out. "It's over." Kurt struggled to raise his head to look at her.

"Anna," he said, his voice hoarse. "I can't protect you like this."

"I'll be fine, Kurt," she said, then lifted her face to the sky as she walked toward the front door. She could make out Mitch's silhouette in an upstairs window, but she felt no fear. Everything she had learned, everything she had been through, all came together in that moment.

She heard Sunshine's voice. "You can do this."

"I know I can," she whispered as she stepped into that home, accepting the possibility that she may never leave again. But somehow right now that didn't matter.

She shouted up the stairs. "Mitch, it's Anna Cunningham. I just want to talk with you." She was prepared to take a bullet if that was what happened. But she also had faith. Sunshine had taught her that. Anna had faith that she would be able to break through to Mitch; he had let her in once before, for that one brief moment on the bleachers in high school, and she knew in her heart that she could find that vulnerable place in him again. And she had faith that everything would work out the way it was supposed to, however that was. "Mitch, come out and let's talk this through."

"There's nothing to talk about," he shouted. "Stay out, Anna. I'll kill her. I mean it."

Anna climbed the stairs slowly, and a feeling inside told her that Mitch had no interest in hurting Cathy. He had lost everything and he was desperate, hurting. Anna knew that. She knew Mitch had suffered because of his father's actions the night her parents died, and she wondered what else he had endured in his life that had filled him with so much rage. She pitied him, but no matter how much pain he was in, what he had done to Sandy, to Taylor, to all those women... to her... was wrong. She moved down the hall toward the master bedroom.

"Mitch, I'm alone. I just want to talk." She still felt no fear as she reached the door; she felt weightless, calm as her steady hand turned the knob. She knew she was exactly the person he needed. She eased the door open and saw Cathy huddled beside the bed, sobbing. Mitch was crouched below the front window; he turned his gun on Anna as she stepped into the room.

Cathy raised her eyes to Anna and gasped. "No," she whispered. "Anna go!" Cathy's eyes pleaded with Anna to run back out to safety. Anna smiled faintly to reassure Cathy, then took a step toward Mitch.

"Mitch, let's talk." The steady feeling in her legs surprised her, and the words came effortlessly. "Mitch," she said, her voice soothing and warm. "It's over. Sandy is gone, and your career is over. Don't make it worse." Anna watched his finger on the trigger as she took another step in his direction. "You can't change the past, Mitch," she said, "but you *can* change the future."

Mitch stared at her through glassy eyes.

"But you have to start now, Mitch, by making the right choice in *this* moment." She took another step toward him and continued. "I don't know everything that happened to you in the past, but I can tell you're hurting."

"Don't psychoanalyze me," he growled, tightening his grip on his handgun.

"Mitch," she continued, taking another step. She now stood less than two feet from the man who had terrorized so many innocent women and shot his own father-in-law, yet still Anna felt no fear. "I know you're hurting," she said. "I can see it in your eyes. But Mitch, you've got to let go of the pain. You can't hold onto the pain of the past if you hope to find peace now." Sunshine's wisdom flowed from Anna's lips.

The gun began quivering in his hand. "You don't know anything about me," he said.

"I know more than you think," Anna said.

Mitch stared blankly at Anna as she took one last step, closing the gap between them.

She locked her gaze on his and spoke. "That day on the bleachers, Mitch. I didn't accepted your apology," she said, "because what your father did was not your fault."

"He was a bastard," Mitch said.

"That may be true," Anna said, "but you aren't your father."

"No," Mitch said. "I'm worse." He steadied his hand and turned the gun to his chest.

Anna's voice remained calm. "You know that's not the answer."

He looked up at her and tears spilled down his cheeks. "Then what *is* the answer?" He pressed the barrel harder into his chest.

"I know the darkness, Mitch. I've been there. I know how it feels to want to end the pain, to make it all go away. I came close to ending it so many times. I've never told anyone that. I hated myself for not being in the car with my parents that night, and I couldn't take the pain any longer." Anna felt Sunshine with her now.

Mitch's eyes widened as if he, too, saw the girl. He sat spellbound as she spoke.

"You've been in so much pain," she said. "It just got too big for you." She lowered herself down beside him and turned to face him. "You can do this," she said.

She saw his shoulders rise, then fall limp as he collapsed into her arms. The gun fell to the floor.

Cathy jumped up and grabbed Anna by the arm.

Anna gently removed Cathy's hand and whispered, "You go. I'm fine." Cathy didn't move. "Please Cathy, go!"

"I won't leave you alone," she said, reaching for Anna's hand.

"I'm not alone," Anna said, and pulled her hand away. "Please go."

Cathy hesitated.

"Go!" Anna hissed.

Cathy saw the fire in Anna's eyes and nodded reluctantly, then ran out of the room.

Anna held Mitch – a broken man who had probably known more pain in his life than even she had. She didn't know the rest of his story, but she did know that he was hurting. Her mother had taught her how to see the pain in others, and how to shower them with love, no matter what they had done. Anna was trying.

"You can do this, Mitch," she said. "You can move forward."

"I have nothing left," he said.

"You're alive," she said. "That's something." Anna thought about the times she had contemplated ending her own life. *What a mistake that would have been.* "You're alive now, Mitch. Let go of the pain. Let go of the past. Let it go and live, *now*."

"I'll be living in a prison cell for the rest of my life," he said, pulling away. He looked down at the floor and whispered, "without Sandy."

Anna couldn't argue with his point, and a little piece of her heart broke for him. "Mitch, what you did to those women, to Sandy, there is no excuse, and you *will* have to face the consequences, but it's not the end of you. You've gotten lost along the way, but no matter where you spend the rest of your life, you can still find your way home." There was nothing more she could say. She waited, knowing he needed to talk.

"Anna," he said. "I have done so many shitty things." He balled his hands into fists and pressed them hard into the wood floor. "I never meant to hurt Sandy. But every time it happened, I got more and more mad at myself, and I was afraid I would really hurt her. So –"

"So you took it out on innocent girls?" Anna said, feeling her own anger begin to boil.

Mitch lowered his gaze and nodded. "I love her. I was trying to protect her."

Anna waited for him to continue.

He dropped his face into his hands. "I wanted to stop," he said. "I didn't want to hurt her anymore. I even made an appointment with a shrink."

"Did that help?" she asked.

Mitch shook his head. "I never went."

You just kept on hurting her, she thought. Anna was struggling. She felt compassion for the hurt child inside Mitch, but no matter how hard she tried to focus on love, her heart kept shifting back toward loathing. *Give yourself time,* she thought.

She closed her eyes and put herself in the dark room as her mother had instructed her to do, so long ago. She allowed the darkness to consume her, then lit the lantern in her mind and opened her eyes. She reached over and took Mitch's hand. "I'm trying to understand, Mitch. I truly am. But there's one thing that doesn't make sense to me." She took a deep breath. She had to know. "Why did you come after me?" she said. "Why me?"

Mitch's head snapped up. "What are you talking about?" He turned and looked directly into her eyes. "I hurt a lot of women, Anna, but I *swear* to you, I never laid a hand on *you*."

Anna felt the chill again and the room began to spin. She leaned her head against the windowsill and took a deep breath.

"Anna?" Mitch said, noticing her face suddenly go chalk-white. "Are you ok?"

She couldn't respond. Her mind raced, her heart pounded and all the fear she should have felt over the last twenty minutes surged over her like a tsunami.

"Anna?" Mitch repeated.

"I'm fine," she said. Mitch's face was a blur. She summoned her will to focus on his eyes. "Are you?"

He took a deep breath and nodded. "I think I'm ready," he said. "I know there's no way I can undo all the things I've done. I'm ready to face the consequences, and I know that includes letting go of Sandy. She deserves better. I honestly do love her."

"I believe you," Anna said.

Anna stood frozen as the officers took Mitch into custody. She stared up at the sky, searching for Orion, for her father. The world whirled beneath her, and her legs went weak. And then everything went dark.

"Anna!" Dan shouted, dropping to his knees and pulling her into his lap. "Oh my God, Anna, are you ok? I need a medic over here now!"

Anna saw the face of a sweet blonde girl in her mind as the small circle of vision expanded and Dan's face came into view. One thought circled around and around in her head as her vision gradually cleared – *You cannot tell him.* If he knew that the man who attacked her was still on the loose, he would never sleep again. She hated lying to him, but then again, she wasn't really lying, was she? Dan would simply assume Mitch was responsible for all the attacks, so she wouldn't have to say anything... until the truth came out. "I'm ok," she whispered.

Dan scrutinized her face for signs of injury, then helped her back onto her feet. "Kurt's going to be fine," he said. "They took him to the hospital, but the wound was not life-threatening."

"Thank God," Anna whispered.

"Anna, you shouldn't have run in there alone," he said, holding her by the shoulders at arms-length. Anna saw tears fill his eyes. He tried to be discreet as he wiped at his eyes with his thumb.

"I wasn't alone," Anna said and touched his cheek, feeling her strength return. "I never have been." She grabbed him and pulled him close.

"So who was that guy at the bar?" he whispered into her ear. Anna pulled away.

"What guy... What? You were there?"

"You didn't think I would just sit back and do nothing while you risked your life, did you?" he said.

Officer Lambert approached the couple. "I had to cuff him to my cruiser to keep him from chasing you into that house," he said, nudging Dan with his elbow before walking away.

"Daniel Why, my bodyguard," Anna said and wove her fingers together behind his neck.

Staring into her eyes, Dan grew serious again. "Anna, please promise me you'll never do anything like that again. You could've been killed."

"Dan," she said. "I'm sorry I worried you. It was just something I had to do." She paused. "For Sandy and for Taylor and for my mother." She took a deep breath. "For myself."

"I understand," Dan said. His fiancée was a strong, independent woman... and the sexiest woman he had ever known.

She pulled his lips to hers, ending the discussion.

"Will you stay with me tonight?" he whispered.

"There's no place I'd rather be."

THIRTY-EIGHT

So that's where the bitch and the cop raced off to, Ron thought, snuffing out his cigarette and clicking off the television. He laid the remote on the end table and pulled the lever on the side of his recliner, laying back and staring at the ceiling. *The imbeciles couldn't catch him on their own,* he thought. *Go figure.* Yes, Anna had stepped in and caught the guy, but still, it pissed Ron off to see what a hero they were making of her. She didn't deserve that kind of glory. He could have done a better job. Why hadn't Malone asked *him* for help. He was the one to consult about men like that. Perhaps he would call Malone and offer his services in rehabilitating the idiot.

Ron thought back to last night, watching Anna race after the police cruiser. He wished he could have been at Malone's house to see the action. He had tried to keep up with them, but driving at such high speeds had been too risky; he couldn't take a chance of getting pulled over chasing after that tramp, so he had returned to Riley's to pay her tab. *Someone needs to teach that bitch some manners,* he thought, as he lit another cigarette and glared at the two photographs beside him.

~

Anna watched Dan sleep and considered how truly blessed she was. She was grateful to have Sandy back in her life, and Kurt and Cathy had been so concerned about her last night. She thought of sweet James and how he had worried about her safety too. She leaned over and kissed Dan's cheek. They might not be blood, but Anna did have her own little family now. "Thank you for not giving up on me," she whispered; Dan slowly opened his eyes.

"Never," he said, pulling her into his arms.

After a moment, Anna spoke. "Dan," she said. "There's someone I need to see."

"Can't it wait?" he said, kissing her neck softly.

"No," she said. "It can't."

Dan propped himself up on his elbow and looked at her. "Can I ask who it is?"

Anna laughed. "Daniel Why," she said. "Are you jealous?"

"Who, me?" he said, trailing kisses down her neck.

She pulled away and sat up. "It's one of the patients I told you about. He's been worried about me."

"Ah," Dan said. "James?"

"Yes," she said. "He really should hear about last night from me, not from the news."

Dan seemed to understand, or else he simply knew that Anna would do what she wanted, no matter what he said. "He's special to you, isn't he," Dan said.

"Yes," Anna said. "He is."

~

It was early, but Anna knew exactly where she would find him. "Have visiting hours started?" she asked, as she wrote her name on the sign-in sheet.

"Not technically," the nurse behind the reception desk said, "but we do have a few family members visiting residents already. Who are you here to see?"

"Ruth Alexander," Anna said.

The nurse looked at her with a confused expression. "Ms…" She glanced down at Anna's name on the sheet. "Dr. Cunningham, there is no one here by that name."

"There must be some mistake," Anna said. "Her husband is a friend of mine. He visits her here every day."

The nurse's expression brightened. "Ah," she said, "you must mean Ruth Daye. Such a devoted husband –"

"Ruth Daye?" Anna interrupted. "Ruth Daye?" she repeated, feeling her legs go numb. "Is her husband's name James?"

"Yes ma'am, James Daye," the nurse said. "Ruth is down the hall to the left through the community room. She's in room 204. James is with her now."

"Thank you," Anna said absently, and moved slowly down the hall, trying to piece everything together.

When she reached room 204, she pushed the door open quietly and found James sitting beside Ruth's bed holding her hand. He turned when he heard Anna enter. His eyes sparkled and he stood. "Anna, what are you –"

"Why didn't you tell me?"

James lowered his head. "Anna," he said. "I was a coward." He looked up at her again. "Anna, you look just like her."

Anna swallowed the lump forming in her throat. "Is that why you made up those stupid excuses to come for therapy?"

"I could never find the strength to tell you," he said. "Before every appointment I promised myself that today was the day, and each time I tried to find the right words, they got tangled up in my head." James took a step toward her, and Anna held up her hands signaling for him to stop. "Anna, please," he said, standing in place. "I knew your mother and father hated me for leaving after Ruth's stroke. They never made an attempt to contact me. I didn't even know they had passed. No one told me, Anna. I would have come for you in a heartbeat."

Anna's own heart pounded in her chest. "But why didn't you tell me who you were when you came back? Why make up a phony last name?"

James looked at the floor. "I was afraid you hated me too."

"I didn't even know about you!" Anna shouted, pounding the doorjamb with her palm. Ruth stirred. Anna lowered her voice. "My parents never talked about you, and I never asked. I just assumed..."

"You assumed I was dead," he said. "I'm sure that was what your parents wanted you to think. They were protecting you, Anna. They didn't want you to know that your grandfather was a selfish son of a bitch who had abandoned his wife and family." James paused again, struggling to slow his breathing. "I suppose I *was* dead to them," he whispered.

Anna continued to try to make sense of everything. "So your first wife..."

"...was Ruth." James said. "I didn't remarry. She has always been the only woman for me."

"But why lie to me about that?" Anna asked.

"I don't know, Anna," he said. "I suppose I was in denial about what I had done. And by the time I came to terms with it, I couldn't change my story."

Anna looked over at the frail woman sleeping a mere ten feet away. "Why didn't my parents tell me about her?" she said.

"Anna," he said, taking another tentative step toward her, "when the doctors told us that your grandmother would never speak again and that she would have no memory of her family, your parents made a decision. They were afraid seeing her in this state would frighten you – you were only three years old when it happened, and you loved her so much. They decided not to tell you about her condition until you were old enough to understand. And then, well..." he paused. "They never had the chance to tell you," he said. "I'm sure it was hard for your mother to see her this way."

"She can't speak? She doesn't know anyone?" Anna asked.

"I'm sorry, Anna," he said.

Anna felt her legs go weak again and she leaned against the doorjamb for support. James was her grandfather, which meant that her mother was his daughter. *He lost his daughter and didn't even know.* Anna felt the tears burn. *How had he coped when he learned the news after his return?* She scoured her memory for clues that he had been in mourning during his sessions. *The poor man.*

She stood motionless in the doorway, and James dropped his hands to his side. They were silent, neither of them knowing what to say next.

Ruth stirred again and slowly opened her eyes.

Anna moved to her side. She peered into Ruth's beautiful blue eyes, a mirror image of her mother's, of her own. She reached down and gently took her hand.

A delicate smile spread across Ruth's face. Her angelic eyes shimmered, her lips trembled and a tear slipped down her cheek. Slowly, deliberately, she opened her mouth to speak – her voice barely audible, hoarse from decades of silence.

"Sunshine," Ruth whispered, and squeezed her granddaughter's hand.

EPILOGUE

Anna smiled as she cleared the plates from the picnic table. *I finally have my family.*

Everyone had raved about her mother's pasta salad, one of the many recipes Anna had discovered while unpacking the boxes in the attic. She and Dan had admired the paper mache carrot costume they had unearthed – the one Anna's father had made her for Halloween when she was five. Dan had tried to squeeze into it, and Anna had landed on her butt when she pulled it off of him. The night she spied Fuzzy Bunny's fur poking through a hole in one of the boxes, she ripped the box in half to free her old pal. She had convinced Dan to allow Fuzzy Bunny to share their bed.

They had spent many evenings in the attic, laughing and crying together as Anna relived the happy times, and the sad times too, with each treasure they discovered. She found her mother's wedding dress and the book of letters her mother had written to her – one for each of Anna's first ten birthdays, scribed in her mother's graceful handwriting with the intention, Anna assumed, of giving them to her when she was older. Dan had held Anna tight as she turned to the page where the eleventh letter would have been.

Anna watched Cecilia and Todd kick a soccer ball around the freshly mowed lawn. Libby sported the monarch butterfly wings, sprinting back and forth across the yard, flapping those wings, trying again and again to fly. *She'll get there,* Anna thought, smiling as she placed two glasses of lemonade on a tray to carry to her guests. Dan and Kurt flipped burgers on the grill, and Dan winked when his eyes caught Anna's. She felt her heart flutter. She had never asked him about the phone calls, but thankfully they seemed to have stopped. Anna had made up her mind to let it go. *I guess we both have our secrets,* she thought, remembering Mitch's words – *"I never laid a hand on you."* She looked at Dan again, admiring the way he and Kurt joked with each other like old friends. *He's a good man,* she thought.

Cathy and Sandy rested on a blanket, deep in conversation beside the fledgling lilac Dan and Anna had planted together. Anna saw Cathy reach for Sandy's hand. Craig had refused to join them today, so Taylor had graciously refused Anna's invitation as well, insisting on spending the day with Craig instead. Sandy had managed to shelter her girls from the news of their father's crimes, but her boys knew and they understood. Craig seemed to be taking it the hardest, and Anna knew Sandy was worried about him. *Thank God he has found a friend in Taylor,* Anna thought. *They have both been through so much.*

She set the tray on the table and carried the two glasses over to Cathy and Sandy. They moved apart, making room for Anna, and motioned for her to sit between them. The three women relaxed in silence, cherishing the sounds of the children's laughter. Anna heard a car pull into the driveway and stood to greet her next guest. Expecting her grandfather, her heartbeat quickened when no one appeared. *What's taking him so long,* she thought. Then she heard his sweet voice.

"Isn't it lovely?" James strolled around the corner of the house pushing Ruth in a wheelchair, her eyes full of joy as Anna approached.

"What a wonderful surprise!" Anna said. She leaned over and kissed her grandmother's cheek, then stood to embrace her dear grandfather. Dan approached with two more glasses of lemonade.

"Don't you have anything stronger?" James said, eyeing the pale ale Dan had set down next to the grill.

Dan laughed. "Straight from the bottle?"

"Is there any other way?"

"Just like your granddaughter," Dan said, winking at Anna before turning toward the house to get James a beer.

Anna hugged her grandfather again, then walked out into the yard. "May I try?" she asked. Libby handed her the wings.

Anna kicked off her sandals, slipped the elastic around her arms and shot off across the yard. She heard the children giggling at her as she ran, her wings spread wide. She felt the warm gaze of all the people who loved her, the people who had always loved her, the broken pieces of her life that had found their way back together again because of one strong, wise, beautiful girl – a girl Anna had come to trust and love with all her heart... herself.

"Love yourself first, and the rest will come naturally."

"You were right, Mom," she whispered...

And then she flew.

ABOUT THE AUTHOR

JEN LABESKY grew up in Indianapolis, Indiana. She met her husband while living in Colorado, and they are now raising their two children on the beautiful Eastern Shore of Maryland.